TIME AERIALS
A Time Travel Diversion

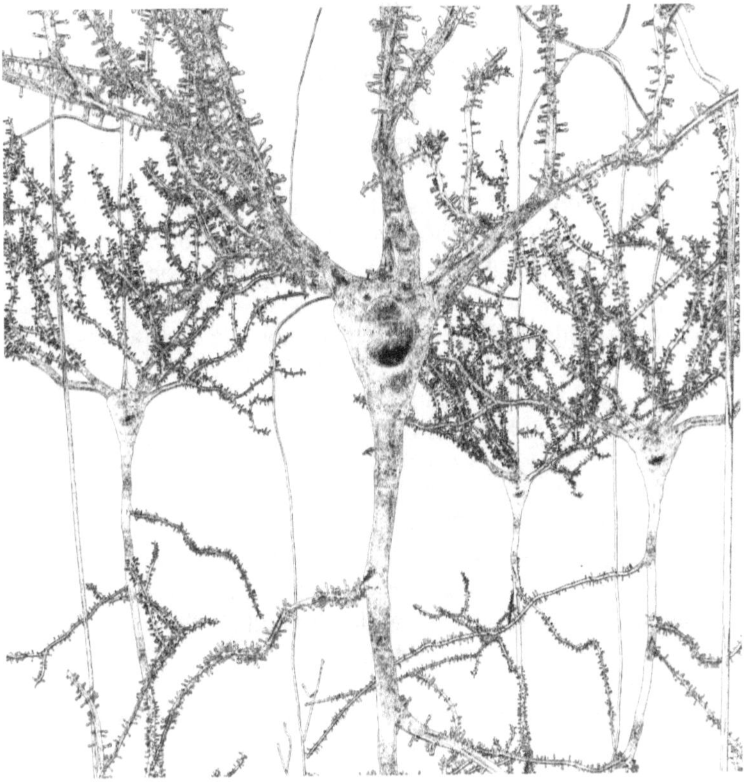

Russell Kightley

Time Aerials
A Time Travel Diversion
Version 1.31

First published by Russell Kightley, Canberra 2015
ISBN: 978-0-9943704-0-2 ePub edition
ISBN: 978-0-9943704-1-9 Kindle edition

This paperback edition, with revisions and illustrations, published by Russell Kightley
Canberra 2017
ISBN: 978-0-9943704-7-1

Cover illustration, internal illustrations, and design
© Russell Kightley

Acknowledgements

Thank you to my wife Lilia, for her endless support and helpful comments throughout the long gestation of this work. Time travel is a shared passion and a great adventure. Thank you to my daughter Stephanie, for her insights, suggestions, and encouragement. And to my daughter Zoe, for her support.

A big thank you to Phill Berrie for continuity editing and advice.

And thank you to the family, friends, and colleagues who have taken the trouble to read and comment on the work at various stages, especially Louisa Barnsley, Reverend Stuart Jenkins, and Donna and Gordon Peachey. Your insights, friendships, and encouragement have been critical.

Dedication
To my family: past, present, and future—in all of your universes.

CONTENTS

PART ONE

TIME AERIALS

Time Grinder

The giant time grinder juddered into orbit around the blue planet. The scene *looked* peaceful, but space had roughened, and nature was misbehaving.

An Extirpator robot watched, waiting for the right moment. It gave the grinder a nudge, and the mass of porous rock accelerated into the atmosphere. The grinder's vast blunt head burned orange, and a tail of blue streamed behind. The juggernaut of oil-drenched stone screamed into the sea like a flying island, punching out clouds of steam. It struck the seabed, and mineral fragments, water, a mist of blue oil, and pulverised life-forms exploded out.

The ashes of the instantly dead scattered across the sky, creating a looming memorial. And the grinder powder, blown in the high winds, cleansed reality. Earthquakes rocked the land and sea, and tsunamis flattened jungles. Huge outgassings wrecked the climate, and terrible plagues spread. The roiling oceans lost their shining monsters, and the blasted plains lost their running birds. And the dusty sky lost its giant bats. And the cities lay smashed, and insects swarmed in the predator-free air.

The battered blue planet recovered, and after millions of years, it again spawned highly sentient creatures. They spread across the continents and grew civilisations. They wrote symphonies, fought wars, built factories, and launched space probes. And the world became interesting again.

In the cramped front room of a small terraced house, a man stared at a time machine.

Time Aerials

The murmuring time field tugged at Harry's thoughts, making his skin tingle, and his heart pound, and his soul ache. The last of the blue oil smoked from the Keystone's surface, and the murmuring became a scream. The sixty smaller aerials, dotted throughout his home like glass bonsai, cried out as the array aimed at seventy-five years ago, when the place was empty, just before his grandfather had bought it.

Harry tapped the pocket of his suit and felt the flask. He held back a tear, grabbed the arms of his chair, and leant forward. His head crossed the focal point, just in front of the tree-like Keystone, and the time field seized his brain. He fought back, teeth bared and eyes scrunched. He sucked in crackling air from the unstable now, and then he sighed. His left arm fell limp as he released an imagined handbrake on an imagined hill, and he shot forward, tobogganing down the years, until the past struck, like a half-buried rock, flinging him into the Keystone.

Harry stood still and blinked. The ghostly Keystone's lower branches penetrated his belly and tingled red like Christmas morning. Its upper twigs brushed his face like a lover's lips, impossibly light and teasing. "Welcome," the aerial whispered, "this is all you've ever wanted."

Harry twisted his head to the left. His wooden chair had gone, and the old-fashioned settee looked new. The large oil painting of highland cattle shone in its golden frame, and the animals peered up at Harry as if he had just disturbed them as they drank at the river. And for a moment, just a moment, the water seemed to flow and burble. Harry stared ahead, past the aerial, at the other wall. The two woodland scenes gained depth and glowed and smelt of autumn. He twisted to the right. The delicate figurines on the mantlepiece, frozen in eternal courtship, looked polished and bright and formal.

Harry frowned and shook his head. He breathed in coal dust and his mind cleared. The house, he realised, should be empty.

It's dangerous to hug a time aerial, even a ghostly one, and he backed away. The fractal branches prickled as they withdrew, making his skin twitch in a million poisonous thrills. He took great care to avoid the aerial's focal point and, keeping his eyes fixed on its glassy twigs, he stepped out of the lounge room.

The hallway had bright wallpaper and freshly painted wood, and slender aerials marched down the passage, bent and twisted as if caught in a perpetual but unfelt wind. Back in his own time, they were bright and solid—*mainly* solid—but here in the past, they looked faint and out of place, like holograms in a tunnel.

He glanced up at the stairs. Brass clips pinned down the thick green carpet, and phantom time aerials shimmered on every step. The lower aerials had rounded heads on long stalks, like miniature orange trees. Higher up, they had shorter stems and fuzzy hemispherical crowns. Right at the top, on the upstairs landing, the lone aerial had a T-shaped stalk, with dual crowns emerging like beams from a lighthouse.

5

I've made the jump, thought Harry. I've actually done it. His grandfather Herbert, from whom he'd inherited this tiny house, and from whom he'd learnt the basics of time-leaking technology, would have been proud.

A rustling came from the middle room, and Harry froze. A scrape on wood, and then a pacing. Harry trembled and held his airless breath.

A thin man, slightly older than Harry and similar in looks, stepped into the hallway, tutting and shaking his head. For an awful moment, Harry thought his time jump had spawned a poor-quality doppelgänger, a weak temporal echo of himself. Then he recognised the man. He should be younger, thought Harry, no more than forty, and certainly not over sixty. And he shouldn't be here. It's the wrong time. No wonder the house had so many familiar things in it—his grandfather had already moved in.

Herbert stared at Harry and frowned as if listening for something. Then he shook his head and walked straight through his time-travelling grandson. He bent to pick up an aerial, but his hands passed through its watery base. He muttered, grabbing again and again at the tiny ghostly tree. Then he doubled back— right through Harry—and stormed into the lounge room.

Harry stood by the entrance, appalled, willing his grandfather away. But Herbert reached out to the Keystone. His fingers brushed its spectral branches, and the aerial sighed. Herbert bent forward, his head passed through the focal point, his eyes rolled back, and he collapsed. Seconds later, he twitched, blinked, struggled to his feet, brushed himself down, groaned, and staggered out of the room. A moment later, the front door slammed.

Harry clenched and unclenched his imaginary fists. This was bad, possibly catastrophically bad. He panted, but no air moved. And he waited for the world to end.

But the past was stable, and Harry remained. He forced himself to concentrate: dates, he thought, I *must* work out the dates. "If Herbert's sixty-five, then I'm back fifty years." Saying the words made the dream logic real. "And I've already been born. I'm somewhere here."

Harry grabbed the front door handle and twisted, but his fingers passed through the brass. He shut his eyes and stepped forward. Glass went through his head and chest, and wood went through his guts, creating an odd sensation, somewhere between a bright light, a tinkle, a dark brown, a fusty smell, a dull ache, and a rough texture. He turned left and strode down the road, towards the corner shop.

Newspapers sat in a rack outside, and Harry strained to read a date. But the little black letters ran like ants, and the headlines blurred and shifted. "Damn coy universe," he said, and continued round the block. He stared at the tiny cinema, all boarded up and covered in graffiti. Its closure was consistent with a fifty-year jump. Maybe next time he'd aim his aerials far enough back to catch a movie, and he could slip in and sit amongst the smokers.

He shrugged and headed back to his home, number 62. The pavement looked level but felt steep, and he leant forward, as if fighting a strong wind, and his feet, although weightless, dragged. Only thirty narrow houses to go, he thought.

Harry pushed through the pain and strode past number 62 with barely a glance, relishing the ghostly freedom and the funny sensations. He enjoyed the walk and felt, or thought he felt, the warmth of the sun on his skin. He would press on to number 145, the house he grew up in.

Harry paused at the curb, looked right and left, and crossed —a smartly dressed ghost that no one could see, taking care on roads that could do him no harm.

The houses here were wider, with bay windows top and bottom, and small front gardens with neat fences, or low walls, or tidy hedges.

Harry stopped at the familiar church. Its tower sat square and squat and reassuring and built, like the hall, from yellow stone. The rooms, a later addition, were red brick. Silver birches with shimmering leaves stood in front. These trees had been chopped down years ago, and it was nice to see them back.

Harry had drawn that church when he was ten years old. He'd sketched it from the bay window of 145, immediately opposite. He remembered outlining each brick, and adding thin washes of colour. And signing it. If the young Harry who lived here now was only eight, then the drawing did not yet exist.

Harry, the discarnate Harry from the future, stood in front of the church and stared at his old house, with its bright pebble-dashed top, and newly painted windows, and recently creosoted wooden fence.

Behind the net curtains, something moved.

Bully for Me

Children ran home from school, chattering and laughing. Harry, who'd moved round the church, backing away from his old house, squinted, forcing himself to concentrate on his surroundings.

Three boys stood on the corner of the next block. Two were big and burly, and one was small and slender. The big ones blocked the smaller boy, adjusting their positions to stop him going past. Something stirred in Harry's mind. He frowned, and his fingers twitched, and he sucked in lungfuls of air tinged with exhaust fumes. Over the years, he'd revisited this moment and imagined it from all viewpoints. He'd endlessly replayed and re-edited the scene, trying to change history. Trying to put things right.

The two bigger boys were at least twelve years old. The little one was Harry, aged eight.

"Where do you live?" asked the nearer thug.

"Over there," said the young Harry, pointing to number 145.

"Well, you're not going," said the other one.

Harry clenched his fists. He'd do anything to materialise and thump the little shits. He marched into the road, aiming for the boys, and oblivious to the approaching car. The sparkling grill and rattly engine passed through his pelvis in a slap of metal and a flash of burning gas. Then a brief, cold transit of glass through his lungs. And the warm wetness of flesh, and the scratch of bone.

The car screeched to a stop at the intersection. The woman crunched into first gear and whined off, indicators blinking.

Harry arrived at the curb, his lips drawn back in rage. He lunged forward, thrusting his face into the skull of the speaking thug, and then he screamed, his words like bullets, polished and sharp and unforgiving. The stupid boy recoiled, like a poked anemone, as he tried to fight the thoughts and make sense of the searing invective filling his head, but Harry's mind won. Harry withdrew and stared at the blubbery face. A tear formed in the boy's eye. It was not as good as beating the little shit to a pulp, but better than nothing.

Harry looked up. His younger self was on the other side of the road, only metres from home. Harry remembered grabbing that same opportunity all those years ago—fleeing without regard for traffic, the moment that one of the older boys had turned away. He was safe now, he knew. Safe as a little boy once intercepted by bullies. And safe as a grown man, since the bully's reaction was always a part of his history. And Herbert's glimpsing of the time aerials must have spurred his grandfather's interest in time-leaking and led to the time aerials themselves. It was all very circular, and dovetailed, and reassuring.

Harry realised that he hadn't seen himself clearly. He'd been so furious, so bent on revenge, that he'd ignored the slender eight-year-old. But he had his temporal fix—it was definitely fifty years ago.

Harry didn't cross the main road to follow his earlier self. His mother would be serving tea and biscuits and asking about school. Nostalgia wrenched his guts, and he couldn't go near her, not after so long. He nodded at his old home—as one might nod

10

to an old acquaintance in the street—and headed back. His steps grew lighter as the aerials in number 62 grew closer. The ghostly Harry was going home with all his worlds intact, and all was well.

62 to 62

Harry edged into position in front of the ghostly Keystone. And stepped over a cliff. Weightlessness, then a jolt through his feet and legs and back, then nausea. He exhaled and stared ahead. The Keystone shone, solid at its base and nebulous at its crown. His back hurt and he took a few moments to realise that the chair was pushing against his spine. He leant forward, and the field grabbed his mind. The room shimmered, and the old stuff reappeared. Harry flung his head back and gasped, and the room settled back, reluctantly, and with a slight hiss, into the present.

Harry pushed the chair away, slid onto the floor, and crawled into the hallway. He stopped at the foot of the stairs, grasped the newel post, pulled himself up, and vomited across the bottom step. He peered up the gloomy stairs at the grey and threadbare carpet. The brass clips had gone, but the pristine little time aerials glistened, as solid as machines that leaked into time could ever hope to be. He scanned the drab walls, the scuffed skirting, and the chipped and yellowed balustrade. There was no smell of coal, but dust hung in the air, and the worn-out house felt safe.

He rubbed his forehead. The array was still connected to fifty years ago, and he had to switch it off. Herbert mustn't get through. Having him preview the aerials in his own time was one thing, having him visit the present was another. Harry shook,

12

terrified that his grandfather might arrive at any moment, glimpse the unfolding future, alter the stable past, and tear Harry's reality to shreds. He went back into the lounge room, planning to douse the Keystone with oil and deactivate the array.

But Harry froze. The oil jar was in the corner, empty and dry. He'd forgotten to reseal it, and the blue liquid had boiled away. Without this oil, the Keystone would go at full power, thrumming and shrieking, and threatening his life—threatening *everything*.

Harry paced, careful to avoid the focal point. The oil supply was an hour away. That meant two hours of driving and some heavy lifting, and he felt too weak for that. But it was dangerous to let the aerials run that long. He stopped and tapped his lip. He *could* point them to seventy-five years ago, when the house was empty—that would be safe. A careful recalibration of the array was impossible, but he could move the little aerials closer to the Keystone and hope for the best. But moving them while the Keystone ran would cause the array to sweep across time, trawling up God knows what from the past. Multiple instances of Herbert, for example, creating a stampede of time-wrecking grandfathers. And perhaps the odd tradesman would walk across the time bridge. And versions of his grandmother might appear, or even Harry himself. He desperately wanted a drink, but he couldn't leave the aerials as they were. And he couldn't move them. And he couldn't run. People from the past waited in the wings, and history itself teetered. His lower body tingled. Harry felt like a boy again, horribly late for class. The school gates were closing, and he wanted to wet himself. It wouldn't matter, because no one would see him dribble. There would be no one left to see the dark stain spread. There would be no history at all...

13

Harry pouted and dug into his pockets. He touched cool glass, and his pout became a smile. He pulled out the flask—half medicine bottle, and half perfume spray—and he weighed it in his palm, and he watched the blue oil slosh.

Harry edged towards the moaning Keystone, holding his bottle out at arm's length, as stealthy as a hunter downwind of an injured bull. He shut his eyes and sprayed, and the sound stopped. He ran to the cellar door, twisted the handle, and pushed, and dank, fetid air—a mixture of mildew and coal dust —spilled out. He flicked the switch, and the yellow bulb sucked out the meagre light. A baby aerial flickered in the corner of the cellar head, and Harry picked it up and carried it to the lounge room, and stood it as near to the Keystone as he dared.

He dashed back, and this time he went all the way down into the cellar, grabbed a sail-like aerial, paused halfway up the steps to collect a conical one, and ran to the lounge.

The Keystone eyed Harry and groaned as he slid the aerials to its base. He sprayed again, misting its branches with blue oil. Its voice dropped, and he returned to the cellar. Down there, it was damp and forbidding, and the clammy air chilled him, but the cheerful little time aerials lit the miserable space, like lanterns in a cave. He walked into the annexe where two globular aerials burned in the corner. The coal dust tickled his nose, and the grimy annexe window made his bowels stir. Windows, he thought, peering through the dirty glass, should have daylight and a view. This one had contemplated a dank cellar for a hundred years. He sighed, picked up the aerials, and left.

The Keystone keened, and blue vapour boiled from its crown. It looked ready to ignite as Harry manoeuvred the last of the aerials, sprayed the last of the oil, and backed away. A final wisp of blue, and the Keystone shrieked, and the aerials sang. And the time-trap reset to seventy-five years ago and an empty house. Or so Harry hoped.

Harry needed a beer. To clear his head. To help him think of a way out of this pickle. And the walk would do him good. He stepped onto the porch, rattled the door to check that it was locked, and peered through its windows. "I should get frosted glass," he said. "Anyone can see in."

Harry had a spring in his step, for he was a real person, going for a real beer, in his own time, and in his own street. He stopped opposite number 145 and thought again of his boyhood attackers. He wondered what they were doing now. Probably nothing, he decided. People like that never amounted to anything.

Coma

The time array at number 62—hastily reset to avoid catching Herbert—now aimed at eighty-eight years in the past, at eleven o'clock on a Tuesday morning.

Mrs Peterson stopped, blinked, and rubbed her eyes. She craned forward, reaching out to the ghostly tree in the middle of her carpet. As her fingers passed through its outer twigs, she heard a faint jingling. She moved closer to the wavering Keystone, and her head crossed the focal point. The time field grabbed her consciousness and flung it eighty-eight years into the future.

Mrs Peterson's Ghost

Mrs Peterson gawped at the now solid Keystone, the unfamiliar furniture, and the altered decor. She screamed, but the only sound was a distant ringing. Arms raised, she ran, and the aerial shimmered in her ghostly slipstream. And its infinite branches sighed as they shook. She pounded down the hallway, through the closed front door, and into the road. Slack-jawed and hunched, she blinked in the sunlight. And as she stood there dazed, a little beige car chugged towards her.

Sid's window was open an inch, his radio played Mozart, and his fingers tapped the wheel. He checked his mirror, squinted down the road, and saw a figure of flapping brown. His withered leg slammed the brakes, and the buggy skidded to a halt. Shaking all over, he climbed out and held onto the driver's door.

Mrs Peterson, still in the middle of the road, gaped at the sky.

"Careful," Sid called. "I nearly hit you."

She turned and stared with hollow eyes. Then she shook her head, continued across the road, walked through a parked car, shuddered, and disappeared into a wall.

The white-painted room beyond the wall had a fat and creamy settee and two armchairs. Cloudy tubing hung from the ceiling, a black oblong stood in the corner near the bay window, and plastic books lay scattered on the timber floor.

Mrs Peterson grabbed at her sides. Her flesh *felt* solid, but she'd come through a brick wall. A *double* brick wall. And it had been peculiar, like eating dry cake, and walking through treacle, and sandpaper.

"What's happening?" she wailed, but her voice drained into silence. Water tinkled in the kitchen, a spoon rattled on china, and someone hummed. Then footsteps padded down the hall, and a girl in a loose and shapeless dress appeared with a mug of tea, and a chocolate bar.

Mrs Peterson opened her mouth. "I'm so sorry..."

But the girl ignored her.

"I *said* I'm *sorry.*"

The girl slumped into a chair, belched, picked up a small controller, aimed it at Mrs Peterson, and clicked. Sound boomed from behind Mrs Peterson, and she span round. Moving pictures of people and machines flared inside the oblong. Booms and bangs thumped through the floorboards, a woman screamed, and guns fired. Mrs Peterson turned back. The girl frowned and stared at Mrs Peterson's middle.

"I said I'm sorry," shouted Mrs Peterson above the din, "and it's rude—"

The girl laughed.

Mrs Peterson sniffed. "This will never do."

The girl rearranged herself and bit into her chocolate.

Mrs Peterson strode across the room and grabbed the girl's shoulder, but her hands sank into jelly, and she felt hard bits, and stringy things, and warm, wet currents. She recoiled and retched. The girl slurped her tea and munched her chocolate and grinned at the moving pictures. Mrs Peterson shook; it began as a tremor in her hands, followed by a twitch in her arms, and then a

18

wobble of her head. She hugged herself and wept deep wracking sobs. "I must be dead," she moaned. "I'm just a ghost." She shuffled to the front door and tried the handle, but her fingers slipped through. "I might have known. Damn it all." With a sniff, she squared her shoulders, walked through the wood, and stepped into a street of hulking cars. Her mouth opened—partly in shock at the altered scene, and partly at the bitter aftertaste of timber, and metal, and paint, and putty, and glass.

Causal Wave

The repercussions from Mrs Peterson's coma of eighty-eight years ago caught up with today, as history rewrote itself in a foaming, thrashing tsunami of tumbling events.

The causal wave had slammed into the present just as Mrs Peterson had crossed the threshold and tasted the door. Almost everyone in this new world was different, although she wasn't to know that.

Back in the house, the walls turned pale green, and the girl vanished along with her chocolate bar, her light fitting, her plump seating, and her big-screen television. A single black armchair faced the restored fireplace, and a glass coffee table sat in front of the chair. A blue box-file lay open on the table, and papers and photographs spilled out. And a silvery machine—part cone and part sphere—squatted on bent legs in the corner where the television once stood. It looked like an alien probe, but it was an audio device of such value that few people from this new history would recognise it. Richard, its owner, was out on business. But at night he would sit in his chair, listen to startlingly clear music, review old documents, and think.

Sid, the elderly driver who had nearly collided with Mrs Peterson's ghost, vanished.

The door of number 62 turned pale cream, and its narrow, clear windows fused into a single sheet of frosted glass. The frames of the bay window went from buff to earthy brown, and the curtains clacked into wooden blinds. Furniture updated and shifted, walls changed colour, new fitments sparkled in the kitchen, and a walk-in shower arrived in the upstairs bathroom. A tinkle, and the time aerials flashed out of existence, severing the time bridge forever.

Along the curbs, the bright-yellow and powder-blue buggies that Harry had known vanished, swept away by hulking things in grey, and black, and dusty white.

The wrinkled barman polished a glass. He smiled, glad to see a customer, and Harry smiled back.

The time tsunami hit the pub.

The velvet wallpaper, with its rips and stains and coiling designs, became cream plaster. Hunting scenes, etchings of cathedrals, and collotypes of cottages—all in matching black and gold frames—appeared on the walls, and ersatz beams crisscrossed the ceiling. And the sticky carpet gave way to flagstones, and the upholstered cubicles and stools gave way to rustic tables and hard chairs. And a girl in black drew a frothy ale. She looked at the dapper gentleman who leant against the bar, and she smiled, her expression demure and knowing. Meanwhile, two elegant ladies picked a corner table, sat down, and stared at their frosted wines.

The man walked over and joined the two women. He pulled out a multi-inked ballpoint pen and a small notepad, looked at

21

the ladies and raised an eyebrow. "Tell me again," he said, "about the disturbances..."

Harry would have loved to drink a pint in this new pub, and Harry—had he ever existed—would have joined the trio for a chat, and explained to them the source of their disturbances.

The Time Machine Detective

Mrs Peterson's coma became the gushing headwater of a new history. Her abrupt departure from her proper time had changed everything.

Herbert survived into the new history because he predated Mrs Peterson's misadventure and, although his life changed in many ways, he still liked time machines.

The causal wave smashed the delicate web of events that led to Harry's conception, and Harry vanished. And billions more became unborn. But billions of different people arrived, including Richard—born in the new history when Harry was born in the old. Richard met Herbert and learnt about time machines. It was as if the universe needed to replace Harry, and Richard—bright new thing that he was—slipped easily into Harry's historical and functional niche. But no one knew. Nobody had any idea that things were different...

Richard's office was a few doors down from number 62—the house of the erstwhile time aerials—and he was alone at his desk, when he heard a cough. He looked up.

A man stood silhouetted in front of the French doors.

"Where are you from?" asked Richard.

"Down the road."

"How did you get in?"

The stranger stepped forward, revealing shadowed eyes and a pinched face. "Never mind."

Richard pushed backwards, casters grating. "OK, *when* did you come from? *Which year?*"

The man pulled out a plasticky gun and aimed.

"Please," said Richard, holding up his hands, "if you're going to kill me, at least tell me *when* you're from."

"Two hundred years in the future."

Richard glanced at the railway clock. The seconds hand ticked round. "What's it like in your time? Are things very different?"

"I don't know, I haven't been here—"

The man vanished.

Richard took a deep breath, stood up, and stepped into a slightly deflected future. He stared through the French doors, and his hands shook, and a thin sheen of sweat coated his brow. The photons that struck his eyes would all be different from now on, and the air that he breathed would contain different molecules, and falling leaves would fall in different paths. It didn't seem like much, not enough to make a real difference, but Richard knew better. He'd obsessed about intervening in history and disturbing the past, and he knew that any change—however small—would amplify. Sooner or later, an egg would meet a different sperm—it took little to perturb a conception—and someone new would grow. Inserting this other person into history would change everything. Someone would glance in a new direction, pause when they should have moved, speak when they should have kept quiet. Made love a fraction later than they did before—and yet another baby would inherit other genes. Fast forward a hundred and fifty years, and no one would be the same. Past wars wouldn't match, and new plagues would have

24

spread in new ways. Bombs that went off in one world wouldn't go off in another. From outer space, the world might *look* the same, but close in—at the granular level, where minds operated, where people actually lived—*everything* would be different.

He wondered what his other self was doing now as he blithely diverged. Most likely, that version was still at the desk, reading through the file, looking at the photo of a mother and her pram—a black-and-white woman, frozen in a black-and-white park. He thought about the future that lay ahead of that other Richard—the future that produced the inept assassin. But that world had sunk below reality—and dragged its gunman with it.

This was the second assassination attempt. Richard had shifted futures twice, and two other worlds lay buried beneath this one. He wondered how far they stretched, those other futures. Did they end when the assassin climbed into his time machine, or did they extend beyond? And what of his other selves? Did those two Richards—insubstantial and unwitting— persist?

Richard was determined to continue his research. This new world would drift from the old, but *he* would stay on track. *He* would be a constant in an updating universe. He had a mission, and he needed an assistant. And quickly, for the next assassin might succeed.

Two months later, he had an intern. The new man was efficient, quick, and keen, and a potential partner for the little firm.

Richard held a police report in his left hand, and the fingers of his right hand drummed on the carved edge of his mahogany desk. "So you think you've found a genuine one?" he asked.

Tim squirmed. "It's not much, I agree, but it fits the expected pattern."

Richard stopped drumming. "Go on."

Tim glanced at his watch and pursed his lips. His face was paler than before, and his eyes darted around, and his slender fingers grasped the wooden armrest. "A man was stabbed, but they found no knife. And the killer vanished—literally."

"Fingerprints?" asked Richard.

"Yes, but the police found no match." Tim shook his crest of blond hair. "It's a classic closed room, with no motive, and no suspect. And it's impossible to solve."

"What amazes me," said Richard, flipping through the typed pages, "is that someone who's smart enough to make a time machine actually *builds* one. It's a death sentence."

The intern fidgeted in his chair, sniffed, and stared at the French doors. Outside, it was a perfect autumn day, and dappled rosy light streamed in and lit the floor.

"The killer's from the future," continued Richard, scrunching a yellowed note. "Or at least he was, before he snuffed himself out of existence."

"How can these things happen, boss?"

Richard smiled thinly at his new intern and wondered again if this pallid man were as naïve as he appeared. Perhaps he was only trying to gain favour. "Time machines always destroy themselves. They alter the past, and then they vanish."

Tim nodded.

"The thing is," continued Richard, "when you make a time machine you want to go back and *do* things. You want to put things right and prevent a catastrophe, or cuddle a loved one. The urge to travel back comes from grief."

"And?"

"They're wrong." Richard leant forward. "Horribly wrong. They always change the past, and people end up never being born. If they go back far enough, they prevent their own conception. Hence no time machine at all. And they all go back. They can't resist."

"With no time machine, they can't go back; hence they *are* conceived, and hence they build a time machine. You get a loop."

"That's where you're wrong."

Tim shook his head. "You've lost me."

"Say you go back and kill your father when he's just a boy. You stab his tiny chest. You've sealed your fate. You'll never be born."

"Fair enough," said Tim.

"But it takes a while for the changes to work their way forward," said Richard. "It's like a cause-and-effect wave spreading from the murder into the future. There's a delay, because the wave's not instantaneous."

Tim frowned.

Richard leant back and sighed. "OK, let's go step by step. The time traveller sticks in the knife and his father dies. Cause and effect domino forward as the new history unfolds. But the time machine is still there in the future—the causal wave hasn't reached it yet. The time traveller stands over the dead child wondering what the hell has happened. He thinks he's made a mistake. Then the new history reaches his time machine and deletes it. There's another lag as the removal of the time machine effects events in the past. Then the time traveller vanishes."

"Assuming that the time machine remains in the future," said Tim.

"Some machines might stay, and some might travel back. Either way, there's a lag. In both cases, the causal wave destroys the future that contains the time machine and the traveller."

"It still doesn't make sense," said Tim. "The time traveller's deleted, so he can't commit the crime."

"The point is," said Richard, "he's not deleted immediately. Say it takes a minute for the causal wave to spread from the murder to the future. When it gets there, the time machine vanishes. Then the repercussions from that take another minute to travel back in time and erase the traveller. So he was there in the past for two minutes. Long enough to kill. And the new reality, which incorporates the murder, has pulled away from the old reality. Meanwhile, the old reality becomes a nether world, a weak and virtual history that lacks the strength to undo the murder. And the old history can't maintain the killer it's spawned. The time traveller doesn't belong in the past, and he can only survive there when he's connected to a valid future. The umbilicus snaps, but the act remains..."

Tim let out a long breath. "So we have time travellers popping up here and there throughout history, buggering things up, and then vanishing. And uncountable snuffed-out time machines."

"Pretty much, but they might not bugger things up. I believe these short-lived, virtual-people could do important work."

"Killing's important?" asked Tim, and he leant forward, his eyes narrowing.

"Maybe. These visitors could do anything. They might kill, or flip a switch, or unlock a door. They might prevent disasters, for all we know." Richard's face burned with a strange intensity. "The universe *needs* them, so it looks away while they dip into the past and break the rules."

"The universe *needs* time travellers?" asked Tim.

"Yes, history needs prodding; reality's not watertight. As you know, the Sun couldn't burn without quantum tunnelling. *Everything* leaks at the edges, and visitors slip through. And stitch new histories."

"That makes me feel better," said Tim. "*Much* better. And to hear it from the master…"

Richard frowned, suspecting that Tim was mocking, but Tim looked serious, and he indicated for Richard to go on.

"These time interventions have a definite signature, and it's those clues that I search for. When I find one, I investigate." Richard swept his arm in a wide arc, encompassing the jumbled stacks of files. "It's all here."

"Very impressive," said Tim, and he peered at his watch. "I have a lunchtime date, so I'd better be off soon." He levered his slender frame from the office chair. "You want anything else, boss?"

"Try looking through the psychiatric reports this afternoon."

"For anything in particular?"

"Unexplained comas, like this Mrs Peterson." Richard slid a manilla folder across the desk. "She fell into a coma for no obvious reason. And it happened in this street. The whole area's riddled with weird stuff. That's why I set up my office here. It's cramped but convenient, and only a short walk from home."

Tim frowned. "Sounds like an interesting case." He glanced at the summary and flipped through the diaries and letters. "It doesn't look like foul play, but I'll go over it carefully."

"OK, take a long lunch. This stuff needs a fresh eye."

"Thanks Richard. You know, I've learnt a lot from you."

"More than I'd have thought possible in a week…"

"Oh, it's been longer than that." Tim's expression hardened. "I've studied you for years. I wrote my thesis on you. I'm an expert on your work. You're a dangerous man. Or you will be."

Richard reached for the desk drawer.

Tim smirked. "No point going for your gun."

"*When* are you from?" asked Richard, glancing at the clock.

"Three hundred years in your future."

"But that would give you less than a minute. You've been here for a week."

"I *left* three hundred years from now," said Tim, "but I took a roundabout route. Before coming here, I went far into what used to be my future."

"And that's enough for a week?" asked Richard.

"Two weeks actually—I managed some sightseeing as well. Anyway, the deal was that I'd get to study you first-hand and live in your time—I'd get to talk to you, and *then* I'd kill you. For a student of history—and of time machines—it was a great offer, and one that I couldn't refuse."

"And if you *had* refused, what then?"

"They'd have sent someone else. You'd end up just as dead, and I'd end up just as non-existent. And I'd have missed this adventure. As I said, I couldn't refuse."

"Why do you have to kill me? Your history's already gone—two weeks of you being here did that. Hell, coming here for a second would obliterate your world. You could walk away, and no one would know."

"Because, Richard, you're persistent. You wouldn't stop your work. You'd keep on going. You'd bugger up all possible histories. Remember, you've met two assassins already—and they weren't sent from my history. So two other futures tried to kill you. As my managers said, and these women are extremely smart, 'We have a duty to the hitherto unborn—from whatever history'. It is a grand vision, isn't it? And I'm a part of it, albeit a short-lived, virtual-part."

"What did I do?"

"Your work laid the foundation for a machine that could see into the future. It saw nothing but a slow extinction, and people didn't react well. You can imagine the chaos. But a device that sees the future…"

30

"...could bootstrap new technologies. And build a time machine." Richard shook his head.

"Yes, and with a time machine we could go back and change the past, and so change our bleak future."

"For God's sake, Tim, it wouldn't be your future anymore. We've been over that: *none of you would exist.*"

"Indeed, but any future is better than none. We chose this one, third time lucky."

Richard nodded. "When are you planning to kill me?"

Tim glanced at his watch, a nice mechanical piece with a glowing blue rim and a heart-shaped window that revealed a blur of cogs and springs. "We don't have much longer, I'm afraid."

For a moment, the watch glass reflected the French doors, and the rosy autumn light beckoned like a hoped-for portal. Tim tapped the glass, and the dial turned black.

Richard slumped forward, and his head, half-full of spiky dust, slammed onto the desk.

Then Tim—student, intern, and assassin—stepped across and inspected the corpse of his hero. Then he checked his killer watch; the dial was back to pearly white, the rim glowed blue, and the seconds hand ticked across the heart-shaped window. "Not long left," he said, as if he were still speaking to Richard. "I think I'll go for a pint."

He strode out into the late morning sun. A ten-minute walk, and he could drink sweet ale and chat to the girl in black. What better way to spend his remaining time? A woman in brown flashed by and disappeared into a wall. Tim shook his head and continued walking. He didn't have long, and the dead were already gathering.

Tim thought back to his briefing. They'd convened in the great cathedral—chosen to add gravity to the proceedings—and they'd told him that two weeks visiting the past would be very risky. "It might be more than the fabric of history can take," the managers had said in their matched high voices, choral and echoey in the vast chamber. "It's not just you, and it's not just your world that will end. It might be their world, too. It might be *all* worlds."

Tim remembered nodding. He'd solemnly accepted his role, like a knight offered a grand errand that was vainglorious, quixotic, and faintly ludicrous. But what choice did he have? Did knights ever have a choice? And he was more than a soldier. He was a tourist, and a student, and an explorer.

Tim leant against the bar and sipped his ale. The pub was deserted apart from a suave gentleman and two smartly dressed ladies in the corner. The man was taking notes, and the women were nodding. The man reminded Tim of his erstwhile boss, and Tim wondered if the universe were fighting back, if destiny had recruited a backup, another Richard to bugger things up—as if it knew about the murder, and wanted Tim to understand.

He put down his pint, watched the beer mat absorb the froth, and smiled at the girl in black. She coyly dipped her chin and reached out. Then she lay her hand on his wrist, as if to comfort him, as if she *knew*. And everything changed.

The Ghost at the End of Time

The solar system looked perfectly normal. The watery world and its far flung companions moved quietly through space. Comets rushed, and rough chunks of debris and streams of fine dust circled. The Sun poured out radiation as it had for billions of years. And a lone craft—on an innocent reconnaissance—approached the outermost planet, caught a few faint rays on its silvery hull, and emitted its regular home-bound signal.

Light stopped. The probe's last message froze at the end of a moment, never to reach home. Then reality exploded. Quadrillions died as space and time were ripped apart. Each dying mind tried to warn its earlier self, and quadrillions of death pulses thumped back through time. But the earlier selves couldn't run from the catastrophe, and they died again, and so the pulses circled in those final moments. They iterated, but they couldn't escape. Instead, the pulses shoaled together and formed the Ghost at the End of Time.

This Ghost, this Great Mind, this Sum of the Dead, coiled against the high rafters of history and peered down into the inky past. Its awareness grew, and it saw deeper into time. It saw the bright traces of earlier minds, for each scrap of consciousness had twisted time and left a gleaming trail. And the wide, frozen tracks of time machines—and the welded folds and buckles in

33

history that they had stapled in their wakes—cut across this glowing scene, but they were rare, like vapour trails in a summer sky.

The Great Mind stared at these tracks in the void and understood its own genesis. Consciousness and time machines had stressed the universe. And the strain on causality had shattered history. Everything had died, and the Great Mind was born. It revolved on the clean symmetry of its origin: consciousness broke the universe and spawned the ultimate consciousness. The Great Mind marshalled its strength, aligned its psychic streams, and reached back in time. It would sequester Herbert and stop the time machines...

Herbert's Double Shot

Herbert sat crouched at his desk and pursed his lips, oblivious to his role in history and his part in its destruction. He grabbed the sandpaper block, sharpened his pencil, blew away the dust, and continued drawing.

Old books, not opened for decades, stood behind the glass of a teak bookcase. A dark and heavy piano guarded the back wall. And a clock ticked away the seconds.

The only sense of movement came from the four hunting prints in their black and gold frames. The hunters raced across pale fields and jumped over hedges and streams. And as the hunt progressed, more riders and horses got maimed or killed. In the chaos of the final print, a triumphant hunter held the fox aloft.

Herbert put down his pencil and leant back. "Good," he murmured, "that'll do." He smiled thinly at the picture of his house, with its arched porch, and its dark front door, and its boxy bay window. He'd drawn himself in the lounge room, busy at work on a miniature version of the scene. The little pencilled man sat in a clutter of detail. But it was a fiction. The real studio didn't face the street—it faced the back garden. But artists can change things.

Herbert stood up and rubbed his back. He glanced at the hunting prints, remembering how his granddaughter had cried.

35

He'd explained them away as dark cartoons against the hunt, but she'd stomped off.

The tinted etchings inspired Herbert. Imagine getting not one, but a whole *series* of pictures published, he thought. And satirical ones, at that. But he knew he never would.

He hobbled out of his studio, through the dark kitchen, and into the greenhouse. The outer door had coloured glass, and he looked through each pane in turn, watching his garden shift from red to green to blue. Then he twisted the handle and pushed, juddering the door. It needs planing, he thought and stepped outside. The yard was dank and comforting. It had been enclosed, like all those in this block, since the houses were built, and it had a time-drenched stillness, like a monastery garden.

He wandered down the path until it vanished under thistles and grass, then he rested his eyes on the greenery and sighed. A fat ginger cat picked its way along the garden wall and mewed. Herbert glared at his neighbour's pet, turned, and retraced his steps.

Something was different in the studio.

He'd only been away for a minute or two, but it felt like years had passed inside. He frowned and scanned the room. The fox hunters still rode across their pastel fields, and nothing had fallen on the floor. And his sketch lay where he'd left it. Herbert walked to the desk and ran his fingers over an image that was far richer than before.

"Who's there?" he whispered, and he cocked his head. "Who put this here?"

There were no footsteps on the landing or thumps from upstairs. There was no smoke in the hall, and no rattle of doors. He tapped his altered picture, and it twitched. His hand flew back, and the drawing rippled and blurred, like a thing prodded in a shallow sea. And then—as if triggered by his touch—delicate fibres emerged from its sides and probed. Herbert retched, afraid that the sheet might scuttle over his hands, like a centipede running from a lifted stone. But the fibres weren't exploring the desk, they were weaving more paper. As he watched, the sheet grew from both ends, and darkness seeped into its fresh weave, and invisible forces pushed the pigment into shapes, and lines, and dots.

At last the weaving stopped. The picture had become a narrow strip, like a length of wallpaper across his desk. Soft inky tones spread over the last few inches of blank paper and pulled into focus. The process was finished, and the silence was hollow as if an unnoticed machine had been switched off. The ends of the photograph swung gently, brushing the floor and sending dust bunnies scurrying. Tiny motes danced in beams of sunlight, and a thin acid smell hung in the air.

Herbert sniffed and inspected the new picture. It showed his entire street, with every house in perfect focus, every brick minutely etched, and every window sharp and glinting. At the left, on the corner of the block, a raggedy boy ate sweets. At the far right, an old man hunched over, his mouth frozen in a gasp. And scores of people stood around, their postures oddly formal, like characters in a frieze, their expressions a mixture of bliss and expectation. Herbert smiled, for the panorama had triggered a memory of when he was twelve and ready for the school photograph. The camera had clicked, and Reggie 'snot-face' Taylor from the year above, had slipped behind the crowd and run like hell—fast enough to beat the shutter and feature twice.

Herbert rubbed his back and scrunched his eyes. A groggy vertigo hit, and he teetered and retched and staggered into the hallway. He banged into the newel post and the building lurched, pitching him into the lounge. The room sighed and threw him back into the hall. He swayed, and his arms ran cold, and his heart thumped. He stared at the bright, thin windows of the front door and forced himself to move. He slid along the passage with his palms flat against the wall, like a sailor edging down a tilted corridor in a sinking ship, until he kicked a light and glassy bush. It fell with a tinkle and lay, like a toppled houseplant, in a litter of icy needles.

Herbert screeched, grabbed the front door handle, pulled, tumbled into the street, and sucked in clean rich air. His breathing slowed, his head cleared, and he blinked. People milled about, and he saw them magnified, like specimens under a lens. Everything about them had a deep and sparkling clarity. He saw each pore, each hair, each thread of cloth, and he almost, *almost* read their minds. But these detailed people didn't see him.

Herbert coughed, and a neatly dressed man to his left stopped. The man turned, looked straight through him, frowned, shook his head, and carried on walking. Herbert took off in the opposite direction. He felt strong and young, and his steps were firm, and his back was straight, and he whistled. He stopped near the end of the block. On the corner—too close to the road—a boy picked sweets from a paper bag. The urchin hummed and munched away, and a bright blue wrapper fluttered to the ground. And he ignored Herbert completely.

Something twitched and sank in Herbert's belly. He pouted, and frowned, and patted his sides, and shook his head. A faint whir started, and the people in the street, including the little boy, turned to face the other side of the road. They stood aligned and expectant, and they smiled in mindless rapture.

The whir became a thrum, and the boy glowed, caught in a band of light. He grew hotter, ready to explode, and then the light swept away. Herbert ran, and the bright band nipped at his heels like a pack of hounds. And it flashed in the windows and danced on the walls, and it lit the bricks like burning coals. He pounded down the street, racing past number 62, and the thrumming became a roar, as if a hellish underground train were cutting a new tunnel beneath his feet. The people waited for the band of light, but Herbert ran. He zigzagged through the frozen crowd, like a demon through a prayer-group, and stopped at the end of the street, where he doubled over, his hands on his knees, and gulped the air.

Nearby, the neatly dressed man was looking in the newsagent's window, and Herbert tried to speak, but no words came. The man bent forward and reached for the newspapers. "Damn coy universe," he said, and he shook his head and wandered off.

The glowing band arrived and burned on Herbert's neck. He turned and gasped, and the light caught him, pinning him there forever.

Iteration

After Herbert had been sequestered, the Great Mind allowed history to unfurl for a few years. It watched as Richard shortened his name to Rick, and then it entered the head of a young girl and left a shard of itself there. The girl grew up to be a demure and perceptive woman. Her mind raced, and her insight deepened. She hid her intellect and took menial jobs and never wore colour. She lived her life below the parapet. But a fugitive sparkle of green light still flashed in her eyes. And if you stared into those eyes, you might see a chink in the world.

The Great Mind shuddered as the universe reset. It awoke to find that the end-of-time had happened slightly later than before. The sequestering of Herbert had removed the time machines and created a new history. But something else had replaced the machines. Something new had twisted causality and shattered history. This latest end-of-time had a new proximate cause.

The Great Mind's memories of the prior history—where Herbert and Richard had run amok—were intact. And it remembered its augmentation of the little girl. But beyond that...

The Great Mind felt different. Its mood had changed, and its power had increased. It had more death pulses, but they were thinner, and harsher, and more driven. And they swarmed in odd

40

ways. The Great Mind, curious about its alien constitution, decided to investigate. It would scan the past to uncover its latest parentage.

PART TWO

SQUAMAFLY

Spider in the Web

Herbert and his works were safely contained. Time machines, for the time being, could be ignored, for this was a different history. And in this reworked place, a spiderweb stretched from a gum tree, looped across the back window of a sporty yellow car, and attached to the hedge that ran down the side of a modest property. The web was like a fairy hammock, loosely slung and glistening, and as Alison pushed her hand through the silk, it collapsed, and a bright insect, like an azure butterfly, zoomed away. Alison only noticed the spider when it swung down, caught in a clump of falling threads, and landed the ground, broken and shrivelled and dead.

"Ali, time for school!" called her father.

She peered at the broken spider and then dashed into the house. She grabbed her bag and thumped down the steps to check on the demolished web.

Keys rattled. "You OK, Pumpkin?"

"Yes, Daddy, I'm fine." She jumped up, spread her arms, and aeroplaned around the lawn and across the driveway, dive-bombing the web.

"Hop in," said her father.

Alison threw her bag onto the back seat and climbed in after it. Her father checked the lock for the second time and ambled over to the car.

"You strapped in?" he asked.

Alison nodded. "I saw a butterfly, Daddy," she announced as the car reversed out of the driveway. "It killed a spider."

"Butterflies don't kill spiders," he said, and they drove off.

Once Bitten

Miles dropped onto the seat, panting and twitching. There were never enough benches in the shopping mall, and this one already had someone sitting on it. Miles nodded at the old man, and the old man smiled back. And as they sat there in their mild awkwardness, the other shoppers staggered around the little upholstered island, pushing trolleys, talking on phones, munching sandwiches, and slurping shakes.

The man was dapper and bright. Tiny, like a leprechaun, with a sparkle in his eyes. He leant across and showed Miles the back of his hand. "I got stung here," he said, tapping his papery skin. "Years ago. It still plays up. *And it's playing up now.*"

"A wasp?" asked Miles, looking away.

"Much bigger, like a giant moth with traces of parrot, and firefly, and scorpion."

"You said it plays up," prompted Miles.

"It itches like hell, then bad things happen."

"Coincidence?"

The old man shook his head. "I take care when my hand plays up. It's a warning, you see."

Miles nodded. "Any examples?"

"A gum tree fell in my garden. If I'd left at nine o'clock, as I usually do, I'd have been right underneath it. And its wood's heavy, like iron. I'd be dead." He sniffed. "But my bite was itchy, so I put cream on it. And that made me a few seconds late…"

Miles frowned. "How do you know that the itch referred to the tree?"

"Because the sore got flaky, like eucalypt bark. *That* was the link. My bite's like an aerial that picks up stuff from the future." He stared into the shop window, cleared his throat, and turned to Miles. "It feels different when someone else has a problem. The pain goes up my wrist." He rubbed his hand. "It happened when my wife got cancer." He smiled. "And we found it in time…"

"So, she's OK?"

"Oh yes, she's fine. We got it sorted. Here she is now."

A stout lady approached hefting a basket of patterned fabrics. "Come on Cecil, time to go."

He rose. "It was nice to chat."

"Wait." Miles grabbed his arm, and the man recoiled. "Sorry, I didn't mean to do that. But you said your sting's playing up now. Should I worry?"

The old man nodded, holding out his scar. "Look."

"It looks like an arrowhead to me," said Miles.

The old man twisted his hand so that the mark was the other way up. "And now?"

"Like a heart?"

The old man smiled. "Yes," he said, and with that he was gone, trailing his wife and her pile of bright cloth.

As Miles stared, the couple shimmered as if they were sinking under water. Then he grabbed his chest and gasped, sucking in metallic air from the mall. And the air brought with it a sharp smell of solvents and a choking stench of plastics. And hints of shoe polish, and dust, and perfume, and sweat. It's not possible, thought Miles, the old man couldn't have known.

47

The shoppers surged around the little cushioned island, munching, and chatting, and paying no heed to Miles and his growing sense of wonder—and his deepening fear of death.

Miles and Miles

Miles was waiting for his wife, so he might as well look at watches. Not to buy, that would be extravagant, just to look. He stood at the jeweller's window and scowled at his reflection. He looked hunched, and dishevelled, and much older than his sixty-two years, and his heart still thumped. He took a slow breath, willing himself to relax, and he tried to forget about the leprechaun-man with the precognitive wound. He wrinkled his nose and peered at a tray of elegant watches. The best one had a single hand and a blank face. Miles pretended to like minimalist design—this was a hangover from his art-school days—but he actually preferred lots of ornamentation. He shuffled along to inspect a range of fat and ostentatious watches. They were red, and green, and blue, and black, and even khaki. And they had mysterious dials, and knobs, and chunky bits. They were designed for another generation, and a different personality-type, and so he moved on to a rack of mechanical watches that were tasteful and *very* expensive. He imagined wearing one. He couldn't imagine actually *buying* one, but the golden watch at the bottom corner suited him perfectly. He tilted his head and pursed his lips.

"Would you like to see some watches, sir?" asked a girl in black. She'd emerged without warning, like something predatory from the coral.

Miles jumped. "Oh, eh, well, I'm not really looking to *buy* anything."

"No obligation, sir."

Miles shrugged and followed her inside, and he blinked at the trays of silver and gold. Everything sparkled and confused him. To Miles, rings, and chains, and brooches were like dresses, and handbags, and fishing equipment: they looked nice in a shop, but they weren't for him. Watches, on the other hand...

"I noticed you were looking at this display, sir," said the girl, pulling out the rack of mechanical timepieces.

Miles nodded and pointed to the golden watch. It looked even more beautiful. Perhaps the lighting was better inside?

The girl took the watch from its stand and draped it across her palm. "What do you think?"

Its rim glowed peacock blue, and its heart-shaped window revealed a blur of cogs. And its tick was soft, like the clicking of a lover's tongue.

"How much is it?" he asked.

The girl's fine fingers turned the watch. Its back was etched with coiling leaves and butterflies, and he was in love.

"The label says ten thousand, but I can do better than that. It's a discontinuous model."

Miles bit his lip. She was gorgeous, but not that bright—or good with words. He moved in for the kill.

"How much better?" He couldn't believe he was haggling over a watch. Life wouldn't be worth living...

She tapped her lips and looked up to the ceiling. "Well, how does *one* thousand sound?"

"That sounds great, but, um..."

"Let me speak to my boss and see what he says. The watch has been here for a while, so he might go even lower."

She stepped behind the counter and picked up a phone, and then she spoke and nodded and smiled. Then she laughed: a lovely, tinkling sound that stirred something deep and dormant inside him. Despite all she did—all the nodding, and talking, and hair twirling, and looking around—Miles had the oddest feeling that she was talking to herself.

"Well," she said, "*that* was odd. My boss said that since that watch has been here for years, and since you're the first person to show any interest in it, then you can have it for two hundred." She gave him the sweetest smile. "What do you think?"

Miles thought it was very good. He thought the girl in black was very helpful and very pretty. He thought the watch was exquisite. And his wife couldn't object, not to two hundred— she'd paid more for a necklace only last week. And the watch had more gold than her necklace, and more workmanship. And it told the time. "I'll take it."

The girl smiled. "Allow me." She slipped the watch over Miles's wrist, and the world jumped, like a film missing a frame.

"That's ten thousand for the necklace, sir," said the jeweller. "Would you like me to wrap it for your wife?"

Miles pursed his lips and shook his head. "No thanks, it looks nice around her neck. We'll take it as it is."

"Very good, sir." The jeweller handed the account to Miles.

The girl in black gave Miles a hug. "You spoil me, Miles."

"Not at all darling, it suits you."

They left the shop, and Miles glimpsed himself in the window. Not bad for sixty-two, he thought, not bad at all. He glanced at his watch. They'd been inside for what seemed like hours, but only five minutes had passed. The seconds hand

51

clicked round. He held the watch to his ear and heard its buzz. The sound was drowsy, like a faraway beehive on a summer's day...

He turned and bumped into a determined looking lady, and their eyes locked. "I'm so sorry," he said, "I wasn't looking where I was going."

The lady frowned and shook her head, and Miles glanced down. The necklace around her mottled neck looked familiar. Maybe he'd seen a picture of it somewhere. It looked cheap—not the sort of thing that he'd buy for *his* wife. And with that, Miles strode off, his heart beating a slow, strong beat, and his wife—dressed in black and wearing her new necklace—followed.

Juanita's Song

It was hot and still, and heavy with eucalyptus, a dry and oily place—a tinderbox forest thrumming with insects. Dr Juanita Pyne crunched through the dry leaf litter in heavy boots, her footfalls, so she hoped, loud enough to scare away the snakes. She took a swig of water, squinted at the flat hot blue behind the gum trees, and sighed.

A rattling hiss dragged her back to the moment. She held her recorder at arm's length and approached the giant tree. And from its base, a screech rose and fell, like an alien lament. Then silence. An egg-sized insect face poked out from a nest of leaves and peeled bark, and it fixed Juanita with an empty stare, and its mouth—ringed with needle-teeth—gaped like a fish.

The face screamed, then its jaws snapped shut, and its silk-wrapped body thrashed about.

Juanita glanced to the right and flinched. A spider, fat and black and furry, like an eight-legged rat, squatted nearby. It eyed Juanita, weighing her up, deciding whose side she was on, and then it shot forward and ran its fangs into the wrapped-up creature's neck. For a moment, Juanita saw a black-caped vampire at the throat of a pale girl, the image as clear as in the movies. Then the spider jumped back, and the creature screamed, and moaned, and sobbed.

Juanita's face turned pale. Insects can't sob, she thought, and she wanted to run, but the suffering made her stay. She put the recorder next to the web, picked up a stick, and prodded the spider. It raised its front legs but refused to move. She reached forward with her stick and pushed the silk that held the victim down. A clump of gossamer white caught around the stick's end.

The spider leapt forward, the creature twisted, and the spider retreated.

Juanita tried again. She lifted a tent of silk from the creature's back and rotated the stick, winding the web like candyfloss. The little animal convulsed and flashed a glowing red. Then it screeched and freed its blue and blurry wings. The remaining silk melted away, and it shook itself and flapped, throwing off leaves and dust and bark, like a dog shaking off water.

The creature that emerged was fat and bright, like a moth crossed with a peacock. And its face was foreign and hungry: part moray eel, and part housefly—with a hint of monkey. Then its wings stilled, and its colours settled to shimmering blue. It cocked its head, as if thanking Juanita, then it pounced on the spider. It chomped, and buzzed, and shuddered. And chomped again. Then it looked up at the frozen woman, like a dog looking up from a bone, and the spider's body fell in half. The insect chewed and swallowed, and Juanita—eyes wide and fists clenched—panted.

The moth-thing grinned. And then it screeched and flew. Rows of thin teeth hammered Juanita's upper lip, and she fell back, smashing her hip on a rock. She moaned and grabbed the insect, but her hands slipped on its downy back. It twisted round and bit her finger, slicing off the last joint, and she squealed and thrashed and kicked.

Her recorder's light was on, and its meter bounced into red as it picked up screams and slurps—and the sound of boots in leaves.

Juanita twitched and then lay still, and the meter fell to zero. The insect extended its legs and peered over the wreck of her face. It crept across her cheek and down her neck, rocking from side to side as it searched for anatomical landmarks. Then it straightened up, parked its antennae, and buried its head in her throat.

All was quiet except for liquid chomps and an occasional buzz of scaly wings. At last, the chewing stopped, and the insect climbed onto Juanita's cooling brow. It looked up, like a raptor over a rabbit, and cried out. The sound wasn't birdsong, but it was pleasant enough.

The creature cocked its head, listening for a response, but the forest stayed silent. Then it opened its mouth—its teeth caked in human flesh, and stained with human blood—and sang again, more sweetly than before. And this time, something answered: a lone, faint cry from deep in the trees. Then other voices joined in, and flashes of luminous blue arced across the pulsing sky. Each fly landed with a feathery thud like a dropped pillow, and soon a mound of flapping, buzzing bodies covered the young researcher, like busy flowers on the hump of a fresh grave.

And then a fly, fatter and brighter-eyed than the others, threw back its head and sang.

Three days later, the search party arrived, advancing like a rank of the blind, their canes sweeping ahead.

Clink.

"Got something," said a sallow-faced man. "Over here." He raised his hand.

Officers approached and marked the area with tape. One pulled the recorder from the leaves and brushed away the dust, and silk, and grit. The machine's lights were out, but otherwise it looked intact, and he popped it in a bag.

They combed the ground and found a mobile phone, a hair clip, a gold ring with a blue stone, a zip, three buttons, and two fragments of cloth—but no corpse.

Months later, in a university lab, a gaunt engineer played a sound file. It had screeching ululations, scuffling, human screaming, something like birdsong, crunching, chomping, and singing. The two speaker arrays punched out every yell and scrape and rustle and sob, and colourful graphs danced on three screens.

He leant forward and thumped a key. "That's it," he said, "apart from hours of forest sounds, punctuated by the odd high note. What do you think?"

"I'd say go for it," said the professor and erstwhile supervisor of Juanita. "We're getting nowhere. But don't release her cries. Out, um, out of respect…" He turned and left the room, averting his head.

The engineer extracted two segments. The tortured screeching and sobbing he named *Juanita's Song One,* and the alien-nightingale voices he named *Juanita's Song Two.* He loaded the audio files onto the Web, along with dozens of keywords. And there they sat, waiting for someone to find them.

And eventually someone did.

Fly Spotting

Don stared at the moon, and a shooting star arced in the west. He put down his binoculars, scanned the horizon, and shivered. A dog barked, something rustled in the trees, and a possum growled. Night was a different world, and he wondered why so few people went out to enjoy it.

Bright blue dots skimmed across the rooftops, turned pink, shot up, sprayed out like fountains, and vanished. Squamaflies were swarming two blocks away. They were nice to watch and very profitable to report, and Don hoped that no one else was looking at the sky that night. He pulled out his phone. This was his second squamafly sighting in a month and at this rate he could go professional.

Squamafly Farm

Tommy the springer sniffed the air and tugged at his leash. But Derek 'Dinosaur' Weedon looked like a concrete toilet, and it took more than a spaniel to shift him. The dog glanced up, whimpered once, and sneezed twice.

That got Dino going, he scrunched up his face and sneezed out a wet thud. Snot splattered the inside of his visor, and he prayed that nothing had penetrated his suit. He gave a little wave. "I'm OK," he said into the mike. He tapped his helmet. "And so's my mind."

The soldiers—autonomous and deadly—were in the bushes. Dino imagined his back in the cross hairs of their guns. A fast bullet was preferable to a fast insect—assuming a bullet could get through—but it wouldn't be clean. If things went wrong, there'd be a swarm of insects and a hail of bullets. And he'd be centre stage—a one-man ground zero. Sweat trickled inside his tightly woven suit. The cloth was heavy, but not bulletproof— that would have defeated the object—but it *was* fly-proof. Or so they said.

Dino stared at the back door. Its paint was peeling, but its window glowed with a stained-glass bird that rose from a nest of flaming yellow flowers. The creature had giant bulging insect eyes, and a raptor's beak, and its golden feathers were tipped in

58

red—*or dipped in blood,* as Dino saw it. It looked like a bird-god in the doorway of a pagan church, and something tugged at his mind, and Dino saw himself—and the image had the quality of a half-remembered dream—with a bottle on his back, and a flamethrower in his hand. And he was hosing flies with fire, and watching them rise endlessly, spewing from the flames, breeding in the heat...

"Phoenix!" Dino exclaimed. "The fucking thing's a Phoenix Fly."

"What?" asked the tinny voice in his helmet.

"Nothing," said Dino, and he tried the handle, frowned, and opened the door. Tommy rushed inside, and Dino followed him in, through the utility room and into the kitchen. Mugs and plates teetered in the sink, empty beer bottles stood on the table, and takeaway pizza boxes lay on the floor. It was a mess, but nobody saw inside. Outside, Dino remembered, the place was tidy with mown lawns, and trimmed hedges, and swept paths. And there was no fenced-in dog to bark and growl. It was a quiet and forgettable house, the sort that neighbours liked...

Tommy sniffed and detected traces of cheese, and tomato, and sausage, and pineapple, and flat beer, and dissecting-room chemicals, an unknown human, and tinned cat-food, and hot plastic, and dusty curtains. And the wet-and-dry stench of insects. Tommy *saw* the smells, neatly arranged like flowers in a garden.

Dino's suit blocked odours, but he *could* hear, and the helmet amplified sounds, and through its speakers, he heard a muted buzz from deep inside the house—a mix of rushing wings and humming electrics. But apart from that, the place was silent.

Tommy ran his nose across the tiles and looked back. His master nodded. The dog walked out of the kitchen and stopped

59

by the lounge-room door. This'll be worth lots of treats, he thought. When I get back, and after my shower...

Dino trudged over, turned the handle, and leant against the door. The buzzing got louder, and Dino entered a sickly semi-darkness, lit only by the orange glow of heavy curtains. His eyes narrowed. There was another sound, thin and insistent, like a mad woman screaming up a lift shaft.

Dino scanned the racks of tanks. The place looked like the back room of a pet shop, but the things in the tanks weren't fish or finches—they weren't pets at all. You'd never press your finger on the glass and say, "I'd like that blue one, please," or, "Can I have that cute one at the back?" Instead, you'd run. And then, you'd run some more.

"Hundreds of bastard squamaflies," announced Dino.

His helmet crackled. "So I see. Get pictures and get out."

The tinny *get out* was as welcome as a lover's hot whisper: *Come back to bed*. Dino thought of his last girlfriend. She'd said, "Come back to bed." She'd said it lots of times in the three weeks they'd been together. Dino wondered if he'd ever have another girlfriend. If the flies escaped, it would be no more *back to bed* for Dino.

The tanks were full of dusty air, and scales and droppings caked their walls. The corner tank was pearly white, like a block of cloud, and a face squashed against its glass, snarled, and vanished, like a ripper in the fog.

The closest tank was clearer. Dino locked his legs and stared at the flies inside. Recording was continuous, and data streamed from his helmet, so headquarters would have pictures even if he never got out. If they got him—if the squamaflies ate Dino *and* his cameras—at least his legacy would include some amazing footage.

Phil sat upright, twitching and grunting. His hands clenched, and shook, and waved about. A black stereo viewer covered his head, and its sounds were clean and loud in his skull, and its images jumped out, sharp, and bright, and all around. The stereo was strong because the sensors on Dino's helmet were further apart than human ears and eyes, and it felt like being there, but more so.

Squamaflies bounced inside the tank, fast, and fat, and red, and rolling-eyed. One hit the side with a wet thunk, smearing its scales across the glass.

Phil pursed his lips. "Great stuff, Dino." He cleared his throat.

"Got enough?" asked Dino.

"Nearly. What's that thing on top of the tank with wires coming out, can you get a closer look?"

Dino advanced. The squamaflies went wild, slamming into the sides. Dino ran his hand across the lid, feeling the collisions, until his fingers struck the black box. The vibrations here were different. He leant over, and his helmet-speakers screeched. The sound, alien and grating, rose and fell, making Dino's heart thump.

"Cut the wires," said Phil.

Dino held the box with his left hand, grabbed the wires in his right, and tugged. The box went quiet, and the squamaflies settled. They weren't happy—squamaflies were never happy—but they *had* stopped bombing the roof.

"They've calmed down," said Dino. "It's amazing."

Phil hunched forward as a memory surfaced. "I'm not sure that's a good thing."

Electric shivers ran through Dino's gut. His scrotum tingled, and he clenched hard. "Before I fill my suit with shit, can you kindly tell me what the *fuck* you mean?"

61

"Look at the tank, Dino."

Dino looked and clenched some more, for the glass now bulged in a dozen places, pushed out by snapping heads. The flies would escape any second. And eat him.

"Reconnect the speaker," said Phil.

"What?"

"Put the wires back. The sound might calm them."

Dino tried, but his hands shook. "It's not working," he moaned. "They won't go back."

The flies had turned a shimmering peacock blue, and they were pushing the glass further out.

Dino shook. *"Phil?"*

Phil bashed on his battle-hardened laptop, searching the internet for *Juanita's Song One*. It was rarely played—squamaflies were bad tempered enough at the best of times, and no one wanted to provoke them—but maybe it would work. He found a governmental copy, tapped the screen, and exhaled as data poured in. He opened the sound file, set the audio player to loop, and turned the volume up to maximum. The tough little machine wailed and Phil barked an order to Jim, the man on his right. Jim launched from his chair, grabbed the computer, and dashed from the van. He had no suit and no weapons, but that hardly mattered—if the squamaflies escaped they'd be furious and kill everything in sight. There was nothing to lose. At least, that's what he told himself as he raced across the road, dashed up the garden path, crashed through the kitchen door, skidded across the tiles, and ran into the lounge room. He stopped behind Dino's massive back. The big man was trembling, Tommy was whining, and the squamaflies were buzzing. It was not a happy sight.

"Step back, Dino," said Jim.

Dino went into reverse, his great boots scraping on the floorboards, like a half-track backing up. He still faced forward, with his stereo cameras trained on the bulging glass.

Jim held out the laptop like a magic shield, and advanced. The squamaflies' eyes widened—impossible for insects, but these little bastards were full of surprises—and they thrashed even more.

"It's not working," said Dino. "Jim? *Jim!*"

"Relax, Dino," said Jim, emboldened by the big man's panic. "Give it time. Phil said it *could* work."

"*Could* work? *Fuck me*. What if it doesn't, what then?"

A squamafly face banged and slammed around inside its glass bubble, like a choking astronaut's head in a helmet. Behind the frantic, straining bulge, its abdomen flapped in the swirling dust.

"Red," shouted Dino. "The little bastards have gone red!"

"That's good," said Jim. "Phil said if they turn red we're OK."

"Well, that's all right then. Well, *fuck* Phil."

"Look at the glass, Dino," said Phil, "and remember we record everything."

Dino looked. And as he looked, the squamaflies pulled back, and their fishbowl bulges flattened, and the glass returned to normal. The insects thrashed in the gritty air, ricocheting off the sides and thrumming against the lid. Juanita's Song had scared them. And in their fear, they'd lost their focus.

"So that," said Dino, "is how these criminal fuckers control them."

"It would seem so," said Phil. "Can you fix the speakers?"

Dino approached the thrumming tank and fiddled with the wires.

"Let me," said Jim, "I'm not wearing gloves." He offered the laptop to Dino. "Hold that up and keep it pointing at the tank. But be careful, it's heavy."

Dino smiled, tickled by the weight warning and happy to have something useful to do. The insect panic cry screamed from the computer. Come to bed, Dino, he thought, come to fucking bed...

Jim prised open the speaker housing and reattached the wires. He laid a finger on the black plastic case and nodded. "It's all good," he said, and he reached for the laptop, but his hands shook, and his eyes stared, and sweat beaded his skin.

"Don't worry, I've got it," said Dino, still holding the screaming machine. "You were great. Now, sit down and breathe slowly, you're in shock."

"OK, but turn it down for God's sake, it makes me feel sick."

Dino poked the keyboard with a fat gloved finger and closed the lid. Jim sank to the floor and leant against the bottom tank. He let out a long sigh and looked up at the big man. "Do you think I breathed anything in?"

"Nah, you're OK," said Dino, and he handed Jim the computer.

"That's easy for you to say, you're in a suit."

"I still think it's safe," said Dino. "The crims manage without them. If you're worried, you can get in the dog-shower with Tommy, he'd like that."

Jim smiled. He *wanted* reassurance, and he knew the precautions were pure theatre. But still...

Phil's voice came on. "Brilliant! Everyone thought Juanita's Song was bad because it made squamaflies angry. But scared and angry flies can't think straight. They can't plan or escape. Trust a lowlife to figure *that* out."

Dino nodded, but he hated the thought of squamaflies thinking. "The little bastards are either angry or plotting. What a choice…"

"I know, Dino, I know," said Phil. "Keep looking, and see if you can find out what's really going on. Somehow, the crims are making money out of this."

Dino returned to the tank. A clear plastic tube, as thick as a finger, emerged from the far corner of the lid. He bent down to trace its origin. A squamafly flew straight at his face, hit the glass, and fell. It shook its head like a person dazed, limped across the grey and knobbly droppings, and slumped in a heap. Dino squinted. The tube hung just clear of the bottom of the tank, and flies crawled all over it. A tight bunch of them probed the mesh ball at the tube's end, and they quivered their wings and twitched their bodies as if they felt a slight breeze. "What the hell *is* that?"

"Follow the tube and see where it goes," said Phil.

Dino went down on one knee—if he squatted, he feared he'd never get up again—and peered behind the tank. The hose, along with others from nearby tanks, fed into a clear plastic box with multiple compartments. One section was half-full of bubbling blue liquid. "Are you getting this?" he asked.

"Yes," said Phil. "It looks like an air filter. Squamaflies are dusty little bastards. They leave dander everywhere. What happens next?"

Jim twisted round to see what was happening, but he didn't stand up.

Dino got down on his hands and knees. "A thick pipe comes out and goes through a hole in the floor."

"OK, it must vent under the house. Have a look in the other rooms. And tell Jim to get out. *And to bring my laptop with him.*"

Dino nodded at Jim and pointed to the kitchen. "Off you go. And take Phil's computer."

Jim got to his feet and dragged away. He turned once, shrugged at Dino, and left.

Dino stepped into the dining room and reached for the light switch. The squamaflies stopped; one screamed, then they all resumed their frantic bashing around. "It's the same in here," he said into his microphone, "there are tanks everywhere. It looks like a pet shop from hell."

Phil jerked upright. "Check for supplies: extra speaker sets, and empty tanks—that sort of thing."

"There are no spares in here; every tank's full of flies, and the bloody things are red and barmy. I'll try the next room."

Tommy snuffled his way into the master bedroom, and Dino followed.

"We've got some interesting stuff in here. The table's covered in black speaker boxes." Dino picked up a tiny blue device. "And there are more audio players. Are you getting all this?"

"Yes," said Phil. "Can you see any empty tanks?"

"No, just electronics."

"OK, everything looks safe. Go through the rest of the house and then try the garage. Keep an eye out for small tanks." Phil pulled off his headset and sighed. He followed Dino's progress on the wall screen, rubbed his eyes, and yawned.

Dino and Tommy toured the building. They found a bed, unmade and stained, a toilet that needed bleach, and three crumpled cigarette packs. Dino opened the internal door to the garage and hit the switch, and lights flickered on, revealing stacks of tiny plastic tanks.

"How did you know about the small tanks?"

Phil smiled. "You said it looked like a pet shop from hell, remember?"

"Yes."

"They're selling squamaflies," said Phil, and he nodded at his own cleverness.

Dino shook his head. "You mean we busted a squamafly puppy-farm?"

"It certainly looks that way. Now, get back and wash."

The reconnaissance was finished, and the house was someone else's problem now. It was time to clean up, and Dino marched up the metal steps of the decontamination truck.

Meanwhile, a man in a white biohazard suit led Tommy away. The spaniel turned and looked up at its big master. Dino waved from the top step, and the dog nodded—like an old friend tipping his hat—wagged its tail once, and trudged away.

Dino took a deep breath and thumped the green button. The truck door unlatched, and he stepped into pale blue light. The door closed with a hiss and a clank. Then came a triple beep. Dino scrunched his eyes, but he still saw the blue flash that was meant to denature the squamafly scales.

A second door sighed open, and Dino stepped into the shower. A click, and he was locked in. The room filled with spray, and he stood there motionless, like a van in a carwash.

The timer chimed, and Dino removed his helmet. He sucked in steamy air and smiled as hot water hit his face. He unclipped his gas cylinder, peeled off his suit, arched his back, and shook his head. And he shuddered and groaned, as needles of scalding water raked his skin.

The spray shut down with a clunk. Dino looked at his fat feet and watched the water drain away, and a powerful sense-memory —of a beach, and tiny feet, and a sucking sea—surfaced from a million years ago. Another hiss, and Dino—hot, and scrubbed, and pink—emerged. He grabbed a fluffy white towel and went into the change area.

Inside the control truck, it was dark, and it smelt of hot electronics. Phil rocked back in his seat, his hands behind his head, and stared at the screens. The soldiers were busy wiring flood lights and erecting temporary fencing. Three workmen bolted a fluorescent sign on a pole, and someone yelled. Forensic teams moved in, a lot of plastic sheeting arrived, and a policeman, hands on hips and chest thrown out, blocked an inquisitive neighbour. And blue lights strobed.

"I should have ordered more decontamination trucks."

"Sir!" agreed the soldier at the next console.

One day, thought Phil, robots will do all this, then I can put my feet up, have a beer, and read a book, preferably a real one with pages and the smell of glue.

Squama Farmer

Three blocks away, under a peeling gum, a grey sedan sat on a nature strip. Its nearside wheels had flattened the dry grass, and above its gunmetal panels, the old tree creaked. A parrot squawked, and something dry fell to the ground.

Randall the insect keeper sat behind the steering wheel with his muscly arm poking out through the driver's window. His other arm encroached on the passenger side—Lucas's side. And Lucas wasn't happy; he sniffed and stared forward.

"Nice parking," observed Lucas, flexing his gloved fingers.

Randall grinned, missing the irony. "They took the bait. They think it's a puppy farm."

Lucas nodded. "If a man has to work for an answer, he'll believe it. The key is to be sufficiently obscure." He tapped his phone, and a front view of the property filled its screen, and he watched as armed men swarmed everywhere.

Randall leant across, invading more of Lucas's personal space, and prodded Lucas's screen. "It's a pity about the house."

"Quite," said Lucas, shifting further to the left. "How much essence have we lost?"

"Two bottles," lied Randall. His job was to feed the squamaflies and collect their weaponised scale-dust. He varied his routine, but he did a run every day—at least that was the agreement. But it was fifty-six hours since the last collection, and now the whole facility was gone. He rotated his right shoulder, winced, and checked the mirror. A cyclist was coming. Fast. Randall forced himself *not* to open the door. The man shot past with a whoosh, and the hairs on Randall's thick arm shook in the slipstream.

"Stupid fucker."

Lucas looked up and smiled. "It's a nice neighbourhood. People *exercise*."

"That's because they don't *work*."

Fifty minutes ago, Randall had been driving to the house when his phone had beeped. He'd pulled over, logged into the surveillance system, and watched a spacesuit and a dog enter the building. Then he'd U-turned, parked, and called Lucas. And here they sat, flicking between channels on their phones.

"Shall we stay?" asked Randall, staring at a close-up of the lounge room.

"No," said Lucas, and he eased his long body out of the car, like a stick insect climbing through a grate. "Give me five minutes and we'll be off. Keep an eye on the phone."

Lucas picked his way around the car, stood next to the driver's door, reached into his jacket, and pulled out a silenced gun. The pistol was long, and slender, and delicate—more like a scientific instrument than a weapon—just like its owner.

Randall's Ghost

Randall hovered near the top of the gum tree. He had no idea why he was up there, but it didn't seem to matter in the least. He looked down at the grey sedan. It was badly parked, he realised, and there were tyre tracks, and a damaged bush. Lucas had been insulting him, not praising him. Irony was no longer lost on Randall.

Lucas's polished head bobbed near the driver's window, like a fussy customer inspecting a new car. Randall half expected him to witter about tachometers, and oil gauges, and leather seats. But Lucas was silent, like an insectile mime with his wispy white hair, and stooped shoulders, and poking-out elbows, and long, lace-up shoes. He slipped something into his jacket, and the object, whatever it was, glinted green. Then he leant into the car, sniffed, retracted his skull-like head, checked up and down the street, sniffed again, and strode off.

Randall followed him round the corner, hovering behind like a pet helicopter, and he watched as Lucas climbed into a white hatchback, started the engine, indicated, looked over his shoulder, pulled away, and disappeared down a side road. Randall knew he'd never see Lucas again. He understood what had happened, and he stared down the empty road for a while, revolving on his peculiar employment, and his even more peculiar termination, and then he zoomed back to his own car. He floated at chest height and stared at the body in the driver's seat. Its fat arm poked through the window, and a slight breeze ruffled the hairs on its cooling skin. Its head lolled, facing the passenger side, and blood dribbled down. Randall, fixer and squamafly feeder and dust collector, was dead, shot by his own spindly boss.

A crack, like the gunshot he never heard, and a section of gum tree, its wood as dense as iron, crashed onto the roof of the grey sedan, heaping a further indignity on the person who used to be Randall. Oddly enough, his death, and his subsequent compression, didn't seem to matter at all.

Squama Pharma

Lucas drove like an old lady out for an afternoon spin. He kept just below the speed limit—slow enough to avoid the police, but fast enough to keep the tailgating idiots off his back. His hatchback was grubby, and its paintwork faded, but every light worked, and its engine hummed, and no unsightly fumes issued from its single exhaust pipe. There was no roof rack, no spoiler, and no stickers. And its windows were clean. It was an entirely legal and perfectly forgettable car.

He rolled into a wide and dusty alleyway and stopped near a group of brick garages. Each garage had an identical roll-up door, and each door was a dull brown. It was a blank and utilitarian place, with no litter, and no graffiti, and no neighbours. He switched off the engine, leant back, and exhaled.

Silence.

He pulled out his phone, tapped in his pass code, and dialled.

"It's secure," he said, and looked up. "No, Rick, nothing leads back to us."

Lucas closed the connection, stared through his sparkling windscreen, and clicked the remote. The leftmost garage door rattled open. Then he sniffed, started the engine, and drove his unremarkable car into its unremarkable garage. A moment later, he came out and shut the door. Using another remote he opened the next garage and stowed the gun in a locked toolbox.

Having deposited his vehicle and his weapon, he aimed a third remote at the third garage, and its door clanked up, revealing a pale blue sports car that was low-slung, and hunched, and glinting. He slipped into its navy-blue leather driving seat and grinned. Then he turned the key, and the dials lit up, and the engine roared. Lucas frowned and, imagining himself to be a fighter pilot, nudged the car's jet-like nose into the dusty alley.

Rick—slender and neat and debonair—stared into the safe's retinal scanner and laid his right hand on its fingerprint reader. Fingerprints are unique, but Rick shared his, and his childhood, with someone else. This other person, another version of Rick— who still preferred the name Richard—was not a security threat, for he was locked away in a history that had detached when Herbert was sequestered, a history that Rick knew nothing about. But Richard was persistent and, as Tim-the-future-assassin had pointed out, he would bugger things up in *all* possible histories. And shortening his name to Rick wouldn't change that.

Rick's far-from-unique fingerprints worked, and the interface turned green, a buried lock clicked, and the door swung open. Inside the steely safe, three racks of tiny bottles glinted, and each bottle contained blue oil that sparkled with fly dust.

He felt a slight breeze ruffle the hairs on his arm, as if someone had walked past, and he looked around, but his office was quiet, and the air was still.

Squamafly Eve

A chrysalis cracked open in Alison's garden and a butterfly struggled out. As it dragged across a leaf, its soft body tangled in spider silk.

The fly flexed and shook and arched, and the spider pounced, and the fly turned.

The spider froze mid-jump and blurred. And hardened silk whipped round and broke its legs, and more lassoed its back, and then the steely noose tugged tight and crushed the spider's guts.

The fly edged away and shuddered—as a person might shudder after touching a spider—and the silk across its own back melted. It crawled up a twig and pumped up its wings and held them out in the morning sun. But there were no sharp patterns as you might expect to see on a butterfly's wing, just a shifting haze, as if the insect were wrapped in a mirage. This was something new, and it came from its scales. Normal butterfly scales have fine ridges and hollows, which help produce the colours, but this mutant fly had spikes. And these spikes branched repeatedly, creating a mist of tiny fibrils—a fractal fringe that leaked into time and blurred the fly.

A child's hand, *Alison's* hand, pushed through the web, and the spider's corpse swung down, caught in a clump of stiffened threads.

The new fly zoomed away and darted across the bushes and around the trees of Alison's garden.

"Ali, time for school!" called a voice.

The fly ignored the human cry and stitched its way from house to house, arcing and pausing and rocketing up. And each time it paused, at each knot in its route, it mated...

Only Alison had seen the *Squamafly Eve*, and that was years ago, and it meant nothing to her then—and nothing to her now.

She remembered the heated arguments in the media and at school on the origin of the squamaflies. The experts believed it was a mutation; they believed in a *Squamafly Eve*. But that was too nebulous a thing for many people. They needed someone to blame and, unable to rage at a chemical change, they directed their anger at governments and scientists.

Alison remembered a special evening when she was ten. Her mother was away at a conference in Europe on Italian painting, and she and her father had finished a takeaway pizza and were waiting for a film on television. It was the tail end of the news, and a politician was skirting around the squamafly problem. Her father had turned puce, crushed his can, and screamed at the TV. He'd turned to her and said, "Just kill the flying bastards." And with that, he'd stomped out to get another beer.

She had no memory of the film, and the scene ended with her father reaching the kitchen. "Just kill the flying bastards," was an off-the-cuff comment, one of a million things he'd said, but those five words had stuck, and she grew up wanting to kill squamaflies. It was a passion, a calling, and something that resonated deep inside. It was something that she *had* to do.

Alison wondered how often a casual remark had changed a person's life. Or changed history.

At eighteen, she'd enrolled in the government-funded squamafly program. Now she wished she'd done art history like her mother and left pest control to others. She could be looking at paintings in Venice instead of growing viruses in Canberra. She hoped that her father was unaware of the power of his words —now that the flies were dive-bombing the lab.

But it wasn't her father's words that had sealed her fate, it was her presence at the hatching of the *Squamafly Eve*.

Through Glass, Brightly

Dusk settled around the eucalypts, and their slender pointed leaves hung dark against the purple sky. Something, perhaps a parrot, flew by. Far away, below the sweeping ramparts, the yellow lights of the sparse city twinkled.

Alison sat hunched with her hands in her lap and stared at the dark laboratory window. A flash of blue and a violent thud. And she twitched as a fat insect spread itself across the outside of the glass. And its broken body—releasing lumps, and drips, and knots, and stringy bits—slid down.

"Daddy," she mouthed.

She rolled closer, crunching her belly against the wooden bench. A fine meteor-tail of luminous peacock blue arced across the lawns, and the glass shook as another insect smashed into the window. A fly head poked through and retracted with a tiny pop. Red and yellow blossomed as guts spread everywhere. And an orange sac slipped out—translucent, and throbbing, and packed with comma-shaped babies—and slid down the glass, leaving a glistening trail.

Alison shuddered and tore her eyes from the escaping uterus and forced them back to the impact point. A dusty imprint of wings framed a stain of gut. And a wisp of scales hung in the air, like smoke from a gun.

Twenty seconds later, another light arced across the gardens, followed by another thud and crunch of insect flesh on glass. Then more dust, and scales, and fluids—and another uterine lifeboat slipped down the window.

Everyone else had gone. The people here had dates, and families, and normal, balanced lives, but Alison was new, and she had no one in the city, and she was staying in a cheap hotel. The lab was better than her dingy room, and she was keen to make a good impression. But the evening was going wrong. She'd planned to catch up on writing and run more tests, but that was pointless now. She'd grown up with squamaflies—and killing them was important—but this was all new, and she wondered what her father would make of it.

A faint whirring, an occasional bubbling of equipment, and every twenty seconds, the crunch of another fly. She tried to picture the lab as an armoured truck ploughing through the darkness— taking her away from this nightmare—and hitting fireflies as it went. But the lab's not moving, she thought. I'm not going anywhere. And they're not fireflies.

She leant her elbows on the bench and rested her chin on her hands. "Incoming," she muttered and flinched as a fly, fatter than the others, hit the window in front of her face. Its domed head forced the glass to bulge inwards, and its jaws snapped, like a giant piranha in a tiny fishbowl. And then it was gone, flipped back by the recovering glass. For a moment, the insect lay smashed against the pane, and then its body fell, leaving a puff of scales and an angel-print of dead wings. "That one saw me," she said. "And it marked the spot."

The flies swarmed in, faster than ever, aiming at the wing-smudge-and-gut-smear target. Body after crunchy body struck the same point. Thud, thud, thud, and the cloud of wing scales thickened, building like cannon smoke on a battlefield. An arc of brighter blue, a crunch and a splash, and Alison screamed. The fly pushed halfway through. The glass snapped shut like a sphincter, slicing the animal in two. Its head and thorax dropped onto the bench, and its jaws still gnashed, and its eyes still rolled, and its wings still flapped. Blood and yellow slime pumped out. And then it died. And a puff of scales rose, like an escaping ghost.

Alison saw herself sliced by a tall and glassy guillotine, she saw her head drop into a bucket of bench-wood, and she saw her headless body pump out blood and slime. She grabbed the back of her neck and clenched. Then she pushed back from the bench and sniffed. The ghostly scales shot up her nostrils—going far too fast for dusty things on gentle currents—and they stuck to the damp lining of her nose. And then they burrowed. Within seconds, they'd reached her brain.

Alison grabbed her phone and stabbed its screen. She sobbed and held it to her ear. Then she frowned and looked around and shook the phone. And her mouth moved, but no words came.

A thud, a snap, and a plop, and a broken fly dragged across the wood, trailing its guts. And an orange sac, full of squirming babies, hauled itself clear. The fly stopped, extended its front legs, lifted its face, cocked its head like a listening lizard, and stared at Alison. And Alison stared back. She pursed her lips and tilted her head. Her arm dropped to her side, and the phone clattered onto the floor. Dying insect and vacuous human— vanguards of a species war—regarded each other. Then the heaving sac reached the edge of the bench and dropped into her lap. Yellow fluid soaked her jeans, and comma-babies wriggled over her thighs.

Alison's jaw fell slack, her head lolled, and she stroked the orange maggot-thing as if it were a cat that had jumped up. Then she squeezed it, forcing out more babies. The tadpole-things, fat and black and drenched in birthing fluid, squirmed across her lap. They had no eyes or legs or wings. But they had mouths. And teeth. And Alison smiled as they bit into her legs.

Flies flew in, faster now, filling the room with fuzzy wings: hectic rainbow streaks of blue, purple, green, red, and yellow. It was gaudy, like an aviary of mad parrots, but without the squawking or trilling—just an alien sibilance and a gentle munching.

Squamafly Lab

The following morning was chaos. People in white coats milled about, poking at equipment, and tutting, and shrugging their shoulders. Five huge wall screens monitored the underground levels. The right-hand screen showed Level Five, the virus factory, where the workers wore full body suits and drifted around, like yellow astronauts inspecting a grey hulk.

"Well, that's no bloody good," said Frank as he hit his unresponsive computer for the third time. "No bloody good at all."

Zoe Martin, the chief scientist, peered over his shoulder. "No, Frank, it's not. What's Jerry got to say?"

"It's only *five* past nine," he said. "It's far too early for Jerry."

Zoe glared, but Frank ignored her rebuke.

"Alison was working late last night," he said, "so maybe she knows something. I'll call her." He picked up his phone. "In fact, I'm surprised she's not here now." After a moment, he shook his head. "She's unavailable, I'll try Jerry instead."

A moment later, Jerry sauntered in, staring at his phone. "Ah, Frank, you called?" He beamed. Then his expression darkened. "What's wrong?"

"We had a break-in." Frank puffed up, preparing himself to deliver spectacular news. "They ruined the equipment, killed the cultures, and destroyed the labs. The project's wrecked." He pursed his lips, forcing away a smile, and jabbed at the screens and their milling workers.

Jerry marched up to screen five and watched tiny yellow figures inspect a vat. Their arms circled, and there was no sound, like a silent comedy.

"And Level Six?" Jerry hissed. "What happened down there?"

"The squamaflies are in their tanks, and the songs are playing."

"Six is newer and more secure, maybe they couldn't get in." Jerry frowned and tapped his lips. "Imagine if they'd let the flies out..." He turned to Zoe. "What about Parks? Has anyone spoken to them?"

Parks was the other Australian lab working on a squamafly virus.

Zoe gave a thin smile. "I can't get hold of anyone there."

Jerry called over to an assistant, "Check the logs, and see when Alison left."

The girl tapped a screen, shook her head, and shrugged.

"I've emailed Clifton in South Africa," Zoe announced, tapping her phone. "It's one-thirty in the morning in Cape Town, but he might be awake. Let's hope to Christ his viruses are OK."

"I'll try Leicester," said Jerry. "They should be all right—they're even more secure."

Zoe stared through the window—Alison's window—but the glass was clean and smooth. And the desk below was spotless. Her hands trembled, so she crossed her arms. "Jerry, in my office," she whispered.

By the time he reached her office, Jerry was shaking uncontrollably.

"Close the door," she said. "And sit down before you fall down."

"What happened to Alison?" he asked, lowering himself into the faux leather chair that Zoe kept for guests. "Do you think she's OK?"

"I hope so. She was working late, wasn't she?"

"Yes," said Jerry, "it's my fault..." He leant forward, hands clasped together between his knees. "I suggested..."

"It's no one's fault." Zoe sat down behind her desk and swivelled, glancing at the framed virus poster. "They look like aquarium creatures," she said, nodding at the pink particles floating in the translucent blues and greens of an imaginary cell. Then she turned to Jerry. "Viruses are, *were,* the best hope. Now it's all gone wrong."

Jerry sat upright and drummed his heels on the floor, and stared ahead. "It certainly *looks* that way. Do you think we'll hear anything from the other labs?"

"I've no idea."

Jerry looked down at his jiggling fingers. "It should be on the news."

"Maybe they're hushing it up," said Zoe.

Jerry understood why. The tipping point had happened six months ago, when squamaflies had attacked cattle in the Northern Territory. He shuddered at the memory of videos of white bones in fields—and they weren't all cattle bones. Sheep were next, so the farmers had herded livestock into sheds, and the flies had moved onto easier pickings. They had travelled south in swarms. But *swarms* wasn't really the right word. The flies were big and bright, and they chirruped like parrots, and so

84

flock was a better word—*a flock of flies*. His old English teacher wouldn't approve. Or perhaps he would...

He forced himself back to the present. "Terrorists?" he asked, raising his eyebrows.

"God, I hope so. It could be an animal rights group. Or an apocalyptic sect—idiots who want us all dead. Give Earth back to nature, and all that crap."

There was a sharp knock, then a security officer in a blue cap popped his head around the door and nodded at Zoe. "The office staff are waiting outside, Professor."

Zoe and Jerry sat there for several seconds, clutching at the moment, unwilling to move into the future, then they left the office, skirted the lab, and crossed the concourse. The inner main doors swished open onto what Jerry liked to think of as the airlock. Then they walked through the scanners, and the outer doors swished open in a perfect echo of their interior counterparts, and the two scientists stepped onto flagstones and into sunlight.

Workers milled about on the sloping lawns, chattering and shaking their heads. They were aimless, and expectant, and waiting for direction, like hotel guests after a fire drill.

Zoe clapped her hands and called for attention. "We have a maintenance problem," she announced. "The machines have shut down, but no viruses or flies have escaped. Once I get the all-clear, you can go home. The scientists are working on it as we speak, and I'll keep you updated. Hopefully, everything will be sorted out by tomorrow."

There was a murmuring, and a nodding, and a stifled laugh.

"Do you think they believed you?" whispered Jerry.

She shook her head. Then she shrugged. "Maybe."

He nodded at the approaching suit. "Here comes the man with the answers."

Zoe held out her hand. "Hello, Daniel."

Daniel Foster was from BiosecuritySquama, the governmental agency that ran the lab. He shook Zoe's hand and smiled at Jerry. Then he turned back to Zoe. "I wonder if I could have a quiet word."

Jerry nodded and wandered over to disturb Frank who was busy comforting one of the junior female staff.

Zoe eyed Daniel. "We have one girl missing, and the entire facility's down. What the hell's going on?"

"We're not sure, but it's not just this place," he waved at the bunker-like building behind them, "the other labs are down, too." He thrust his hands into his pockets and stared across the lawns. "You say you've lost *one* person?"

"Well, we can't find Alison. She's new and keen, and she was working late last night. Her phone's dead, and there's no sign of her."

"Sorry to hear that. Cape Town lost thirty, Leicester even more. When I say lost, I mean gone without a trace." Foster pursed his lips. "It happened at the same time, which meant the other labs were busy." He sniffed. "Time differences, you know…"

Zoe gaped at him.

"Time zones," he continued, pressing the point. "They were all at work."

She shook her head as if to clear it. "Yes. No, I understand that. I mean, how the hell can people just disappear?"

Foster shrugged. "The equipment's gone, too. It looks OK, but the insides are wrecked. And the viruses are dead." He stared at the horizon as if expecting an air invasion. "It's a sophisticated attack."

"What about the Americans?" asked Zoe, and she scanned the perfect lawns. The grass was newly mown, and sharp bands of pale and dark striped the artificial hillside. It all looked so normal and contained.

"They're OK. It's all non-viral weapons in the US. They're interested, though, very interested."

"Let's walk," said Zoe. "I have to let the staff know what's happening. What should I tell them?"

"Say it's a terrorist attack. That way, everyone will expect secrecy, and they'll know not to ask questions."

"What do *you* think it is?"

He shrugged. "I'm keeping an open mind. So far, it's just the SquamaVirus labs. What does that suggest to you?"

Zoe raised her eyebrows. "I'll send everyone home. Then we'll talk."

Zoe strode into the crowd of office workers and support staff. "OK everyone, please listen," she said, and the murmuring stopped. "We're not the only ones with problems. Parks and two overseas labs got hit last night. They think it's terrorism, and I'll be liaising with Mr Foster from Biosecurity. That means that the facilities are now a crime scene, and you can't go back in. Please go home, and we'll call you with any news. Any questions?"

"What about our cars?" asked a large administrative officer, sitting on the low wall that skirted the road. Her face was red, and she was panting, and tapping her chest.

Zoe looked at Foster. He smiled. "That's no problem, madam, the parking areas aren't part of the investigation."

"Is anyone hurt?" a woman called.

"No injuries have been reported," said Zoe. "Now, if you'll excuse me, I have to help Mr Foster."

The office staff nodded and grinned. The large admin lady waddled to her car and chatted to a stooped and attentive coworker.

Zoe watched them go, and wished she knew as little as they did. "Let's get out of here," she said.

Foster pursed his lips and followed her down the slope. "I have a briefing at eleven thirty, and I'd like you to come."

"I'd love to, and Jerry should come too. He's very discreet. And terribly smart. His ideas might be crucial."

"OK, I'll get him cleared."

The meeting room was large and grey and hushed. Zoe drummed her fingers on the polished concrete windowsill and stared at the city below. A radio tower dominated the landscape from the top of a wooded hill. Wind ruffled the lake and bent the sails of faraway yachts. Tiny cars dotted the thin ribbons of road that skirted the water and fed the centre and outlying suburbs, and a distant plane inched across the impossibly blue sky, leaving a white trace. The scene was clean and measured and tranquil, like a watercolour of a perfect city.

Jerry stared out. "It's the apocalypse, but everything looks the same—at least it does from up here."

"An Ebola outbreak looks fine from the air," said Zoe.

"It's like being in a flying saucer and hovering over a doomed planet," said Jerry. "We're watching *Invasion of the Squamaflies,* starring—"

A clink cut Jerry off, and a wooden wall opened. Daniel strode in, followed by three women and four men. These seven people were smart and fit, and they radiated power—but not, thought Zoe, understanding.

Daniel handled the introductions, and everyone shook hands and sat down. Small talk washed around the oval table, but Zoe kept quiet and she ran her fingers across the silky oaken desktop, and she stared at the hard edges of the chairs, and the textures of the clothing, and the colours of the ties, and the funny shapes that people made.

"Dr Martin."

Zoe jumped.

Reid, thickset and polished and ministerial, leant forward, his teeth and cufflinks glinting. "Please summarise the situation at your lab," he said, and as he spoke, his blue tie bobbed.

Zoe forced her eyes from the minister's throat and took a deep breath. "The lab *looks* fine, but nothing works. The insides of the machines have turned to dust. All the squama-killing viruses are dead, and a girl's missing. The scientists are working frantically, and the office staff went home. I used the terrorist story, to keep—"

"Story?" Reid interrupted, raising an eyebrow. "If it's not terrorism, what is it?"

"Squamaflies."

"I see," said Reid, leaning back. "I imagine they were concerned about your new virus."

"Yes, they're evolving—"

Reid coughed. "My money's on environmental activists."

"No," said Jerry. "They lack the means."

Reid rotated to face Jerry and frowned.

"Please go on," said Daniel.

Jerry looked at each face in turn. "There was no sign of a break-in. A worker's vanished, and something destroyed the equipment from the *inside*." He cleared his throat and stared at Reid. "No one has the technology to do that."

"Assuming your..." and the minister paused, and he drew circles in the air as he searched for the right word, "... *theory* is correct, what are the implications?"

"Things don't look good," said Daniel, moving in to support Jerry. "Squamaflies are breeding fast, destroying one food supply after another. First they sucked nectar, then they munched fruit, now they like steak." He spread his hands like a boastful fisherman. "They grab salmon from farms. Last week, someone saw a fuzzy eagle dive into a paddock…"

It went on in this vein for a while—punctuated by coughs, and laughs, and finger-drumming, and a fit of hiccups—and Zoe nodded as the room pulsed with colours and sounds and shapes.

Eventually, Reid rapped the table. "Thank you everyone. We'll issue a press release. I'd like us all to meet again tomorrow, and review progress. Thank you, ladies and gentlemen."

Chairs scraped, and the bureaucrats filed out.

Zoe, Jerry, and Daniel remained seated and exchanged glances.

"How bad is it?" Jerry asked, looking at Daniel.

"They've taken elephants…"

"Elephants?" said Zoe. "God help us. And how come we didn't know?"

"They blamed poachers," said Daniel. "It's one cover-up after another. Cattle got plenty of attention because they're farm animals. And there are lots of cows, and farmers talk, so the authorities couldn't hide it. But while everyone was watching livestock, hundreds of other species vanished. Wild losses aren't being reported—particularly the extreme cases, like the whales…"

Jerry's jaw dropped. *"Whales are extinct?"*

"No, but they've been attacked." Daniel twisted his lips as if he'd been presented with rotten food. "And a whaling boat got taken out. It was found abandoned like the *Mary Celeste*."

"With its radio turned to dust?" asked Jerry, and he giggled in a suppressed, slightly hysterical way.

Daniel nodded. "Squamaflies don't like competition, but they minimise human casualties—they're keeping a low profile until there are enough of them..."

"Until now," said Zoe.

Daniel shook his head. "Not now, not yet—there are still too few of them. But our viruses scared the squamaflies, that's why they took out the labs—but they did it cleanly."

"How long have we got?" asked Jerry.

"The world's got five years, maybe less," said Daniel.

"OK, let's get lunch," suggested Jerry. "While there's still food."

"And virologists to eat it," added Zoe, and she made a call.

Last Orders

Zoe and Daniel and Jerry were in a café in the city, near the law courts. The place was bright and metallic, and it smelt of fresh coffee and rich cake. Two policemen sat by the window, gazing at traffic, and three pin-striped lawyers huddled in a corner, braying, and slurping milky coffees.

"Three long blacks coming up!" announced Jerry, bearing a tray. "Food will be here shortly."

"I miss my lattes," said Zoe, stirring sugar into her treacly brew. "After the cattle attacks, dairy stuff is too expensive for people like us."

"We can adapt to anything, given time," said Jerry. "People are good like that. There was rationing in the war, and my folks got through it."

"Except this war won't stop," said Daniel.

A buzz, a screech, and a terrible thump. The café door shook, and Zoe jumped, sending coffee over the table. She looked up. A man was beating his fists on the glass, but no one moved to let him in. The chatter had stopped, and even the lawyers were quiet. Everyone was watching the man who thrashed outside in a haze of colour. Part of Zoe's mind saw a circus act, a street performer, or a fire-eater, but the rest of her mind floated off and whispered, "It can't be Frank."

A chainsaw squeal, and a yellow fly streaked onto the man's hand. It twitched and shook, and its head burrowed into his flesh. He screamed, and a trail of sizzling blue shot into his mouth. A fat abdomen flapped from his lips, like a swollen tongue. Then it disappeared, like a rat down a hole. The man stomped and waved and grabbed his throat, and his eyes bulged, like a choking diner. Then he fell limp, like a puppet with cut strings. He slid down the door, leaving a glistening trail on the glass, and the skein of lights tightened around his body in a throbbing, blurry corset.

A lawyer retched. Crockery smashed behind the counter, and the waitress stumbled out, keening like a witch, and vomited.

Zoe tried to stand, but Daniel grabbed her arm. "Not yet," he hissed.

"That was Frank," Zoe moaned. "I rang him. He was coming to meet us."

"Did anyone else see that?" asked Jerry. He grabbed his head and rocked. "Has someone put something in the fucking coffee, or what?"

Sirens started, and a policeman edged forward and peered out, but there was no corpse on the ground, and no smears on the glass—just a few wisps of colour coiling down the road. A patrol car screeched up, and the two café policemen ran outside.

Jerry twitched, and his hands shook. "They'll kill us all, won't they?"

Daniel looked calm. "They might." He glanced at Zoe.

Zoe forced the pieces of her mind back together. She gobbled two white tablets and took a swig of water. Then she stared through the window as the four policemen wrapped things

93

up. The taller one from the café had his hand hovering over his gun, and he was looking at the sky.

Jerry grabbed the sides of the table. "Can't we just nuke them or drench them with pesticides?"

Daniel leant forward. "No, *nothing* will work—it's too late. The government knows, but what can it do? Maybe if they'd acted sooner, when the warning signs first appeared..."

"What about the public? Didn't anyone guess?"

"You didn't," said Daniel, "and you work in the field. And things don't look too bad to the average person: they hear about attacks, but they don't understand the implications. The mainstream news is bland, and the rumblings on the edge get drowned out. *Or howled down...*"

"*You* knew," said Jerry. "*You* saw it coming."

"It's Cassandra's curse, and I hit a brick wall—again and again—so I gave up."

"What's next?" asked Jerry.

"The virus was our last hope. And the flies *knew*. The bastards *knew...*"

Zoe was staring into space.

"What is it?" asked Jerry. "What's up?"

Zoe turned to face him, but her eyes were blank. She waved at the general outdoors. "The world's got a few years left, but we're finished. It looks safe, but they're biding their time..."

"They won't smash themselves against the café windows if they don't have to," observed Daniel. "They'll get us in the street."

There was a shout from the kitchen, metal crashed, and the waitress swore at the cook. And something blue zoomed from the back, buzzing low like a model helicopter.

Crushing the Squamafly Eve

The Great Mind looked back over the awful rise of the squamaflies. Time-leaking scales had made the insects precognitive and fast-evolving, and they'd evaded all predators, and bred until the food ran out. Then they had turned on each other, and the resulting time-vortices had torn reality apart. Quadrillions of flies had died and...

The Great Mind, fast and insectile, enjoyed the symmetry: squamaflies had broken reality and created this latest version of the Great Mind, a *Squamafly* Mind. There was no blaming time machines this time; nature had done it alone.

The Great Mind sifted through history and then, with great precision, and a shudder of dread, it killed a butterfly.

Fly in the Web

Alison was mere inches from the spectral finger. She pushed her hand through swaying silk, and the web collapsed. And a butterfly fell out, broken and shrivelled and dead.

"Ali, time for school!" called her father.

Alison dashed to the house, grabbed her bag, thumped down the steps, and checked the body.

Keys rattled. "You OK, Pumpkin?"

"Yes, Daddy, I'm fine."

"Hop in."

Alison threw her bag onto the back seat and clambered in.

Her father rattled the front door and made his way to the car. "You strapped in?"

She nodded. "I saw a dead butterfly," she announced, as they reversed out of the driveway. "He was blue."

"Things die, Darling; nature's cruel."

"A *spider* killed the butterfly, Daddy. *Spiders* are cruel."

He twisted round and raised his arms. "I'm a spider, and I'll get *you*."

She squealed. "No Daddy, don't." And then, she laughed—a happy, tinkling, girly sound.

Drive Away

Seven years had passed since the Great Mind had crushed the Squamafly Eve, and Alison was now fourteen, and her future was bright. But changing history strains reality, and little worlds bud off. Quiet sidings open up...

Alison stepped off the school bus and blinked. Behind her, there was no strain of engine, no grind of gears, and no smell of diesel. She turned and squinted down the road. The bus had vanished, and so had the thin girl and her young sister from next door. And the lanky, funny, mop-haired boy from the other school had also gone.

Black parrots chased across the perfect sky, squawked, and shot off. A faraway dog barked, and another one answered. And a warm breeze blew her dress and ruffled her short hair. She cupped a hand to her ear, frowned at her lack of curls, and listened. But she heard no chatter, and no cars, and no drone from the highway.

The house behind had a nice lawn, several bushes, and a big shady tree. Fresh paint glistened from its planks, and its windows sparkled. But it had no garage, no driveway, and no car. And beside Alison, there was no bus stop and no bench. And the concrete bus shelter on the other side of the road had disappeared. The houses beyond were prim and painted and carless. She scratched her head and frowned. "I've had a haircut and got off at the wrong stop, that's all."

She pulled the straps of her backpack, grunted, rolled her shoulders, looked both ways, and walked into the road. The blacktop had gone, and so had the white line. This was a road of pale grit, like a country lane.

A buzz made her turn. Dozens of butterflies zinged above the gravel, and the heat haze made them ripple, like fish in a shallow sea. Alison giggled, and the insects danced away and sang a high and haunting song. Butterflies don't sing, she thought and shrugged.

She reached the pavement and stood in front of a garage-free house and squinted at its windows with their delicate net curtains. Then she looked back, shielding her eyes, trying to glimpse the butterflies. But nothing moved in the road, and nothing flew in the air, and nothing cried in the trees.

She walked down the narrow lane between the houses and peered over the wooden fence. The shed was there with its cream walls and green roof.

"It *was* the right stop," she muttered. "I *am* home."

A magpie, perched on the shed's ridge tiles, eyed her knowingly.

"I'll get you some cheese, Maggie," she called.

The great black bird took off, screeching.

The shed was her father's studio. Perhaps it had survived *because* it had no car inside. Or maybe only *other* people's garages had vanished. Maybe *her* house was OK. Lost in thought, she rounded the corner and stumbled into a new hedge. She yelped and brushed herself down. And her fingers caught in silk. Alison tore at the spiderweb, and something crisp and dusty-blue fell out. She stared at her house. It was definitely *her* house,

98

but the driveway had gone. Her memory might be playing tricks
—she'd forgotten her haircut, after all—but she *did* remember
the driveway. She remembered it being laid, for heaven's sake.
She'd pressed her nose against the dirty glass and watched them
dig the earth. *And* pour the concrete. *And* smooth it out. *And* hose
it down. It *had* been real. It *had* been there—for years.

A new path cut to her front door; it was wide, with a neat
border of flowers. They don't just *take* things, she thought as she
stepped over the polished stones, they *make* them, too. She
stared back across her altered garden—with bushes where its
driveway should have been—then she sighed and climbed the
steps to the porch. And there she froze, for the front door's
window was new, and huge, and bright, and multicoloured—and
filled with a stained-glass, angry eagle.

Alison swung the schoolbag off her back, grunted with
relief, and dug inside amongst the books. She pulled out a
woollen purse with tassels and stitched flowers. "You're not
mine," she muttered. But she knew it was. It wasn't plastic, and
there was no grinning monkey printed on the side, but it *was*
hers. She poked inside her altered purse, but there was no key,
and no bus pass. "I suppose," she said, "if there aren't any buses,
then I don't need a bus pass. But I *do* need a key."

"That you, Pumpkin?" her father asked from behind the
stained-glass eagle. And as he moved he rippled—and the eagle
rippled, too.

"Yes, Daddy."

The door rattled open, he stood aside, and she shot in,
dropping her bag in the hall.

And as her bag hit the floorboards, the world missed a beat.

"What's happened to the car?" she asked as she pounded into the front room.

"I washed it, that's all. And Alison, *put your bag in your room!*"

"But Daddy—"

She stared through the grubby window at her old driveway. The little car shone red in the afternoon sun, and the concrete underneath was damp.

She scratched her head and felt her long and curly hair. "No haircut, after all," she said. Then she looked at her purse, and a happy monkey looked back.

PART THREE

INDUSTRIAL REVOLUTIONS

Parallelograph

Her mother had rarely ventured more than a few blocks from this house. And in her later years, she hadn't left the place at all, confined to the ground floor, shuttling from bed to lounge to kitchen, like a human locomotive shunting along a forgotten siding. Maybe she'd travelled in her mind...

And with that comforting idea, Rose levered herself from the bed, grunted, and stepped into the living room. I must return the walking frame, she thought, but not today. She dropped into her father's winged armchair and stared across the coffee table, with its piled-up magazines, and past the potted plants, and through the net curtains. The church opposite hadn't changed, and the traffic still flowed. Everyone's dead, she thought, but everything looks the same. She stroked the diary's cover and squinted at the golden numbers. The little book was sixty years old, five years older than she was.

Rose flipped through pages of left-leaning scrawl; she understood most of it and she smiled at the names of her aunties and grandparents. Her mother's words crammed the days of January and February, but they stopped in March. Then, halfway through April, her own handwriting took over. She tensed, adjusted her glasses, and read about the last few weeks—the period since her mother's death. Some details were wrong—she hadn't gone to the local pub or swum in the town pool—but overall, the story was accurate.

The blue writing—*her* writing—stopped on today's date. She shook her head, blinked, and massaged her neck. Outside, the traffic roared. She drew the curtains against the evening rush and she shivered. The ornaments, the books, the furniture, and the framed prints on the wall—all so familiar—had shifted to the wrong side of normal. The house was breathing. And it wanted her out.

Rose checked her watch. Her friend was due in twenty minutes. But twenty minutes was too long. She slipped the diary into her pocket, picked up her bag, and grabbed her coat. She stopped in the hallway, and the upstairs darkness called. *Come up,* it seemed to say. *I'm waiting.* The back window creaked, the just-swept chimney howled, and a dog barked. She grabbed the wine from the hall table, stepped outside, struggled into her coat, and locked the door. She put the bottle on the shared wall of the porch, buttoned up, and checked her watch: fifteen minutes to go. She shivered as cars roared past. "It's not my time," she mumbled, "or my place."

"Hi," said Sylvia from the street. "I'm early."

"Thank God. It felt like midnight in there," said Rose, and she hurried to the gate. "Where did you park?"

"Miles away, up Percy Street. Come on, let's go."

Twenty minutes later, they were sharing the bottle of Shiraz, dinner was on, and rich tomatoey smells floated in from the kitchen.

Sylvia leant forward, and strings of wooden beads knocked across her chest. "Are you OK?"

Rose shrugged. "I was. Until today. I suppose it's finally sinking in. The house seemed…"

"Haunted?"

Rose took a gulp of wine. "Yes, and I had to get out. It must be guilt."

"You think your mum resented you being away?"

Rose nodded.

"It's all in your head," said Sylvia. "Your mum didn't mind. Children move on. I should know, Liz is in America. And getting married."

"Sorry, I didn't know," said Rose. "I mean, I'm glad she's getting married, just sorry she's so far away."

"I miss her, but I'm OK—happy for her, and happy for myself. I'm sure your mum felt the same."

"I hope so. She wanted grandchildren, but…"

"Right," said Sylvia, slapping her thighs and jumping up, "enough of that. It's time to eat."

Rose leant forward.

"Sit down, it won't take long."

Rose slumped into the fat cushions with their thick-stitched monkeys and looked around. The mantlepiece had a carriage clock, a brass microscope, and a sandy-coloured ammonite the size of a dinner plate. Books were everywhere, and some she recognised from years ago. As teenagers, they'd scoured the discount sections of bookshops, competing to build their libraries. In the end, Sylvia had won. But their tastes had diverged. Here, in Sylvia's house, were classics, high literature, history, and politics—topics of no interest to Rose.

A new television filled the corner. Rose couldn't remember Sylvia ever watching TV, but things change. And people change. Think of the books. Rose dug into her pocket and fished out her mother's diary. She flicked through to today's date and stared at the blue words. Then she rummaged in her bag and pulled out a pen with four inks. She selected red and wrote, *"Hello diary."*

"What's that?" asked Sylvia.

Rose jumped, and the diary flew out of her hand. She grabbed it and knocked her drink. "Shit, I'm really sorry."

"No harm done. I'm used to wine stains, hence the red carpet." Sylvia went back to the kitchen and returned with a damp cloth. "Well, what is it?"

"Just Mum's old diary."

"You've read it?"

"No, I just skimmed it. It's mainly boring lists and notes. I'll go through it later." Rose shrugged and popped the little book into her bag.

A few minutes later, Sylvia dumped a pan of bubbling puttanesca on the table. Rose tossed a salad of rocket, olives, and avocados, and they helped themselves to pasta.

"Cheers," said Rose, "and thanks."

Glasses clinked.

"No more death and diaries and house clearing," said Sylvia, "let's talk about work, *or men.*"

Rose blushed.

"OK, tell me about the world of physics…"

After dinner, they cradled brandies and reminisced. They were lost in the past, when the carriage clock ticked hard, as if to rouse them, and Rose looked up. It was eleven-thirty. "The hours have flown," she said, "and yet…"

"Go on."

"Look at that fossil. The hours mean nothing to it. The thing's ancient…" Rose trailed off, unable to finish the thought.

"It's made of stone, and it's been dead for millions of years. Death messes with your sense of time."

Rose nodded. "It's not just a change of perspective, though, is it? The dead are different. To them, a minute or a million years are just the same. Time vanishes. It's an absolute change. Time—feeling time pass, feeling it flow through you—is what life's about."

"Enough about death, it's time for bed."

Sylvia fussed, bringing towels and showing Rose where everything was in the spare bedroom.

"Thanks for putting me up. I couldn't have stayed in the old house."

"This place is lived in, that's all," said Sylvia. "I hope you're cosy here."

Rose nodded. "I am. It's lovely. Thanks."

"OK," said Sylvia, "good night."

"Good night," said Rose, and she snuggled under the duvet and imagined her mother's house. She pictured herself walking around upstairs. And in her mind, she entered her remembered teenage bedroom and she stroked the long-gone posters and the old ornaments. From the safety of Sylvia's bed, she pulled a thrown-away book from a taken-down shelf. And leafed through it. This was an expedition into the past, a private archaeology. Her mother's house—and Rose's childhood home—was a shipwreck, a forbidden place, something swallowed by history. *Move on,* it said, *you're not welcome. I want to sink in peace.*

Morning came, and sunlight filtered in. Rose groaned, turned to face the wall, and pulled up the duvet.

Sylvia tapped on the door. "Tea?"

"Oh, thanks." Rose forced herself upright and took the cup. She rubbed her forehead and groaned. "I had too much wine last night."

"Tell me about it. I've put on coffee, eggs, and toast."

"Perfect." Rose slurped her tea and grinned.

As soon as Sylvia had gone, Rose put down her cup, grabbed her glasses, and reached for the diary. In yesterday's space, the words "Hello Rose" had appeared. In blue ink.

Forking Out

Back in her mother's house, Rose surveyed the overstuffed front room, as Sylvia clattered down the garden path. A metallic click, and more footsteps, and a bang as the gate slammed shut. Then came the roar of a heavy truck, and the tinkle of a bell, and a sparrow's twitter. Rose felt like a sudden invalid who was straining to hear the world outside.

"You can't stay here by yourself, it's not *healthy*," Sylvia had said, before sweeping out. "I'll pick you up at five."

It was already eleven in the morning. At one o'clock, she'd run to the deli for a sandwich. At three, she would go to the corner shop for more wine. At four, she'd stroll around the block and window-shop the past...

Sunlight poured in through dirty glass. She walked over, sniffed the net curtains, and got a sharp and dusty smell from childhood. The old house had recovered from its bad mood and was chatting to her about the past, and it felt like home again.

Rose climbed the stairs with only the slightest tingle in her gut. She padded down the hallway carpet to the front bedroom, walked over to the window, and stared at the church. Cars and trucks ground past, and a memory surfaced of dark Saturdays, when football crowds had surged by, and she'd looked down and felt safe and thrilled. It was, she recalled, like being on safari and watching a stampede from a tree-house.

Rose thumped onto the double bed, which creaked and shot out dust. She opened the little diary and stared at the neat blue words in tomorrow's space: "A jet exploded over London today. Has it happened in your world?"

She selected red ink and wrote, "I'll check the news. You can be Blue Rose and I'll be Red."

Rose glanced at her watch, walked downstairs, switched on the TV, and flipped to news. But there was nothing about an air crash. She stared through the bay window, listened to the murmur of traffic, and wondered about Blue Rose. Had their lives diverged that much? Was the jet safe in this history? Then she remembered that the message was in tomorrow's page.

"What day are you?" she wrote in red ink.

"Wednesday," answered the diary in blue ink.

"It's Tuesday here," she wrote in red.

The diary pushed against her fingers, as the invisible blue pen wrote, "We're drifting apart in time."

"What do we do?"

"We wait," said the little book.

"OK, let's talk tomorrow." Rose snapped the diary shut and gazed at the busy day beyond her window.

Ahead of Myself

Late Wednesday evening, Rose sat in the winged armchair and watched an emergency worker pointing at a smoking building. Blue and red lights strobed across concrete, then a graphical plane exploded. Blue Rose had watched the same pictures, on the same screen, from the same chair. And she'd done it first, in what was now her yesterday.

Rose opened the diary and wrote, "The plane blew up here at 9.08pm."

"Same time here," appeared in blue ink.

Rose massaged her brow. Pain clouds gathered around her skull as she tried to make sense of things. The blue words dated from her arrival at her mother's house, she realised. That was when they'd split apart. But Blue Rose was travelling faster in time.

She wrote in red, "Since we're drifting apart, please write your messages in your current date."

Blue writing appeared in the space for the day after tomorrow: "No problem."

"Dear Blue Rose, you're speeding up. We can measure how close our histories are. Let's use exchange rates as a proxy. The pound is worth $1.702."

A few minutes later, in blue: "3.30pm, 3 May. The pound is only worth $1.655. It dropped after the crash."

At half past three on Friday afternoon, Red Rose sat in the winged armchair and wrote in red, "3.30pm, 3 May, my time. The pound is worth $1.653. We've diverged by $0.002."

The diary jerked, and blue words scratched themselves across the page: "Look at 31 December. Now!"

Rose tore through the pages and gawped at the final entry for the year: "I've just found the diary. I'll send you stuff! Look back twelve pages. TAKE CARE. Love Rose." It was written in green ink.

Red Rose flipped back, but the pages were blank. Then something tugged at the diary as if a ghost child were grabbing it. Rose swept her arm across the table, sending stacks of letters flying, and a biscuit tin clattering onto the floor. She held the diary open, pinning down its corners with her fingers and thumbs. Neat green words appeared, and her cheeks tingled, rushing sensations coursed down her arms, and shivers ran down her back. These were stock prices from late December. The invisible green pen added currency values, lending rates, commodity prices, and house values.

The diary stopped vibrating, and Red Rose looked up, groaned, and massaged her shoulders.

Another jerk, and the green writing started again: "You'll need capital. Be discreet and don't be greedy."

It wrote names, dates, times, football results, winning horses, and cricket scores.

"Oh, and register these domains." Fifty confected words appeared. "Just the dot-coms."

The diary went still, and Red Rose wrote: "Thanks Green Rose."

"Yes, thanks Green Rose." Appeared in blue ink. But Green Rose didn't answer.

"She's gone," wrote Blue. "I bet this diary only works for this year, and Green Rose has already moved into next."

"How did she get so far ahead?" wrote Red Rose.

Blue writing appeared: "We discovered the diary early, and that kept us close. But Green Rose found it much later, so her bond with us was weaker, and she flew ahead."

"How many are we?" wrote Red Rose.

Blue writing started in next week: "There could be millions of us, and those who never found the diary must be years ahead by now..."

Rose frowned and took up her pen: "I feel that I'm the one and only me, and I assume that you feel the same about yourself. Maybe we're the same person, but divided by the moments."

Blue Rose wrote, "No, our exchange rates differ. And we write different words in different inks. You won't grow into me. We're NOT the same."

Rose sniffled. Blue Rose had moved into next week, and Green Rose had gone into next year.

She thought about her other selves—the ones who'd missed the diary. They could be decades ahead. They could be dead of old age.

She shook her head, grabbed another notebook—one that wouldn't change—and copied everything from Green Rose.

The next day, the blue and red and green had gone. She flipped back to her mother's slanting script and closed the book. Outside, the traffic hissed.

Bad Luck Café

January the fifth was bad luck for Rose, and so was The Lookout Café.

"A table for two, please," said Rose, and she fingered the black and gold card. "I'm responding to your invitation."

"Certainly, madam," said the silky voice. "We look forward to seeing you at seven-thirty on the fifth."

Rose hung up. Maybe all the negatives will cancel out, she thought. Maybe the invitation was a good sign. She called Sylvia. "Hi, I've booked the restaurant. It's time to face my fears —and who can resist a free dinner?"

"Great, let's live dangerously."

The Lookout Café is not a café, and it has no view. Thirty years ago, it *was* a café. It sold milkshakes, weak coffees, cakes, biscuits, and chocolate bars. It had plastic chairs, and its tables wobbled. And it closed at five. It had sweeping views, and you could sit near the window, cradling your drink, and look across the park lawns, and glimpse the artificial lake through the ancient oaks. You might see a toy yacht bob over tiny waves, and a boy squat on the bank. On the path outside the café, there were mothers with prams and people slurping ice cream. If you craned your neck, you could see the little church and its private graveyard. The whole span of life was there. And you could still see red squirrels.

Then the Council ran out of money, and luxury apartments grew where the flower beds had been. The café lost its view, then it lost its customers. It closed, got boarded up, and graffiti spread like ivy. And broken bottles, and crushed cans, and sweet wrappers collected outside.

One windy autumn afternoon, as the light drained from the sky, a dapper man came past and stared at the sad café. He stood with his collar turned up, and his hands lightly clasped behind his back, and he inclined his head and sniffed. He had the air of one who'd been away, learnt many things, and then returned. And the man, whose name was Rick, felt his bowels stir. And he always listened to his guts.

The next day, he bought the building and the name. Now you had to book weeks in advance to get a table at The Lookout Café. And it didn't open until seven.

Rose had christened it *The Bad Luck Café* when she was still a teenager and it still sold milkshakes.

At thirteen, she was slurping a strawberry shake and enjoying the sunshine at an outdoor table, when her cat, Horace, went under the wheels of a car. She hoped he wasn't trying to reach her—cats rarely follow their owners—but you never know. Cats do strange things.

A year later, Myrtle, her bouncy spaniel, had twitched and died at home while Rose ate crisps at the café.

At fifteen, she'd met a boy there, her first date, a slender mop-haired kid from school. He'd arrived late and drummed his fingers and stared out of the window. She'd tried her best and asked him things, but all she got were grunts and *maybes*. Then

114

he left without offering to pay. Outside, he'd teamed up with a friend. And laughed. And shaken his head. And slouched off.

She'd sat there, hot and seething, with her throat in knots. "You're fucking bad luck," she'd moaned. *"You're the Fucking Bad Luck Café."* After that, she stopped going.

When she was much older, and far braver, she'd returned. By then, the rubbish bin outside was wonky and the ice cream sign —with its faded rocket-lolly—was rusty and bent. Inside, the place smelt milky and rancid, and the counter was smeary, and the cakes were few. The waitress, greasy-haired and grubby, surged forwards. *"Yes?"*

"Coffee, please."

"That with milk?" The girl sneered and cleared her throat.

"Just black, thanks."

"Sugar's on the table," said the girl, handing her a chipped mug.

Rose paid, ignored the tips jar, and picked a table near the window. She cradled her coffee and stared at the bleak park. Outside, a woman pushed a pram, and a toddler ran beside her, muffled up and pulling a toy. It was January the fifth, so the toy was a Christmas present. Rose took another sip and groaned. A pimply youth in the corner smirked, belched, and returned to his comic.

Four blocks away, her father clutched his chest.

It was a quarter past seven on January the fifth, and Rose and Sylvia stood at reception. Rose sucked in the fragrant air and tried to calm herself, but her hand twitched.

The manager looked up and cocked his head like a mantis. "Dr Rose Ferrel and *partner.*" He grinned. "Your table will be ready shortly. Perhaps you'd care for a cocktail while you wait." It wasn't a question.

Rose stared at his face, and the pimply youth stared back—straight from the day when her father had died.

"Thanks," said Sylvia. She took Rose's elbow and guided her to the bar. "What would you like?"

"Whiskey and soda, please."

"Two please," said Sylvia.

The girl in black nodded and turned to prepare the drinks. She was slinky and slender and deft, and she glanced at her watch, as if she were expecting someone. She handed the glasses to Sylvia. "It's an unusual malt, and a specialty of the house. What do you think?"

Sylvia smacked her lips. "Smokey."

"I think it burns," said the girl. "And it has a high cost."

"Don't you mean price?" asked Rose.

"Quite." The girl frowned at her watch as if it had stopped. She tapped its glass. "It plays up sometimes."

"It's very pretty." Sylvia leant across. "And it glows."

"Useless for keeping time, though." She extended her wrist. "Listen."

Sylvia put her ear to the warm glass. "It's buzzing."

"Sometimes it buzzes and sometimes it ticks. And sometimes, it sings—you can never tell. I like holding it against my ear because it reminds me of faraway seas."

Rose stared. The slinky girl wavered and became the sneering girl—with apron smeared and hands on hips, and a cheap watch on her wrist.

"Ladies," said the dapper man, resting his hand on Rose's shoulder. "Welcome to my café." He fixed Rose with a stare. "I'm Rick, and I hope you enjoy your meal."

Rose's jaw dropped. "Thank you. And, er, thanks for the invitation."

116

"My pleasure," said Rick, and he nodded and stepped away. He held himself like a cavalier, and his jacket was finely cut, and his voice was soft and strong—like the murmuring of a distant ocean—and he radiated power. He should have held a cane or a sword-stick. And for a moment, he seemed to.

"You're shaking," said Sylvia. "Look at you, like a teenager with a crush."

"I'm not," said Rose, wringing her hands and blushing. "Not at all."

Pete Misses His Appointment

Pete wandered up to his old laptop, pressed the power button, and sank into his chair. A green light twinkled, then came a worrying grind and a bright chime. He hunched forwards and glared at the flat and graphic landscape. Another chime rang out, the fan screamed, and he was in. A few quick clicks, and the emails appeared. There was nothing of interest except a reminder about the dentist the following day. He opened it, but there were no details, just *"DON'T GO!"* all in caps. He frowned, the fan stopped, and the screen went blank.

"Bloody thing," he muttered, and he slammed down the lid. He stood up, arched his back, thought about virus protection, and completely forgot about his dental appointment.

At 9.40 the following morning, in the centre of town, Pete was swimming in the fifty-metre pool, as was his custom. The water was warm and clear, and he peered through his goggles, pretending to be a submarine. It was his final lap, and he was looking forward to a hot shower. He touched the tiles at the end of the lane, swam to the steps, and grasped the handrail. At the instant his hand touched the metal, a slate grey car hit a petrol tanker.

Pete staggered from the pool. He enjoyed the heavy, muscular sensation of emerging from water, and he stood dripping on the side, savouring the moment. Then he struggled into his flip-flops, picked up his bag, put on his glasses, and blinked. Across town, less than a mile from the dentist, the car and tanker went up like a bomb.

After a leisurely shower, he dried off and started another fight with his clothes. Dressing would have been easier had Pete been normal, but he liked to put his pants and shorts on together, and then wriggle into his tee shirt while it was still inside his jacket. It was the reverse of how he got undressed. He thought it saved time, but he usually stumbled or poked his arm through the wrong hole. Today, he stubbed his toe.

There was no rush, so he took the lake road home. He flipped a switch, and his window opened, letting in warm air and bird sounds.

Close behind him, an enormous woman, crammed into a rounded miniature car that was more kitchen appliance than vehicle, glowered and gibbered and shrugged and waved her paper mug. Pete dropped his speed and clenched his wheel. She pulled out and an oncoming car flashed and screeched to a halt. The woman swerved back, and her drink—which Pete sincerely hoped was scalding coffee—flew everywhere.

He was still shaking when he arrived home, and his key missed the lock and clattered onto the tiles. He picked it up, swore, and tried again.

He dropped his bag in the hall, grabbed an iced coffee, and slumped in front of his unreliable computer. Five minutes later, two emails appeared. The first was an overdue reminder about his dental appointment at ten in the morning. The second email used his full name as the subject line. He opened it and scanned the introduction which promised vast wealth via a certain foreign stock. Feeling prudent, he hit delete before he read the rest. And so he missed the details about himself that only he could have known. And he missed his own name at the bottom. And he missed the future date...

The computer's whine became a shriek, and it shut down. Pete called the dentist, apologised for his failing memory, and rescheduled for the following week.

He swigged the last of his coffee, swore at his crippled laptop, and then loaded it, along with an old printer, a tape player, and a scanner, into the boot of his car and then he set off for the waste facility.

Pete hated the tip. He resented the drive, and he worried about punctures from screws, and metal, and broken glass. He stopped to read the signs and as he did so, the car behind, with a trailer full of branches, hooted, then shot past in a cloud of dust. Pete turned left when he should have turned right, backtracked, circled twice, and finally arrived at a bin full of computers, televisions, cables, and keyboards. He stared straight ahead, clenched the wheel, and took a deep breath. He hated driving, he hated other drivers, and he hated the tip.

After taking a moment to compose himself, he climbed out, opened the boot, and scratched his head. He eased the printer out and threw it in the bin, returned, grabbed the laptop, and span round.

"I'll take that," said the attendant. The man had perfect teeth, a smooth complexion, piercing green eyes, and a spotless uniform.

"Good luck," said Pete. "The bloody thing barely works."

"I love a challenge," replied the grinning man. Carrying the computer as carefully as a new mother carrying a new baby, he walked to a purring maroon car, doffed an imaginary hat at Pete, and climbed into the back seat. There was a flick of blond hair in the driver's window, and the car scrunched off.

Rick sank into rich leather, hummed an old tune, brushed the dust from the laptop's lid, and watched the bins and cages and trees roll past. He pictured the rig that waited at the lab with its freezing plate, and its clear plastic hood, and its cylinders of cold gas. With this level of cooling, Pete's computer could run for two minutes at full temporal extension—enough to reach far into the future and receive emails from an even older version of Rick...

Cataphractal Corporation

Dr Rose Ferrel sat in her office, flicked the buttons of her multicoloured pen, and revolved on her peculiar introduction to Rick. A lot had happened since that fateful night at the Bad Luck Café, and they'd become entwined, personally and professionally. She tapped the pen against her teeth and thought of her mother's diary, and the secrets that it held, and the riches that it brought.

She gazed at the rig in the adjacent lab, with its bottles and fans and tubes, and wondered where it would all end. They'd built the cooling system for Rick's computer, and they'd glimpsed the future. But now he wanted more, he wanted to see further. And seeing further was crucial because now they had competition.

"They're losing years of work," Rick had explained, referring to well-placed friends. "They do all this secret stuff, only to find that their ideas have already been patented…"

They had to shield the future, but protecting tomorrow's ideas was impossible with existing technology. They needed something new. She pushed the pen's red slider and drew a circle, then added a box in black, an arrow in green, and a note in blue. She drew in red again and grinned: the impossible anti-spy device could invent itself. If she *wanted* the machine, iterating time-loops would build it. And Rick's precognitive computer, weak though it was, could start the loop.

She reached for the phone.

The following day, Rick arrived at Rose's lab and gave her a peck on the cheek. He laid his padded bag on the bench, unzipped three sides, and withdrew Pete's laptop. "Your call was timed to perfection," he said. "This is a magnificent machine—vastly more powerful than my last one. It reaches years into the future—more than enough to make your loop. Problem solved."

"Let's hope so."

"Is the cooler ready?" he asked.

She nodded and opened the door to the lab. The refrigeration machine filled the wooden island bench. Its clear plastic hood was two metres across, with hinged openings front and back. From the sides, thick tubes snaked into the floor, and bottles of gas stood waiting by the bench. Fans hummed, and timers ticked.

Rick smiled. "Perfect. Let's go!" He leant through the front opening and put the laptop on the cooling plate, taking care not to touch the freezing metal.

Rose reached through the back of the hood, plugged a power cord into the laptop, attached a data cable, and nodded. "All done."

Rick opened his new machine and pressed its button. There was a grind and a chime. He tapped in his password, stepped back, and shut the hood's front flap.

Rose closed the back, checked the seals and turned the knob. Gas hissed, and fans hummed. "All set."

The laptop shimmered.

"It's connected to the future," said Rick. The gauge jumped ten degrees. "Hold on, it's burning up. *Quick!*"

123

Rose twisted the knob and slammed the slider, and the gas jets screamed, and the fans roared.

Rick peered through the rattling, frosting hood at the laptop's tiny screen. "Something's happening. Have you got anything?"

Rose checked the external computer—the one linked to the laptop by the data cable—and shook her head. The screen flashed. "Wait, there's writing." She leant closer. "And pictures!"

Rick checked the dial. "Are we done yet?"

Rose scrolled through six pages of text, and two diagrams. She peered at the end of the document and pursed her lips. "Looks like everything's here."

Rick kept his eyes on the rig as the laptop's casing dulled, and its screen went dark, and it shut down.

Rose reached across, twisted the knob, and pushed the slider home. The gas stopped hissing, and the fans slowed. "Come and look."

Rick trundled over in his chair, leant his chin on her shoulder, and gaped at the screen. "Well, bugger me."

The instructions looked simple enough—they could easily build the device with what they had in the lab—but what held their attention was the date at the bottom. They'd signed it two years from now. The time loop was set.

For two years, they worked on the gadget, honing its design, and tweaking its components, and updating the instructions as they went.

It was five to midnight, and tomorrow was the deadline, *Loop Time,* as they called it, the date of the first signing. The machine sat on the bench and blue lights flickered down its edges. It hummed and hunkered down, turned glassy, shimmered, and flashed. Then the humming stopped, and the device became solid again.

Rose faced the giant screen of the main computer, scrolled through the pages one last time, and then she changed the document's version number to two.

"That's it," said Rick. He pressed the laptop's power button. A tiny green light came on and a chime rang out. He logged in. "Send the instructions through."

Rose transferred the data, all the words and pictures, from the main computer to the laptop and gave Rick the thumbs up.

Hulking refrigeration units screamed, and ice sparkled. The laptop shimmered—and connected to its earlier self.

"All done," said Rick, "let's hope our earlier versions are ready."

Two years in the past, another Rose and Rick received the instructions as planned. Like their counterparts, they slaved on the technology for two years, updating the text and pictures as they went. And just as before, and just prior to *Loop Time*, Rose changed the document's version number to three and sent it back in time.

And another Rose and Rick received the improved instructions and repeated the process...

The billionth iteration of Rose checked the seals and turned the knob. Gas hissed, and fans hummed. "All set."

The laptop shimmered.

"It's connected to the future," said Rick. The gauge jumped ten degrees. "Hold on, it's burning up. *Quick!*"

Rose twisted the knob and slammed the slider, and the gas jets screamed, and the fans roared.

Rick peered through the rattling, frosting hood at the laptop's tiny screen. "Something's happening. Have you got anything?"

Rose checked the external computer and shook her head. The screen flashed. "Wait, there's writing." She leant closer. "And pictures!"

He checked the dial. "Are we done yet?"

Rose scrolled through hundreds of pages. "Yep, got everything."

Rick grinned. "See, it worked first time. No need for loops."

"Mmm," said Rose, selecting the last line of text. She pressed delete and *Final Version, Edition 1,000,000,001* vanished.

The laptop exploded with a dull thud, shaking the rig, and filling the icy dome with a snowstorm of metal and plastic.

Rose fumbled in her bag and pulled out the diary. Her mother's scrawl remained, but all the extra stuff—all those coloured messages from herself and her other versions—had long since gone. But she loved it as a talisman. Like the laptop, it was a humble thing that hinged—a thing that opened a gateway and worked miracles. And died. "Where have you all gone?" she mumbled, stroking the blank pages.

"What?" asked Rick.

"Oh, nothing, I was just thinking aloud."

Rick stared at the document. "There's a lot to do."

"I think most of the work's already done," said Rose, and she peered at an empty November—blank pages that another Rose had once filled with tiny writing from the future. Rose had grown rich, but she never became that other Rose. She never wrote those lines. She gazed across the lab. Those other diary-selves lived, she presumed, in private histories, diverging forever. But what happened to the billion time-loop Roses? Had they survived or had they vanished after each cycle? And had they dragged the whole world with them when they looped? How many people had died a billion deaths to create this technology? How many babies were born in loops, never to reach their second birthdays?

Rose stroked her belly. She'd never had children—her womb had never stretched—and it was too late now. She thought of Rick and their sterile couplings—hundreds of billions of heated fornications—erased by the loops.

Rick fussed over his exploded laptop. "I hope it was worth it."

"We'll build something better, I'm sure."

Just beyond the lab, a machine stopped running. In the recoil of the new silence, Rose shivered and remembered that Liz was three months pregnant, and that Sylvia was thrilled to be a grandmother—for the billionth time.

Rick and Rose spent the next two years building a suitcase-sized machine that was crammed with heat sinks, fans, and pumps, all focused on a dark core that hummed and flashed.

"Not exactly pretty," said Rick, rocking on his heels as if he were appraising a new sculpture. "But I love it."

"Let's hope it works," said Rose. But she knew it would because the plans from the future—a billion iterated futures— were perfect in every detail.

They installed the machine in the dismal cellar below the lab, where it was cool and quiet and out of the way. And there it sat, humming and twinkling and warding off future snoops.

Upstairs, in the airy front office, they created Cataphractal Corporation to commercialise the technology. Money poured in, the spies were blocked, and business became fairer.

But free enterprise abhors equality and looks for an edge.

"They want more," said Rick, clattering around the vault like a petulant jailer. "I have three major clients bending my ear for self-spying."

Rose shrugged. "You think it's safe to release that technology?" She stared at the flashing green light. It was hypnotic, and the white-noise-hum of the cooling systems relaxed her, blocking out the world, blocking out *all* the worlds.

"A glimpse into your own future can't be *that* bad." Rick slid an arm around her waist. "We achieved all this with just one look. And nothing's gone wrong..."

Rose imagined the snuffed-out babies, and she thought of Liz going through a billion labours. Rick still talked as if it were a single iteration, and she wondered if he were that naïve. Perhaps he didn't care. Or didn't know. "Even a crippled version could be risky..."

Rick grinned. "Blocked, crippled, enfeebled, whatever it takes to make you happy..."

The green light flickered, the hum became a roar, and it was done.

An industrial revolution followed and altered the world. Diaphanous ships hung in the sky, and wide-eyed passengers peered down on impossible cities. Bubble-submarines took children into ocean trenches. Glinting engines wrought sculptures from dreams. And portable ecstasy boxes held the populace—at least those not cruising the skies or oceans—enthralled.

"Doesn't it bother you?" asked Rose.

"No, the machine—augmented though it is—looks just the same, and it still chugs along. And the money rolls in—even more money, now. What's wrong with that?"

"We trust it too much," said Rose.

"Businesses can only spy on themselves—there's no way to cheat."

"But that creates private futures," said Rose. "It partitions time. *It isn't safe...*"

"But the world," said Rick, "is fabulous. Why would you want to change it?"

The Great Mind hovered over the planet and saw the swirl. Time surfaces flexed and twitched, and tore like silk, and shrieked in brilliant yellow. Regions froze and fractured in sparkling showers of crimson. Colours ran, and burning lines whiplashed across the dimensions. This was Art on a grand scale. But, aesthetics aside, it was a worry.

Time had honeycombed into discrete columns, where private ideas shuttled from the future to the past. Rose was right: partitioning time *had* stressed reality.

The Great Mind tried to repair the damage, but twisted time-lines flung it back.

Down below, the planet prospered and spewed out radiant temporal pollution.

A deep sadness welled up in the Great Mind, for it hated to kill an innocent person, even to save a galaxy. It steeled itself, and then it reached back several years and destroyed an alien time-circuit in a humble laptop...

Pete Keeps His Appointment

Pete wandered over to his useless computer to check his emails. It always took ages to start, and it only worked for five minutes before overheating and shutting down. He had to get a newer model. But today, without its power-hungry time-circuit, the veteran machine sprang to life. His electric diary appeared, and the fan stayed quiet.

"Life in the old bugger yet," said Pete, and he nodded and noted his dental appointment.

The following day, he drove to the dentist, distracted by his throbbing tooth. A slate-grey coupé with no lights tried to edge past. Pete leant on the horn and the camouflaged car dropped back. Shaking, he checked his mirror and saw the other driver, and his swarthy passenger, give him the finger. "Stupid bastards!" he screamed.

In that exquisitely engineered moment, a petrol tanker barrelled through a stop sign. Pete slammed into its steely side, his foot still on the accelerator. The tanker driver wrenched his wheel and slammed his brakes, and the tailgater hit Pete, completing his compression. And everything detonated.

Big Flossy & The Giant Loom

Jenny called it her studio, but it was a dingy back room that stank of dust, damp timbers, and something recently cooked. She dumped her coffee on the desk, leant back, pouted, and grabbed her midriff. It's getting worse, she thought, and her mind drifted to the local gym with its dusky windows and sleek machines. Behind its glass, elegant women strode on treadmills and sipped from water bottles. She imagined swiping her card, and marching in, and nodding at them. And losing herself in that private, public space. And toning up. But she had no card...

A toilet flushed upstairs, and footsteps thumped across the ceiling. The old bastard didn't wash his hands again, she thought. TV sounds boomed down. One day he'll wash his hands, get a job, and fuck off.

There were two office chairs of the swivelling kind, with plastic frames and fabric cushions. Warren sat in the broken one, slurped his coffee, and licked his beard. His pink tongue looked like a newborn thing writhing in pubic hair, and for a moment, Jenny thought it might detach and crawl up his face, and search for a teat. He smacked his lips and slammed his mug on the table. "You couldn't *give* these chairs away," he said, and he thrust back, rattling the casters on the boards. "Especially not

131

this one 'cause it's got holes." He inserted a finger into his seat cushion and poked about. *"Something* might be living in it."

Jenny's throat tightened, and she glanced at her sketches. "Everything's crap."

"What we need is bubbly fabrics," said Warren, and he extracted a nugget of yellow foam from his chair, rolled it up, and stared at it as if it held the secrets of the universe.

The man lumbered overhead and slammed a door. And then, of all things, he began to sing.

Jenny snarled at the ceiling. "Fuck off, you silly old bastard."

Warren flicked his gaze to her breasts.

She looked down and caught him. *"Yes?"*

He sniffed the foam and flicked it on the floor. Like a schoolboy flicking snot, she thought, a stupid kid.

Warren frowned, grabbed the armrests, rocked, growled like an engine, pushed off, dropped tone to change gear, then squealed to a halt. He grinned at Jenny.

"Get to work," she said. But she smiled. And he laughed.

Jenny returned to her pad and scribbled for half an hour. "Bollocks to this, I'm getting nowhere. Let's go for lunch and you can tell me your theory. Then we can look at new chairs."

The corner pub—all red brick, and blue tile—had sash windows, heavy curtains, and faux-wood decor. The warm lounge smelt beery, with a background hint of grease. Warren sipped his pint, and Jenny stared at her half, while they waited for their order.

"Foamy fabrics," he said, "would have fabulous properties. We'd be rich."

"Fabrics are not the problem, they're cheap. *Design* is where the money is—"

"No, Jenny, *listen...*" and he explained how such materials could seep across dimensions and change fashion—*change everything*. And in the midday twilight of the pub, his words made sense...

Warren spent the afternoon hunched over his little computer. At last, he looked up. "I'm thinking feathery rather than foamy."

"Mmm." Jenny nodded and returned to her sketching. She thought about the gym again, and wondered what a suitable outfit would cost.

Back at his flat, Warren's headache threatened to become a migraine. He threw the remains of his curry into the bin and rinsed his fingers under the kitchen tap. He climbed onto a bar stool, rested his chin on his hands, and stared at the tank on the counter. An aerator spewed bubbles, and as he watched the silver stream, his head cleared. Tiny red fish darted like sparks, something like a lobster scuttled over the coloured stones, and a snail made its winding way across the glass.

And then there were the sponges, yellow and throbbing. Five huddled on the dark slate, three jiggled in the currents, held by glistening cords like underwater kites, and one bobbed free in the bubbles. They had come with the fish, these funny blobby things, hitchhiking as unseen babies on the rock. Now, they were as big as tennis balls...

One of the limpet-five detached from its slate and floated to the surface. It bounced in the bubbly waves, and it reminded Warren of a just-landed space capsule. He scooped it out, and blue oil drained across his hands, and ideas flooded his mind.

The next morning, Warren arrived at the studio with a bag of balsa wood. He tipped rods, blocks, and sheets onto his desk and grinned. Then he set to work with a knife and glue. As the week progressed, he brought in various cogs, batteries, wires, tubes, sandpapers, an electric motor, and a bottle. And with these things, he built a mediaeval-looking toy.

"It's working," he said, as Jenny arrived the following Monday. "Look."

The device, no bigger than a ream of typing paper, had a delicate open frame packed with spindles, wheels, levers, and cogs. An electric motor was bolted to one side, and a medicine bottle full of blue oil was strapped to the back.

"That's lubricant," said Warren, tapping the bottle, "for the thread. The rest is a grinder. Watch this." And he fed a length of cotton through the front slot, then he reached through the open top to pull it into the guts of the machine. He wound it round the spindles, passed it under a wire, and through several tiny gaps. Then he knotted the ends to make a loop. "Fingers crossed," he said and flipped the switch. The motor buzzed, a bulb twinkled, cogs turned, and the thread circled through the machine. "I hope the knot doesn't get caught," he said and rubbed his hands.

The gadget hummed and ground for ten minutes. Warren peered in, smiled, and switched off the motor. "It's done," he announced, as if it were a cake that had risen. He snipped the loop, pulled it out, and draped it over Jenny's hand. "Well, what do you think?"

Jenny stared. "It looks the same to me."

"Here, try this." He handed her his illuminated magnifying glass.

She peered at the glistening filament, pale blue against her palm, then she tilted her head, and squinted. "Your magnifier's no good," she said, "everything's blurry."

Warren beamed. "See?"

134

She frowned. *"No."*

"It's not the lens, and it's not your eyes. It's the *thread*." He jiggled about. "The thread *itself* is out of focus."

Jenny brought her hand closer, shut one eye, and poked the wavering filament. "It's not possible."

"Fantastic, isn't it? What you're seeing is *temporal blur:* the thread as it was, is, and will be. Each time it goes through the machine, it gets a gentle sanding. After ten minutes, the surface is all teased out and shredded—crinkly enough to spill into time. The thread should snap, but the blue liquid holds it together."

"Bloody hell," she said.

Warren smiled. "Impressed?"

Jenny nodded. "What would happen if you made cloth from this stuff?"

"I've no idea." He took the string from Jenny's hand and waved it, and it kinked and twisted and hung and sagged, as if tugged by invisible forces. He flicked the curious fibre, and it thrashed like a bad-tempered snake. "But I can't wait to find out."

A week later, he stood by his desk, grinning and bouncing. He'd trimmed his beard, put on a clean shirt, and washed his hair. But his eyes were puffy, and he looked thinner.

"Well," said Jenny, "let's see."

With a magician's flourish, he pulled the bed-sheet back. "Behold," he said, "mark 2—bigger and better than ever." And he set it running. The new machine, the size of a laundry sink and made from pine, took twenty threads at once.

"Let's call it Flossy," said Jenny, as the little engine scraped and grumbled. "It looks like it's flossing all its wooden teeth at once."

That night she cooked him dinner. Three courses and two bottles of wine later, they slumped in front of a muted TV. Warren took a bite of dark chocolate and a sip of brandy. "I could do this for hours…" he said, and his head fell forward.

"Take two days off. Minimum," she scolded. "I'll keep an eye on Flossy while you rest."

Warren managed one day.

At mid-afternoon on the third day, they contemplated a pile of glistening fibres.

Jenny stood with her hands on her hips, like a disapproving governess inspecting a child's gift, and she inclined her head. "We couldn't make a handkerchief with that lot."

"It's enough for proof of concept," said Warren. "All we've got to do is knit it into a sheet."

"*Weave* it," corrected Jenny.

Together they built a tiny loom, a Flossy's cousin. And after many hours of work, and lots of eyestrain, they produced a tiny square of cloth—a shimmering rag the size of a piece of toilet paper. Warren poked it with a pencil, and it recoiled, like a stingray in the sand. He grabbed a corner and held it up, and watched it flick and billow, as it tugged and twitched in an unfelt breeze.

"We've got a winner here," said Jenny. "Imagine an evening gown made of this stuff. A girl could ripple, like a movie star by a wind machine."

Warren stared into the distance. The little piece of cloth had behaved as expected, judging from how the single thread had acted, but he'd hoped for more. "It would take a hundred years to make a dress at this rate," he said. "We have to scale up production." He tapped the delicate loom. "It's OK for fairy clothes, and that's about it."

They needed guidance and money. They needed Rick. But they didn't know about him and, until Warren had prodded his tiny sheet, Rick hadn't known about them. Warren's fractal fabric had acted as a baby transmitter, and Rick had picked up its signal and engineered a meeting.

A few days later, Rick tripped on the pavement outside Jenny's studio. He tore his suit and gashed his knee.

Jenny rushed over. "I'll get you cleaned up," she said, fussing over him. "I work here."

Rick groaned and pushed himself up. He held out his hand, and Jenny helped him across the path. She kicked away litter, fumbled for keys, dropped them, picked them up, and unlocked the door. Rick hobbled down the passageway and into the dingy back room.

"Welcome to my studio," said Jenny. "Please take a seat."

"You're an artist, how nice. I'm Rick."

They shook hands.

"I'm Jenny, and I'm more of a designer than an artist. Clothes and, well, just clothes, really..."

Rick smiled and lowered himself into Warren's excavated chair. He glanced around, while Jenny washed his wounds and gave him a pint of water.

"Hungry?" she asked.

Rick nodded.

"OK, I'll be back in five minutes."

They sat munching doughnuts and sipping long black coffees from the café on the main road. Rick explained that he'd been rushing to a business meeting, hence his haste and fancy suit. "I've postponed the meeting. I can't go looking like this…"

"What sort of meeting?" asked Jenny, and then she blushed. "Sorry, I didn't mean to pry."

"Not at all. It's a small electronics firm. I can't go into details, but they want to scale up production and attack new markets. They need capital and expertise. That's my specialty, you see. I arrange money and know-how."

Rick hoped he hadn't overdone it. He hadn't.

"Interested in the rag trade?" she asked, with a glint in her eye.

"Absolutely! I love the fashion business, although I'm hopeless with clothes myself. My advisor chose my suit, tie, shirt, shoes, and even my watch." He held out his wrist, and his windowed timepiece leaked blue light and buzzed. "I have to look good in meetings, as you might imagine."

A door slammed, footsteps clumped down the corridor, and Warren stumbled into the studio, carrying an even bigger version of Flossy. He gaped at Rick and put the machine on the bench.

Rick introduced himself and apologised for the intrusion. "Jenny's been telling me how you make these fantastic models. I might be able to help—with the business, not the models."

Warren nodded and mumbled, and turned away.

"I'd like to take you both out to dinner," said Rick, "it's the least I can do to return your kindness."

"We'd love to come," said Jenny, and she beamed.

Warren froze.

"How about the pizza place around the corner," said Rick, "say tomorrow at eight?"

Jenny looked at Warren and gave a little nod. "Perfect, the food's great. We go there for lunch sometimes."

138

"I'll reserve a table," said Rick, and he smiled and hobbled out.

After the front door had slammed, Warren grumbled. "What if he saw my machines, or the thread?"

"No one could *possibly* understand your machines," said Jenny. "And the cloth was in the drawer. He could help us, Warren, he really could. He likes fashion, and he helps businesses to scale up, which is just what we're looking for. We're stuck, you know we are."

"A fairy blanket and a baby flossing machine won't persuade your new mate to give us money, you know."

"He's the best hope we've got," said Jenny.

Warren nodded, and together they planned how they might interest Rick in their little venture.

Midnight settled, and Rick was in his penthouse study, slumped in his chair, with his feet resting on his vast mahogany desk. The ceiling lights were off, and the computer screens were dark. A green-shaded banker's lamp provided the only light. He looked through his picture window at the factories outside, and he let his eyes defocus. And a distant motorbike accelerated through its gears, as if taking a series of breaths. And a dog barked.

Rick had spent hours trawling through the dark zones of the web, and now he knew private things about Jenny and Warren. And he knew about Frank, too—the gentleman upstairs with employment and hygiene issues. Rick's eyes closed, and he let the information simmer and connect. Apart from his gentle breathing, the only movement came from a thread caught in the lamplight. The blurry fibre flexed and arched, like a worm on a hook, trying to escape from the glass paperweight. Rick lifted the crystal, and the stolen strand scuttled across the desk and disappeared into the shadows.

The following evening, at precisely eight o'clock, Jenny and Warren arrived at the restaurant. The place glowed, beacon-like, amongst the dark showrooms, and the closed shops, and the empty offices. Warren shivered, checked his watch, took a deep breath, nodded at Jenny, and opened the door. The little pizzeria smelt of fresh herbs, and olive oil, and onions, and garlic. Behind the counter, the owner span his dough and nodded to an unheard aria. Rick sat in the corner, sipping a glass of wine. He acknowledged them with a small nod, then he stood up and smiled.

Jenny and Warren walked over and sat down. As soon as the greetings were finished, the owner, sporting a clean apron, strolled over with a carafe of Sangiovese.

Rick poured. "To the rag trade," he said, and their glasses clinked.

"To the rag trade," echoed Warren and Denise.

For ten minutes, the trio chatted, keeping the conversation light and general. When the owner returned with a notebook and pencil, they hadn't even glanced at the menus.

Rick looked at his guests and raised an eyebrow. "How about getting three different pizzas to share?"

Jenny and Warren nodded.

"You choose," said Rick to the proprietor. The man smiled and returned to the kitchen area. He dipped one hand into a giant jar of anchovies and the other into a bowl of sliced onions, then he sprinkled them across the dough in a series of short wavy motions, as if he were still listening to his silent opera.

Jenny felt her head spin, and Rick's voice washed over her, ebbing and flowing, and smoothing away her worries. The wine

140

was so strong, and the anchovy jar was so big, and the room was so warm, and the lights were so low…

"Ecco!"

The pizzas landed and Jenny pulled herself together. The food was delicious, and throughout the meal, Rick cajoled, and flattered, and left time for Warren to talk. It was masterful. By the time the zabagliones appeared, Rick had all the information he needed. And he'd promised them the world.

They staggered into the cool night, and a dark red car hissed up. Rick offered them a lift, knowing they wouldn't accept.

"A walk will do me good and clear my head," said Jenny.

Rick climbed in and waved from the back seat. The car pulled away and purred down the shining asphalt.

"Bloody hell," said Warren, staring at the tail lights. "I never expected that. It seems too good to be true."

Jenny nodded. She linked arms with Warren, and they headed back.

Rick, who was not a man to waste time or settle for half measures, bought a disused factory in the centre of town. While the architects and builders worked on the renovations, widely spaced equipment manufacturers built different parts of Flossy and the loom.

At last, the building work was done, and the machine parts were delivered. On a damp Wednesday morning, Jenny and Warren arrived at the factory for an inspection. Watery, workaday light seeped in through the high windows, and ranks of electric lamps—chosen to match the Victorian factory style— lit the ceiling, like an armada of flying saucers.

Rick paced the floor, inspecting piles of equipment, and nodding and tutting and twitching. Boxed components of a massive Flossy stood on one side of the room, and the parts of a giant loom on the other. "Let me show you around," he said, dusting himself down.

"I love the exposed bricks," said Jenny, rubbing a wall. "And the ironwork's fantastic. It's like a real factory."

"They did an excellent job," agreed Rick. "It's very authentic." He led them up to the next level and slid open an iron door that ran on rails. "Voilà!"

It was a great hall with long benches, like a refectory, but without the chatter of pupils or the clink of cutlery, and the tables were covered in equipment, not food. Warren approached a squat and reinforced Flossy.

"This level's for research and prototyping," said Rick. "For testing new machines, and fibres, and printing techniques. For trying out dyes and stitching. And for making mock-ups."

Jenny shook her head. "Brilliant, absolutely brilliant."

Rick smiled. "Upstairs again. The next level's all offices." He marched out and pounded up the metal steps. "Administration's not as exciting," he continued, as he led them through a suite of rooms, "but it *is* essential."

"It's beautiful," said Jenny, stroking an antique bureau. "This is a fabulous place to work."

"This typewriter's *fantastic*," said Warren, punching two keys at once. The machine clattered and jammed.

"I have a weakness for old office equipment," said Rick, wincing. "I find it comforting. Don't get me wrong, I like computers, but they're not the same as typewriters with ribbons, and filing cabinets that squeak."

"They're just for show, right?" asked Warren. "You *will* use computers, won't you?"

"They're already here, but they blend in. I prefer the antique style."

Warren stared at what looked like a giant black telephone. "Is this a fax?"

"One of the earliest, and I've owned it from new."

Warren nodded, doing his best to look impressed. He reached out.

"Don't touch, it's delicate. Now, let's go to the Theory Room."

They trooped into the dark passageway and up more metal stairs. Rick stopped in front of a reinforced wooden door. The sanded timber had flecks of white paint embedded in its grain, and the iron bands had remnants of pink.

Jenny ran her hands along the timber, feeling its age. "Is that red lead and white lead?"

"Yes, it's what's left of the undercoat, I'm afraid," said Rick. He shrugged. "It's an old factory."

"It's not a nursery," said Warren, and he smirked. *"Don't lick it."*

"This is yours, Warren," said Rick, sliding the door.

A huge workbench—a wooden island piled with computer equipment—stood in the middle of a glassy room with city views.

"I've never seen so much computing power. Never." He dashed to the biggest screen, tapped the keyboard, and grinned. "This is amazing."

Rick gave a slight nod. "And now for Jenny's studio," he said, and he led them up several flights of stairs, and then he stopped at a heavy green door. "After you."

Jenny stepped forward and pushed, and she entered an airy studio that filled the entire top storey. Skylights and wide windows lit the tailors' dummies, and easels, and computers, and drawing boards. She gasped and clapped her hands. "It's bigger, and better-looking, and *far* better equipped, than my old art

143

school. It's like a garret reimagined as a cathedral. Thanks so much."

Rick stood back and smiled. "It's my adventure, too."

It took five weeks to assemble Big Flossy and the Giant Loom. The great machines had heavy planks, and cogs, and brass controls, and glassy tubes, and squat, enamel feet. They looked like mediaeval war machines crossed with beam engines.

Dust, and tools, and polystyrene littered the floor. And the room was quiet except for the background hum of fans, and the occasional gurgle of blue fluid. Jenny and Warren and Rick sat on wooden crates and admired their work. And then they left, and as they left, Rick made a call.

Jenny and Warren returned the next day to find Rick standing in front of the engines, grinning like a kid. The rubbish had gone, the windows sparkled, the floor shone, the control panels winked, the gauges twitched, and spools of thread crowded Flossy's wide and wooden mouth.

"Time for a test run," said Rick.

"You do the honours," said Jenny.

Warren sniffed and nodded. "Go on, Rick, you start it."

Rick marched over to Flossy and flipped her switches, and twisted her dials, and pulled her levers. Then he squinted and scratched his head and cleared his throat. "That should do it," he said and stepped back, as if he'd taken a match to the touchpaper of a rocket, and was afraid it might fizzle or explode. But the extractor fans roared, the oil gurgled, and Flossy sucked in ten thousand threads. She thumped and squealed and clattered for ten minutes, then shimmering, blurry fibres wound out, ready for weaving.

The Giant Loom's first run produced metres of time-leaking cloth, and at this size, the fabric did more than shiver and flex. Like a slow-motion flag in a changing wind, it froze and folded and billowed and twisted and jumped. And sometimes it lay still, breathing gently.

Jenny's first designs used autumnal colours shot through with brilliant reds, yellows, and greens. There were rich swirls, thin radiating lines, hints of strange alphabets, and bold and abstract eyes. The eyes, and the cloth's slow-breathing movements, gave the prints a watching and predatory look.

"Like cats in the leaves," said Rick.

They began with headscarves, since they were easy to cut and stitch and print, and any rippling could be blamed on breezes around the wearer's head. Rick called in favours, and the scarves appeared in fancy stores. Their striking designs and constant shimmer attracted buyers, and Big Flossy and the Giant Loom ran twenty-four hours a day.

Demand was so great, even without advertising, that Rick ordered three more grinders and two more looms. The two men assembled the great engines while Jenny worked on fresh designs.

Late one Thursday afternoon, as it was getting dark and as rain flecked the skylights, they met in the studio to plan their clothing range. Jenny flipped a switch, and rows of lights came on.

"Ties?" asked Rick, as the mannequins looked on.

"A bit obvious," said Warren. "But they don't need much cloth, and you can charge a lot."

"Jackets are fashionable and profitable," said Jenny. The others grunted.

145

"Your turn, Warren," said Rick.

"Underwear. You know, *lingerie*."

Rick grinned, and Jenny nodded.

"It shimmers and, well, it *moves*," Warren explained. "It would be continuously stimulating."

Rick grinned. "Have you been experimenting with offcuts, Warren?"

"Yes. I mean no." He blushed and dug his hands in his pockets. "Fuck off, both of you."

Lingerie needed little cloth, and shipping was cheap. It was pleasant to wear at home or in the office, but it excelled on the dance floor or in the gym, where fast bodily movements made the fabric jerk and twitch, as past and future versions tugged and twisted the cloth.

"Your lingerie's a *sensation*," said Rick, as he tapped the sales graph.

"You're just jealous," said Warren, but this time he didn't blush.

"Warren," Rick continued, "has not been sitting on his laurels." He held up a heavy pair of underpants. "More thread, more lubricant, more transits through Big Flossie, more…"

The pants twitched on cue, and everyone laughed.

The following month, on a drab Wednesday morning, Warren called Rick into the research area.

"I've put threads through the test-Flossy five hundred times," said Warren. "They needed lots of oil, but they held together, and I made up a sample weave. What do you think?"

"It looks very nice." Rick folded a corner of the creamy linen. "But it's very stiff."

Warren handed him a knife. "Try cutting it."

Rick stabbed at the fabric, but the knife slammed into an invisible wall and clattered onto the floor.

Rick massaged his wrist. "What the hell just happened?"

Warren grinned. "It leaks more into time, and that makes it far tougher."

"Let's try shooting it," said Rick, "and see how it copes with a bullet."

The next day, Rick arrived at the lab with a spivvish grin and an army rifle.

"I'm impressed," said Warren. "Let's pop it here." He tapped a stout bench, crossed his arms, and nodded his approval.

"Do you know anything about guns?" asked Rick, as he fiddled with the stand and sight.

"Nothing whatsoever, but this one looks powerful."

"It is. I hope your cloth's up to it."

"It is, assuming it stays put." Warren walked the twenty paces to his sample and re-centred the framed canvas on its easel. Then he pulled out a marker and drew a red circle in the middle of the creamy cloth. The canvas shifted an inch to the left, and Warren moved it back. "Stay," he ordered and backed away, glaring at the arrangement. He re-checked the cameras, wagged his finger at the canvas, walked over to the gun, put his hands on his hips, and sniffed.

Rick adjusted the weapon and peered through the sight. "OK, it's in the cross hairs."

Warren smiled and started the video cameras.

Twenty minutes later, they sat in darkness staring at a huge screen. Warren shuttled back and pressed play. The bullet hovered in front of the cloth, caught in a resinous time field.

147

"It's beautiful," said Rick, "look how it hangs in the air."

The bullet fell with a clink.

"Let's watch it again," said Warren, "but slower."

The speakers roared, and the bullet stopped by the red circle, bobbing like a bumblebee inspecting a flower.

"You're right." Warren stepped back from the video screen. "It *is* beautiful."

"This material's perfect for soldiers, police, and politicians…"

"I can tune it," said Warren, "to balance mobility and protection. I can even mix different grades, like blending whisky."

"I'll make some calls," said Rick.

The car—with chequered tape, and painted marks—rocketed at the steel barrier. A hollow thump, and everything blurred. The car pulled back into focus, and four technicians approached and unclipped the netting. Not a dent or scratch. And the dummy sat unbroken in his chair.

Warren rubbed his hands together. "Perfect. Can you imagine how much money this will make?"

Morning coffee was over, and conversation had petered out. Warren leant forward. "What about offcuts? It seems such a waste to throw them out."

Jenny frowned. "You can make paper from bits of rag. It's easy, I did it in Art School. You bleach them, soak them, and press them. That's all there is to it."

Rick raised an eyebrow. "By hand?"

"Yes, I can do it in my studio."

"We'll use the spare room on the second floor," said Rick. "And keep the studio as it is."

Jenny grinned at Warren.

"OK," said Rick, and he levered himself out of his saggy chair. "I'll get the plumbing organised. Let me know what else you need."

"I'll make a list," said Jenny.

The room was ready in a month, with new paint, and brass plumbing, and it was filled with vats, and presses, and drying racks.

Jenny stood in the middle of the floor and shook her head. "My God," she whispered. "It's amazing."

She soaked the offcuts, stirred the pulp, spread it, pressed it, dried it, and admired it. And then she stacked it. She patted the top sheet. "I'll draw on you on Monday."

All weekend she wondered about her paper. It took huge amounts of willpower, two dates, and a major shopping spree to keep away from the office—but she needed balance in her life. At night, she lay awake and mulled over her magic paper, and when sleep finally came, so did the paper dreams.

Rick didn't take weekends off, and he was in the factory on Saturday evening when normal people were out drinking. He pulled out a sheet of Jenny's handmade paper from the stack, ran his fingers over the soft grain, and smiled. He took five more sheets, rolled them up, slipped out through the back door, and set off to his downtown flat. *Then* he went to the pub.

Jenny stared at her screen, unable to write another word. She'd spent the first hour of Monday morning trying to catch up with office tasks. But the paper called. *Draw on me*, it said. *And I'll show you magic...*

"I'm coming," she muttered. "I'm coming."

Jenny dragged her pencil over the rough tooth of the new paper and sat back. The grey line wavered and twisted, pushing and pulling across the sheet, and thin washes of colour soaked into the weave, creating a beautiful sketch of a girl in a light and airy dress. Jenny held the paper at arm's length, tilting her head left and right. "It's the best I've ever done," she mumbled. "But I didn't do it."

She tried another sheet, and the result was even better. She took the pictures—half-alive with winking girls and shimmering cloth—and slid them into her plan chest. "No one must know," she said. *"No one."*

Thursday afternoon brought squalls, and the milky light from the high windows cast soft shadows. Jenny stroked the creamy, defocused fibres of the latest batch and smiled.

Rick popped his head round the door. "Can I see?"

Jenny handed him a sheet.

"Lovely. I've never seen paper like it."

"It turned out better than I'd hoped," she said. *"Far better."*

Rick sniffed. "I have a friend who runs an art shop, and I'm sure he'd love to stock it. He carries the finest papers, and the best artists go there."

"I'd rather keep it, if you don't mind. I can use everything I make."

"OK, it'll be our little secret." Oh well, he thought, I'll tell him it was a one-off.

They were alone in the pizzeria on a chilly Tuesday evening, sitting at their favourite table, right at the back. A battery-powered candle flickered in a ruby pot, and they stared at the dancing light and sipped their wine.

Rick was in the corner, his face was flushed, and his arms were splayed on the chequered cloth. He took a swig. "I'm pleased to report that our fabrics are selling as fast as the Flossies can make them." He topped up their glasses with sparkling red. "And, as of today…" He raised his eyebrows waiting for a response.

"Yes?" prompted Warren, whose face was redder than Rick's.

"…we're officially billionaires."

Jenny grinned. "Yay! Cheers to that!"

Glasses clinked, the pizzas arrived, and Jenny dug in. The men stared at their plates and drank more wine, then they tore at their food. The anchovy special was superb, and the wine was heady and divine. They were rich and drunk and happy and fulfilled. And they thought that nothing could go wrong.

Extirpators

But things always go wrong when you meddle with time. Warren's first tiny square of fabric had sent out a signal strong enough to attract Rick, and now the world was a giant transmitter, and millions of moving sources were radiating time waves. These emanations were faint, but modulated. The lingerie picked up the complex movements of its wearers and soaked up their erotic energy, while the military clothing absorbed the stress of battle. Vehicle nets were fast moving transmitters at the best of times, but in a crash their broadcasts were flushed with panic. And all these subtle time-waves—stained by orgasms, and panic, and mortal dread—radiated into space. Someone was bound to notice.

The Great Mind noticed. It saw the disturbances ripple out from the planet, forming delicate intersecting shells of clear purple, shocking red, iridescent green, and hundreds of other colours that only it could see. Such gossamer waves were—so it thought—far too attenuated to threaten reality. So it indulged the entertaining Rick, and the Flossies continued to run.

The other entity that noticed was a malign space destroyer, a wandering Extirpator. This protein robot hunted sources of time disruptions. Destruction was total, and the machine left no tracks and no memories—at least none in the modified reality into which it shifted after doing its duty.

This robot was an escapee from an ancient intervention of the Great Mind. Hundreds of millions of years ago, in an obscure edition of history, an earlier iteration of the Great Mind had tried to automate the smoothing of space. It did this by beaming expertise into the minds of the gentle and inquisitive Uadromorphs, who responded by building a space probe to investigate nearby worlds. The Great Mind captured their probe and altered its structure, and the reconfigured object hurtled across vast empty tracts of the universe. As it travelled, it recruited other machines, and these altered things spread across the stars. The Great Mind thought it had saved itself a great deal of work. It had smiled at its clever intervention, and then it had returned to its introspections.

Extirpators deleted egregious time disruptions by travelling into the past and undoing crucial events. But they didn't stop there. Propelled by hard imperatives written into their structure, they developed into grotesque extremists that destroyed anything that disturbed time. Minds leaked into time. And so minds, like tiny time machines, ruffled reality. And this space-roughening attracted the Extirpators. The radical robots deleted trillions of species, stripping whole galaxies of sentience. But Extirpators were themselves time machines, and so they too corroded reality. But they missed the irony, for there was no room left in their poisoned intellects for reflection.

The earlier version of the Great Mind woke up to its awful mistake. It returned to the moment before it had fathered the Extirpators, and it watched the newly launched probe glint in the light of an ancient sun. It tracked it to the dark side of an alien moon and destroyed it. The probe's countless rogue progeny, chased by a flashing causal wave, like a sword across time, flipped out of existence. Trillions of victim species that were made unborn returned, and consciousness survived.

But a lone Extirpator, wrapped in multiple layers of history, like a thief in many cloaks, evaded the purge. It arced into meta-time and as it flew it replicated and seeded countless histories. One of those machines was here, now. And it was about to annoy the Great Mind, like a mosquito that had squirmed through a fly screen.

The Great Mind watched the celebration dinner. It watched Rick announce their great wealth, and it heard the clink of glasses, and it watched them eat their pizzas, and it saw them smile and chatter.

Then the lights went out, and the restaurant vanished. The Great Mind stared at a gnarled tree in a dank forest. A light wind rustled the leaves, but no birds called, and no animals scurried in the undergrowth. It pulled back and scanned the planet. All sentient beings had gone, and so had their nests, hives, burrows, tools, and buildings. There were no factories, and no looms, no art, no music, and no science. No vapour trails crossed the sky, and no fish swam in the sea. A cooler and less interesting Earth span slowly, unremarked upon and unloved.

The Great Mind recognised in this abrupt extinction the dread signature of an Extirpator. In a rare moment of extreme fury, caused partly by having its entertainment interrupted, but mainly by realising that an Extirpator had escaped, the Great Mind tracked back down the moments and destroyed the guilty robot.

The world was restored. Rick's factory reappeared, and the Big Flossies resumed their thread-roughening labours.

The Great Mind settled back to watch the meal from a few moments before the Extirpator's attack.

Rick was in the corner, his face was flushed, and his arms were splayed on the chequered cloth. He took a swig. "I'm pleased..." He frowned and rubbed his forehead. "Sorry, I've completely forgotten what I was saying. It must be the wine..."

Jenny and Warren laughed. They were drunk, and happy, and they thought that nothing could go wrong.

Sponge

In shallow water, where a wide slow river mingled with the Pacific Ocean, in the shadow of an iron bridge that carried an endless succession of cars and trucks, a sponge bounced against a rock, waiting to be found. It was an aberrant species, unknown to humans, but a favourite of the Great Mind, and the vast intellect swirled above the rippling waters, enthralled.

Across the water—just little coloured dots from this distance—chattering holiday makers munched on fish and chips, ate slices of pizza, and clinked glasses. Couples and small family groups meandered along the distant promenade. An elderly cyclist wobbled past a small dog, and a skateboarder stopped, flipped his board with a fat shoe, caught it with a thin hand, and wandered off down an alley.

One of those bright dots was the young Dr Olivia Fox. She was wearing bright pink shorts and a pale green top. She stood on the promenade, near the fish and chip shop, and her tanned legs continued to flex, and her red trainers tapped the concrete. Her lips pursed, and she stared down into the water at a stingray that lay in the shallows. To her left, a little girl shrieked and pointed, and a small crowd gathered.

Olivia glanced up at the bridge. A grocery truck rumbled across, puffing fumes and shaking the struts. A pedestrian on the bridge's walkway stopped to watch a dinghy putter along in the river below. A pelican flapped above the water, ungainly and out of place, like a lost pterosaur. And a small plane, on the lookout for sharks, droned in the distance.

Olivia peered down into the water, but the ray had gone, and the crowd had dispersed. She sighed and set off, skirting the car park beyond the fish shop. Fifty metres later, she stopped opposite the discount store, waited for two cars to pass, and then crossed.

The shop was full of irresistible and gaudy plastic things. Two minutes later, she emerged with a bright red bucket, grinned at the day, and made for the bridge.

The Great Mind returned to its contemplation of the yellow blob. As if to repay the attention, the wobbly sea creature clenched, pumping blue oil through its body, bathing and refreshing its myriad glassy cells.

Olivia reached the far shore and stared back across the bay. The Great Mind, still admiring the sponge, hovered over the water, directly in her line of sight, making the air shimmer. She blinked and frowned and rubbed her eyes. Then, as if drawn by a mirage, she paddled out, squinting at the wavering glare. A splash and a stream of bubbles further out drew her attention, and she waded over and looked down. The sponge clenched— this time for Olivia's benefit—and blue trails shot out. She grinned like a toddler, bent down, and scooped it up. "You're beautiful," she said to the pulsing thing in her bucket. "I'll show you to Tim." She arched her back, brushed her hair from her face, and stared at the far shore. But the Great Mind had gone, and the air was clear, and the spell was broken.

She trudged out of the river and onto the sand, and frowned at her ruined trainers. Then she squelched over to a rock, sat down, swore, and untied her laces.

She walked away with the bucket in one hand and her shoes in the other. It would take half an hour to get home barefoot, and she wondered how much Tim, her fiancé, would have drunk by then.

Tim was on the balcony of their little apartment, slumped in one chair, feet on another. He took a sip of beer, dug into a bowl of peanuts, and stared across the river. A jet ski thudded into the water and cut a broken foamy trail beyond the moored yachts.

"Hi, Liv, wanna beer?"

"I'll have tea. Here, look at this."

Tim, still munching, gawped into the bucket. "What the hell's that?"

"It's a sponge—unusual, though. I'll send a sample to Kevin; he'll know what it is."

"Kevin," said Tim, "is an arsehole."

"You're just jealous because he's a marine biologist, and you're not."

"I wanted to be a marine biologist when I was fourteen. I'm grown up now."

Telepathy Box

Rick stroked the little box and smiled. "How much?"

His visitor shrugged. "Nothing up front, I was thinking more of a percentage—once you get it working, once you make a profit." The visitor held out his hands, showing he had nothing to hide.

Rick pursed his lips and let his eyes flick from the rumpled man to the polished box. "Fair enough. Ten percent of profits?"

"Fifty," countered the visitor, struggling to his feet. "It seems only fair."

"OK, I'll have my lawyers do the contract," said Rick, and they strolled to the door in silence.

The man smiled. "I'll be in touch." He waddled down the corridor, opened the blue door, and disappeared.

Rick ran back to his desk, sat down, and examined the box. There was a black on-off switch on the back, and a silver power dial on top. "Make sure," the rumpled man had said, "to face the machine *away* from you—keep the switch towards you. *That's critical.*" Rick ran his fingers over the surface, but found no opening, and no panel, and no screws. He leant on the intercom.

The speaker crackled. "Yes, Rick?"

"Come and get this thing X-rayed, will you?" He held the box to his ear and shook it. From inside, came a slush, a sigh,

159

and a tinkle. He put the mysterious cube back on his desk and rubbed his oily thumb.

Penny popped her head round the door. "Rick?"

"Forget the X-ray, I was being over cautious." He wiped his hand on a tissue, making the paper translucent and blue. "But I'd love a coffee. Get one for yourself and join me."

At the front entrance of Rick's building, two glass doors slid open. Street sounds intruded, and a rush of air disturbed the monstera's leaves. A dark-haired girl, dressed entirely in black, looked up from the reception desk. The rumpled man smiled, slipped through the doors, and ran down the steps. The doors closed, the lobby regained its composure, and the girl returned to her book.

The rumpled man waited by the kerb while a delivery truck drove past, then he looked both ways and crossed the road. He turned and squinted at Rick's building. Distorted traffic raced across its windows, but nothing was visible behind the glass. He slid his hand into his pocket and stroked slick metal. There was one more delivery to make. He walked past a small pizzeria and disappeared up a side street.

The rumpled man was still smiling when he returned to his nondescript hotel. He took the back stairs to his room and locked the door. He peered through the window at the alleyway, drew the curtains, stripped, showered, shaved, and changed into fresh clothes. Then he stood in front of the mirror. An upright man, dapper and bright, stared back. The rumpled man had gone, and Kevin the marine biologist was back. He put his razor into his washing kit, taking care not to nick the third ball of yellow foam. Then he folded his old and crumpled coat, put it in his suitcase,

160

and laid the grey wig on top. He opened his document wallet, removed his passport, and slipped it into his jacket.

Rick held down the box with his left hand and rotated the dial with his right. He leant back and waited for Penny.

"Here Rick," she said, handing him a frothy coffee. She pulled up a chair and chatted away, but her voice was different; it sounded as if she were speaking inside his head.

Rick touched his ears, checking for headphones.

"Take your eyes off my tits," said the Interior Penny, "and fuck off."

"Thanks Penny, you're a dear."

Penny grinned. "You're welcome."

"Arsehole," continued the interior voice.

Rick drove his legs together and fought to keep a straight face. "I've no idea what this thing does," he said, nodding at the silvery box between them and clenching his belly muscles.

They sipped their drinks for a moment.

"OK, I'm off," Penny said.

"Send Ron in, will you? I'm dying to get his thoughts on the new project."

"Will do," replied Penny in her normal voice. "Now fuck yourself with the box," added the interior voice.

She left, and Rick giggled, then he laughed. He was still wiping his eyes when there was a light knock at the door.

Ron's round and placid face poked in. "You wanted to know what I think, boss?"

Sponge-Books

Kevin tapped his lips. The telepathy box was brilliant, but it had to stay niche, because all hell would break loose if too many were sold. Unfortunately, Kevin needed money, he needed something to sell in the millions, and so he had to apply his sponge technology to the everyday needs of ordinary people. He thought that a telepathic book would be ideal—a device that would rescue publishing and protect authors. And he smiled and set to work.

A year later, he rocked back in his chair and stared out at the late afternoon. Something called from the woodland beyond his window, and something answered. Something bright and blue arced across the lawns and flew up into the gloom. It was nearly five, and Rick would be here soon.

Kevin reached for the slender volume on his desk. The cover was dusky pink and had his name, with drop-capped *Ks,* etched in gold. He opened the book and stared at two spongy surfaces. They were pale cream, and silky, and blank. He looked like a man staring at the middle pages of an ordinary book. But this was a sponge-book, and its contents, the actual words, were encrypted and impossible to hack. The sponge decrypted the words and projected their meaning straight into the reader's mind, so that the text was never visible. And the book would lock onto one brain, like a dog with one master.

Reading a sponge-book was like dreaming. Some people read normal books that way, but Kevin's books made the dreams real—for everyone. Even the illiterate could enjoy the sponge-stories, because everyone can dream.

There was a firm tap on the door.

"Come in," said Kevin, "and have a seat."

Rick nodded, took the chair, swivelled, leant back, and pursed his lips.

"This is it," said Kevin, handing Rick a pale green sponge-book. "You'll love it."

Rick opened the device and stared at its blank interior. "Now what?"

"Relax and pretend to read."

Ten minutes later, Rick closed the covers and gave a long, deep sigh. His face was flushed, and he smiled. "That was truly magnificent." He blinked. "I'll take as many as you can make."

"That could be thousands every week, once the sponge farms are going full tilt."

"Thousands, tens of thousands, millions, I don't care. I'll take them all," said Rick. "In fact, I insist."

"Well, if you're sure. At the agreed price?"

"Absolutely, but the deal has to be exclusive."

Kevin nodded. "Sounds fair enough."

"Excellent, I'll have the papers drawn up."

A year after Kevin and Rick had made their pact, a truck backed up to a loading dock. A grind, a squeal of brakes, and the huge diesel shuddered and died. The driver heaved himself from the cab, broke wind, coughed, and headed for the canteen. Behind him, a metal roller door rattled up, and forklift trucks arrived to unload pallets of dream-books.

This was Rick's warehouse, and it stood on the edge of town, and it was nearly full. He strode down the main walkway, with tiers of shrink-wrapped books on either side, and the grate and strobe of forklifts filtered in from the other aisles. His left hand rested on the shoulder of a slender man, and his right hand swept a wide arc, indicating the mountains of stock. "Your story could be on every book; you'd have a best seller."

"No one has ever shown the least interest in my book," said Thad, as they walked in step. "Why would they buy it now?"

"Leave it to me," said Rick, and he held out his hand.

"OK," said Thad, and he handed Rick a tiny flash drive.

"You'll be happy," said Rick. "You'll be rich."

Six months later, they met in Rick's office. Rick put his feet on his desk, and his mahogany chair creaked. He sipped his brandy, making his cut-glass tumbler glint in the afternoon sun.

Thad hunched forward, stared at his untouched glass, and pursed his lips. "I never believed it would happen, you know. I really didn't."

"It couldn't fail, not with your story and my sponge-books."

"I have a friend…" said Thad. "Would you be interested?"

"Is his book any good?"

"She," corrected Thad. He frowned. "I think her work has merit—and broad appeal."

"You're a famous author now, your opinion counts," said Rick, and he took another sip. "I'd be happy to see her."

The stories came out as sponge-books, but Rick made old-fashioned copies of each one. He had them printed on archival paper and bound in green leather. And he had them displayed in his office, like a runaway set of encyclopaedias. No one would ever read them, but they looked nice on their custom-built shelves, and they intimidated visitors.

Rick sat at his desk and tore at a brown paper package. It was another green book, thicker than the last. He stroked its spine, running his fingers over a golden logo of a spiky lizard that was biting its tail. Then he opened the book, grimaced, and flicked to the end. He slammed it shut and massaged his forehead. All the stories were awful, but the buyers—who were dreamers not readers—thought they were brilliant. That was because sponge-books by-passed language altogether, and turned text into dreams, making anyone a top author.

He wandered out of his office and into the foyer, where he paused by an architectural model of a warehouse. The little building was ugly and blank, but the miniature landscape was delightful. Plastic trees marched down one side of the warehouse, and a toy truck was backed up to a dock, where tiny figures directed the unloading. Rick smiled at the details, remembering his childhood train set, and its bushes and buildings and rolling stock—and the thin, sick smell of ozone. He breathed in the remembered gas and sighed. Then he walked over to the reception desk, exchanged a joke with the girl in black, and strode out through the glass doors. He stood squinting in the sun, his hand shielding his eyes, and his chest thrust out— like a captain scanning for enemy ships from the prow of a concrete destroyer.

Rick returned to his office and massaged his temples. He sat in his chair and span, and as he span, he stroked the cover of a pale blue sponge-book. He smiled as he remembered the bookish girl, the one that Thad had introduced. She was his second signing, and only twenty-five, with thick dark hair, and heavy glasses. Her face was clear and delicate and full of hope, and her fingers were impossibly long. Her stories—her *written* stories—were enjoyable to read, but as dreams they were gorgeous.

He stared at the churned fields beyond his window and realised that he'd become a pornographer.

A loud knock broke his reverie.

"Come in," said Rick, composing his face.

"Thank you for seeing us, Rick. We appreciate your time." Harry was sixty-three, tall, grey, and dressed in casual but expensive clothes. A stocky young man followed him in.

"Not at all, it's good to see you again. You too, Joe." Rick pointed at the two hard chairs that faced his desk. "Please, have a seat."

"It's getting worse," said Harry, "much worse."

"What can I do to help?"

"Can you limit the number of sponge-books?"

"The technology's out there, I can't turn the clock back." Rick waved at his leather-bound volumes, which stood as a proxy for the relentless march of his sponge-stories.

"It's not just books, they're destroying film and television. Theatres are empty, and no one goes to concerts."

"I know, Harry, I know, but book-dreams are better than movies—better than real life." Rick shrugged. "Better than sex."

"Everyone stays at home and dreams," said Joe. "Sponge-books have ruined all the comedians and artists and musicians. Not to mention the actors. Even prostitutes and porn stars…"

Harry leant forward. "There are suicides, Rick. I've lost three friends. No one can compete with you and your plastic dreams."

"It's mayhem out there," added Joe. "People have lost their jobs—*and* their urge to create."

Rick fidgeted and glanced at the blue sponge-book. He wanted to get back to the story—back to the castle, and the

166

tapestries, and the four-poster bed with its cushions and silk sheets. And the long fingers of the bookish girl. He looked up. "I'll see what I can do."

An hour later, Rick forced his eyes from the book and stared across the fields. The ground was being dug up to build another warehouse. He flicked a switch, and a window opened, and the rich sweet air poured in. He glanced at a glass-fronted bookcase. Inside, were relics of an earlier time—forgotten imprints with faded spines. They made nice pastel patterns in the sunlight, but no one would ever read them again. And their symbolism had grown tired. Eventually, he'd throw them out. Or move them to a vault.

He leant on the phone. "Bob, is there any way out of that bloody sponge-book contract?"

Rick's chief lawyer searched for the right words. "No."

"Surely you can do *something?*"

"You wanted an unbreakable contract. You were afraid someone might get to you, remember?" said Bob.

"What happens if Kevin gives up or retires?"

"You covered that, too. If he dies, or resigns, or retires, or goes insane, then the technology passes to a new entity—and that entity is obliged to keep producing sponge-books. There's no way out." Bob coughed. "But I inserted a clause that releases everyone in ten years."

"OK, so we wait ten years."

"The clause only operates if the books get superseded. You thought they'd be outdated by then..."

"And?" asked Rick.

"The scientists are stuck in sponge-books, too. They dream but they don't innovate..."

Rick stared at the great excavators churning the lawns for warehouse number four.

"Rick?"

Rick blinked. "I'm still here, Bob."

"I have the papers for you to sign—the ones for warehouse six. And the studio bosses are agitating about that buyout. You're locked in. There's no backing out of that one." Bob cleared his throat. "Congratulations, Rick, you're a media king."

But Rick wasn't listening; he was stroking the pale blue sponge-book. He wanted to dive back into the dreams of that very attractive young writer, the one with the impossibly long fingers.

Sequestering Rick

The Great Mind watched the glazed-eyed Rick. It watched him pant and twitch.

Rick was a problem in many worlds. He was Harry's functional replacement, and he'd popped up in all subsequent histories. In a faraway reality—where he was still known as Richard—he'd developed time-technologies so disruptive that assassins had come from several futures. Herbert's sequestration had taken care of that career, but Rick was born before Herbert's containment, and so he had survived into the squamafly world, where he had dabbled in time-leaking dust before succumbing, like everyone else, to the hunger of the flies.

But Rick was persistent, and the crunching of the *Squamafly Eve* had unleashed something of a career frenzy for him. Again and again he popped up, involving himself in one enterprise after another, until his own cleverness trapped him. The sponge-books had tranquillized the world, removed the urge to invent, and captivated Rick. They held him in their thrall, in a mental prison where he could do no damage—Rick had sequestered himself.

The Great Mind relaxed. It was time to reflect. Time to review old encounters, and to imagine new ones. Time to live in the mansion that was the Mind Library...

PART FOUR

THE MIND LIBRARY

Inside the Mind Library

My secret house is ramshackle, and the passages don't run straight. And it's always big with lots of unvisited rooms. The architecture changes, and the location shifts, but it's always my house. I'm invariably showing someone around. Last night I said, "This is the library." My companion wasn't in view, but I knew he was impressed, for the place was magnificent. It sprawled in all directions and the floor was tilted and uneven, as if several misaligned rooms had been knocked together to create a single space. Carpets were scattered everywhere, sometimes three or four deep. They were faded and threadbare, and some were as thin as bedsheets and just as plain. Others had a compressed pile, and a light wash of colour, like Persian rugs left for years on a damp lawn. Beneath the carpets, the boards creaked, and some had rotted away, so it was wise to tread carefully.

Dr Walden sat still. Then he jotted something down. "Please go on."

Thousands of mouldering books sat on sagging shelves. The large ones had spines of sun-washed leather, pale pink or green. The small ones—paperbacks, I suppose—were black, or white,

172

or red, or blue, and they were cracked and broken. Big or small,
I couldn't make out their titles.

The windows were secure—by virtue of an exterior mesh—
but partly open to keep the place ventilated. The library had a
nice view, but the fields outside had been dug up by great
ploughing machines, and the earth was wet, and brown, and
furrowed. The ploughs stood idle, and the scene reminded me of
roadworks on a Sunday. But the turning wasn't for a planting,
the machines were digging something up—bodies, or a
foundation for another house, I couldn't be sure which. And I
knew that I wouldn't be around long enough to find out.

The library had a small upper section, like an observatory,
poking through the roof. I climbed the helical stairway for a
better view, and I scanned the torn-up land. The windows up
there were wide open, and the air rushed through, carrying the
sweet smell of perfume or decay. My companion stayed down in
the main library. I assume that he was leafing through a book
that had taken his fancy. I don't know. I've never seen my
companion, and he never speaks.

Dr Walden nodded. "I see."

That was last night. In earlier dreams, the house was different. It
was often much bigger. Sometimes, more like two houses—
perhaps joined by a corridor or a tunnel. Or quite separate.
Often, they were at different elevations, as if carelessly built on
the side of a hill. In those cases, the second house was even more
secret, and even more dilapidated—a place that I had only just
discovered, although long suspected to be there.

I remember a multi-lobed kitchen attached to what looked
like a derelict ballroom. Shrivelled bags hung from the

173

ballroom's vast ceiling. I've forgotten what they were, but I think they were once alive.

Walden squirmed. "Alive, you say?"

A long time ago. But in my secret house, I'm always drawn to the library. It's hard to navigate, whether it's spread out or compacted, subterranean or winding up a tower, or projecting over a cliff, or spanning a wide and lazy river, or sinking into mud. And the books are always impossible to read. I know they contain real thoughts though, those books. The library's mine, but the books come from elsewhere.

"Are they other minds?" asked Walden, but no one answered. He checked the windows of his office, slipped out, and locked the door.

Star Book

The Great Mind reached out and pulled a book from an impossibly high shelf. The book was new, not soggy and faded like the others, and its cover was midnight blue with a splatter of silver stars. Golden lines traced out a constellation in the shape of a lizard, and golden letters named it in an unknown language. To the right of the star-group, alone in dark blue space, a red circle framed a tiny planet...

The Queen in Check

The Bizzling Jee fixed her subordinate with nine of her twelve eyes. The other three remained focused on the wall display to her left. As she watched, the imagery expanded, seeping across the ceiling and touching the ornate pillars.

"Tell me again, Grimbolicus Nex, and this time, try to keep most of your arms still."

Nex squirmed. Purple worry patterns formed at his head and travelled down his glistening thorax. Orange throbbed at his rear as he clenched. He was always nervous in front of Her Majesty, especially when he had bad news. True, the bad news filled the walls and ceiling, and the swirling imagery carried his signature, and the story was self-explanatory. But still…

He suspected that she enjoyed his discomfiture, but he was wrong. The Queen was playing for time, putting off the moment of acceptance, hoping it was all a terrible mistake. She recruited a fourth eye to watch the expanding images.

"Well, Your Bizzling, as I, er, intimated, and as the display clearly shows, we, that is to say, I, think that the, er,—"

"For God's sake, get on with it, Grim!" bellowed the Queen. Her voice made the display flicker. She knew she'd get a crisper account if he focused on her anger. It was a fiction that rulers used: keep your subjects in awe of your power and they missed the fragility of the world. A skilful monarch could weave her lines of influence around her subjects. Comfort from power, process, and protocol. If the court were properly regulated, then so were the heavens. Old magic, but it worked.

Grim twitched and looked around the giant chamber, all of which now carried his story. Tortured figures animated the vaulted ceiling, the pillars ran with streaming numbers, and the floor tiles flashed in blue. His worry patterns had stabilised to throbbing standing waves of pink, as he fought to stay continent. "The problem, Your Bizzling, is that time's rotting." He gave a weak smile and relieved himself over the tiles.

The Queen stared at him with her two central eyes, stalks at full stretch. The other ten swept the chamber, informing the ninety-five percent of her gigantic distributed mind that now concentrated on the disaster story.

"Thank you, Grimbolicus Nex. That will be all!" she roared.

He backed out of the room, leaving a trail of pungent green fluid, and the Queen alone with her nightmares.

She retracted her eyes with a wet kissing sound and concentrated. The chamber dissolved, and her mind grew. First it probed a few moments into the future, and then it scanned a few minutes into the past. In a dazzling flash, all instances of her mind—from its earliest stirrings of consciousness six thousand years ago, to her fabulous death mind—coalesced into one giant super brain. The Queen saw this as a huge corrugated tunnel whose slender luminous ribs marked out her various selves. Her central being shuttled back and forth down this vast cloister and cried for answers. Side tunnels appeared as other minds joined hers, and strange celestial chatter filled the air. The tunnels merged, creating a high and expanding vaulted dome. She was in the mind cathedral. She knew this and much more.

Another entity approached, far more powerful than the others. It made the walls thrum and the vault burn with golden light. The Great Mind arrived in all its glory and explained, in singing tones, that free will and temporal meddling had undermined reality and rotted its fabric. It told the Queen that the problem was ancient and inevitable, and that everything would be destroyed. The Queen's mission was to help slow that rot. Not to stop it, that was impossible, but to delay it so that the universe could hold itself together long enough for them to live out their lives.

Much to her annoyance, the Queen discovered that she was only one of billions recruited for this vital task. Those other minds were spread across time and space. They ranged from the long extinct Gnonglocks, a strange race that, though microscopic, had developed hive minds that outshone the fabulous silicon brains of the dust-dwelling Jellarks, right up to the Gnayans, limbless aquatic forms that wouldn't evolve for another three million years. This information did not sit well with her sense of privilege and self-importance. But she was a pragmatist and realised that you just don't argue with a mind as big as the one occupying the roof of the luminous cathedral.

The Great Mind had told her to reach back in time and intervene in twelve separate lives. These rogues had learnt to communicate with the past. They'd sent messages back to themselves and become rich, but they'd corroded time.

She hoped that the Great Mind knew what it was doing.

Her extended mind telescoped down to its normal size and its inner light went out. Her dozen eyes popped out through puckered portals and scanned the chamber. Little had changed, but Grim's green trail had gone. The display had shrivelled to a respectable size and now showed a nature program on flower-mimicking spiders attacking perfumed blue butterflies. The Queen sent out an annoyed pulse, and scores of waiting drones fussed around her, adjusting her robes and lubricating her eye holes.

She waited until they'd fettled her, then she slid over to the main balcony and surveyed the glistening city that stretched as far as her twelve eyes could see. Winged carrier drones flitted about, and the hum of commerce rose from the streets, and summer scents filled the air.

The Queen frowned. How could she do the Great Mind's bidding? She did a quick mental check of the palace's advanced temporal machinery and decided than none of it was up to the job. A few minutes ago she'd been a formidable queen. Now she was a minion with an impossible task and a cellar full of useless equipment.

A vast and boggy depression engulfed her. As queen, she'd always channelled such moods into violent rages, but this new feeling was too dark for that, and screaming at underlings wouldn't help. It was all too much, and her eyes streamed scented tears.

A flapping and scraping came from behind. Queen Bizzling Jee retracted her eyes, wiped her head, and turned to face Grimbolicus Nex. She poked her eyes out one at a time, plop, plop, plop. "Yes?" she asked imperiously.

"Your Bizzling?" asked the puzzled subject.

"What do you want, Grim?"

Grim didn't understand why the Queen had summoned him, and he didn't like the flaming red across her carapace. He glimpsed her drying tears and clenched. He waved his forward arms in the universal symbol of deference and hoped he could pacify her.

But the Queen was not pacified. She took his arm waving for insolence and was about to explode. Her invective engine thrummed out a list of insults powerful enough to crush a king. But something stopped her, a faint voice from deep inside sang out, and she listened, and her anger drained away like dirty oil. "Why did I summon you, Grim?" she asked, forcing her colours into neutral tones.

"I've no idea, Your Bizzling. As you know, there's been no news for three hundred years, at least nothing worth reporting. I assumed you had a project for me."

"Indeed, I do," beamed the Queen. "Grim, I need a visualisation of the high-level perfume trails, something dynamic and colourful. Would you oblige?"

Grim smiled and tried to hide his disappointment. He executed a creaking bow and reversed out of the chamber, forward arms still windmilling.

"I've done it," she muttered. "I've set things right with a mere command." She swept from her chamber and thundered down the stairs. "To the time engines!"

The Great Mind was proud of its deft handling of the Queen. Left to her own devices, she'd have grown desolate. She'd have done terrible damage as she meddled with history to distract herself from the pain. In a brilliant move, the Great Mind had given her a meaningful job and let her glimpse its ineffable power. The Queen felt that she had kept the universe safe and done so at a serene and regal distance using invisible servants. Although deluded, her perspectives had sharpened, and her miseries had gone.

Compared to the Queen, the twelve time rogues were a minor threat, and the Great Mind had dispensed with them during Her Majesty's anaesthesia. It had also sabotaged the palace time engines. They still worked—there was no point annoying the Queen—but they were crippled and aimed at safe places.

The King's New Codes

King Bozzling Jee had grown an idea, and his twelve eyes streamed at the beautiful prospect. He stared through his tears at the scattered tomes and open scrolls that lay scattered across the tiles of his room. And his fabulous multi-flapped carapace glowed a happy orange, and blue streaks rippled across it, making him look like an overcooked lobster in a shallow sea.

The King was an avid reader, and he'd recently devoted himself to the study of biology. Minions had ferried countless books and manuscripts, and he'd read them all. He preferred to read in the conventional manner, eschewing the great expanding screens so beloved by the Queen. It was, he felt, more scholarly and fitting for a philosopher such as himself.

His fourteen neural bundles, each five times bigger than a human brain, had organised his learning, and his mind hummed with evolutionary theory. What he realised—and the realisation had upset his sense of order—was that organisms were compromises, great bundles of historical accidents; hostages to archaic body plans, evolutionary tramlines, and weird embryologies. It was a wonder that bodies worked at all.

He saw that living things, including his own royal personage, were designed by a fumbling committee. This was an anathema to the King who much preferred a single architect, generally himself, to oversee any project.

The King's idea was to redesign creatures from scratch, to start with a clean slate; to remove the accumulated genetic debris and make sleeker, more efficient, beings—fabulous creatures no longer heir to the many debilitations that plague animals evolved in the normal way.

And so the King sent for his chief librarian, Lexis Grozzle.

A loose nest of elbows with a long neck and a tiny head arrived. Its wings were parked, and its forelegs flapped, and its head bobbed, and its three bulbous eyes scanned the chamber. Its face —a small triangular patch between its eyes—searched for an expression to please the King. "Your Majesty?"

"I propose," said the King, "to create another me, engineered from the ground up with no compromise." The King eyed the librarian. This would have been disconcerting with two eyes, but with twelve it was terrifying. *"What do you suggest?"*

The librarian, with his microscopic head, looked incapable of answering such a question. But his sixty brains weren't in his head—they were bundled in his barrel chest. He might look like a pot-bound snake in a leg farm, but he was a genius.

"I'll need a sample, Your Majesty."

The King twisted round and a lateral scale hinged up, like a luggage flap on an armoured bus.

The librarian approached and, using his delicate mouthparts, extracted a gelatinous blob. "I'll take it to the fabricator in the main time engine before it dries. The engine will work on your genome and iterate under my personal direction."

"Lexis, you're a genius!" He closed his scale. "But remember that the Queen's playing on the engines, and your fabricator sucks a lot of power."

It was rare for the King to use anyone's first name, so the librarian was flattered. And relieved. And emboldened. His facial expressions settled, oscillating between smug and apprehensive. "I'm sure that Her Majesty will understand," he said and left with a rustle of jointed limbs.

The King moved to the great window and stared at the placid city. The rippling blue lines coursing over his back grew thicker, and the fringes of his carapace glowed a poisonous yellow. He was ecstatic, and he smiled as he extended an ear and planted it on the stone floor.

There was the crisp crackle of librarian legs going down the stairs, then silence. The King repositioned his first ear and extended two more. The floor rumbled. A deep bellow came through the stone, and a fraction later through the air. The King smiled, picturing the Queen's fury. The librarian shrieked. This was playing out just as he'd expected. A deep pounding shook the chamber, louder and louder.

The door flew open, and the Queen stood there, quivering with rage. Her body remained on the threshold, but her eyes extended into the room. "What," she demanded, "is going on?"

The King detached his ears from the floor and grinned. He was rewarded with a glare. Then he raised five legs in appeasement, but the Queen was not amenable. She surged into the room and leant forward, meeting him eye to eye, their combined eyestalks creating a basket between their faces. The King's eyes retracted first. He backed away, mumbling to himself.

"My time," bellowed the Queen, "is always valuable. My time on the time engines is sacrosanct. You *know* that."

"Yes," conceded the King. "But this couldn't wait. This is an idea you'll approve of."

"Go on," she said. "Convince me."

The King explained his grand scheme, shrugged, and waited.

"Am I to understand," said the Queen, "that you are planning to create a better version of yourself?"

"Yes, a new and streamlined me, a shining and genetically concise me."

"And about time, too. If you need any suggestions for improvements, just ask." And with that, she swept from the room.

Many floors below, in the dingy vaults, Librarian Grozzle—still ruffled by his confrontation with the Queen—brushed down his leg hairs. He approached the main time engine, inserted the King's bud into the fabrication port, and then he applied his tiny head to the opening, like a stopper. Grozzle concentrated the full force of his mind and imagined the King redacted. And his imaginings impelled the great engine. It thrummed and glowed. No wonder the Queen loved it so much. Then silence. Not only had it computed the King's new code, it had synthesised it too.

Grozzle extracted his head, blinked his three eyes, and pulled out the modified bud using his softer mouthparts. He wrapped the bud in his bounciest silk and he began the long ascent to the grand chamber. With each step, the little bud swung in its harness.

Grozzle took a deep breath and scratched the dark wood of the great door.

"Come!" boomed the King.

Grozzle stepped in, like a stork delivering a baby. "Your Majesty."

The King stared at the little bundle hanging from Grozzle's mouth. A happy grinding came from his lateral carapace scales and his entire back turned yellow. "Ready so soon?" he cooed.

185

"The time engines work fast," said Grozzle. "Here, Your Majesty." The librarian's mouthparts telescoped forward, dangling the silk-wrapped bud before the King.

"May I?" he asked, as if he wanted to kiss the baby of an awed subject.

"It's you, I mean it's yours, Your Majesty."

"I conceived the idea, but you conceived the baby, Librarian Grozzle." He cradled the bud. "You and the time engine."

"That's very kind, Your Majesty, but I assure you—"

"Nonsense," said the King. "Take credit. You're a genius."

"Thank you, Your Majesty. Will that be all?"

"Yes." The King loaded the bud back into the recess from which it had emerged less than an hour before. The bud would have to go to the Royal Nursery tomorrow, but tonight he wanted him close. The King slept in the great chamber that night, grinding away and dreaming of his little creation.

Two weeks later, the glistening juvenile popped from his oversized nursery cell. He was fat and sleek on royal jelly, and as tall as the monarch himself. His colours throbbed, and his brains raced, and his claws snapped. Cleaners fussed and fettled and rubbed him down, and sang him songs.

He clicked, and the cleaners ran. The infant prince gathered himself together, like a duchess gathering her skirts, and took his leave. Nurses, feeders, and minstrels trailed him out and followed him down the halls to the great chamber.

There was a rustling on the corridor tiles, and a firm knock on the door. "Come!" roared the King, echoing his first words to his reworked bud. The door creaked open.

"Ready so soon?" asked the King.

"Yes, Your Majesty." The prince waved a leg and his support staff scuttled away. The senior minstrel strummed a chord, bowed, exited, and pulled the great door closed.

"Come closer. Let me see you properly."

The creation slid forwards and extended its twelve young eyes. Crisp images of the King fired up in the infant brains, and young glands clenched.

The King leant forward. "Just like me!" He sniffed and shed a perfumed tear. "I'm told your genome is fifteen times smaller than mine, and that you have learnt faster than I ever did, and that you've matured in only weeks. What do you say to that?"

"I would say I'm a worthy successor, Your Majesty."

The King's twelve eyes widened, bulging at full extension. His ears shot back into their pots, and something green dripped from a widening gap between his end-plates.

The prince shot forward, and his young mouthparts clamped on the ancient, armoured neck. They cracked the shell and sliced the glistening cords that linked the King's brains into a single coherent mind.

The prince vomited gallons of stomach juice into his father's gaping interior. Then came an insistent chomping and rustling, and an occasional crack of a carapace scale. Royal fluids poured out, and chunks of meat went down. The last bit of the King, a withered tail, flapped from the infant's mouth and vanished.

The prince dragged his bloated belly around the chamber, sucking up the last drops and fibres. His twelve bright eyes scanned the room for debris, and then he sagged and belched.

He planted an ear on the cool floor, as throaty grunts and mechanical whirring sounds came up through the tiles. Deep below, in the vaults of the castle, the Queen had disengaged from her time engine. Then came the sound of pounding feet.

187

He heaved himself to the back of the chamber, rearranged his mighty gut, belched, stared at the door, and waited.

Queen Bizzling Jee surged into the great chamber. "Where is he?" she demanded.

The swollen infant twitched. "The youngster left, Bizzling. He felt—how can I put it?—*constrained* here."

"I see," said the Queen. "Constrained, you say?"

"I do," replied the pretender. Hectic patterns raced across his back, and hot pink throbbed across his gut.

"Feeling well?" asked the Queen.

"Never better. In fact, I want to bud again."

"In that case, I'll alert the nursery." She turned away, and tears welled. Her jaws clenched, sending jagged yellow stress lines across her neck.

The Queen had known the King was dead the moment his nerve cords had snapped apart. His death pulse had struck her like a thunder clap and propelled her from her time engine. And she had wanted to confront the juvenile, to see for herself how the experiment had failed. Or succeeded too much.

The King's genetic adventure adjusted himself and broke wind with a wet splatter. The Queen huffed and marched out. As soon as the door had closed, she barrelled down the hall to the Royal Guards. They nodded and gasped as she explained the situation. And then—as a solid wall of scales and chomping teeth —they advanced on the chamber. The pretender was fast, and his mouthparts were sharp, but he was bloated, and young, and stupid, and no match for the massed guards.

Delirium Tempus Virion

The Great Mind poked around on the high shelf, amongst the drab and speckled books, until it found a glowing red volume with a machine—part steam engine, and part aquarium—drawn in gold leaf on its cover. The book's spine was stamped in silver foil as if it had a publisher, but the logo—a spiked icosahedron—was an imagined time virus. And there was no title or author's name.

The illustration sputtered into life. Its cogs turned, its tubes bubbled, and smoke spiralled from its tiny chimney. Behind the moving drawing, the leather changed from red to green to blue. And then the book vanished, leaving a dark night with stars above, and a twinkling city below.

A Moment's Consideration

Dr Olivia Fox twirled a lock of dark hair between her ringless fingers and peered down at the golden lights of London. The huge plane banked, and she turned to look across the aisles, catching fractured views of the city through the windows on the other side.

"I still get excited," she said.

Lisa grunted and continued reading the novel she'd bought at the airport. The cover had golden lettering, and an etching of a steam-driven machine.

Olivia settled back, smoothed her khaki pants, and let her thoughts wander. She'd made several useful contacts at the conference, and her paper had done well, and she might collaborate with the German group. All in all, she had a solid career; there was no prospect of a Nobel prize, but it was still something to be proud of.

She glanced across at her companion, but Lisa—eyes wide and lips twitching—was in another world.

"Leeese," complained Olivia, "you're no company."

"Mmmm."

Olivia turned away and stared out at the blackness. She thought about Timothy, her *fiancé*. She mulled over the word. It sounded fraught, and archaic, and wrong. Tim was an artist, so nothing was ever definite—promising maybe, but never definite. She released her hair, leant across the armrest, and poked Lisa's paperback.

"Don't—"

The plane's midsection shattered. For a cartoon moment, the head and tail sections flew on, then the explosion swallowed everything in a ball of light. The shock wave pounded out, refracting the city lights for an instant.

Olivia saw no flash and heard no explosion, but her death pulse—a furious, thwarted bundle of energy—understood far more. It shot back in time, screaming out a warning, and crying for revenge.

A hundred years before Olivia's jet exploded, and directly below the future detonation point, two gentlemen stared at a home-made device. It was part clock, part aquarium, and part steam engine, and it covered the desk, and its wires and tubes coiled and ran across the floor. And discs span and cogs ticked. Hunched and happy, the time machine—for that is what it was—clicked and gurgled.

Walter, who'd built the device and in whose study they stood, was tall with thinning grey hair. He was clean shaven and precise, but his skin was waxy and mottled, giving him a frail and cadaverous look, like a diseased stork. He sniffed every few seconds—a childhood tic from a half-remembered trauma—and shuddered. And cleared his throat.

Reginald, his friend and visitor, was round and florid and calm. He leant forward and squinted, working his ginger whiskers. "Very impressive," he observed at last.

Walter tilted his head and peered down his curving nose. "Indeed."

Fire crackled in the grate, but the study felt chilly. And above the house—in this younger London—no jets flew.

Walter picked his way across the study carpet. He grabbed a newspaper from the chair by the fireplace and held it out to Reginald. "Turn to the racing section and choose a race. Note the winner's name, but keep it a secret."

Reginald ran his finger down the page and stopped at a horse called *A Moment's Consideration*. "Done," he said.

"Now, write me a note urging me to bet on this horse," said Walter, and he sniffed and held out a creamy sheet of bond.

Reginald took the paper and wrote down names, and times, and places.

Walter hopped from foot to foot, twitching and sniffing. "Very good, now please sign it, date it, fold it up, and pop it in the slot."

Reginald inserted his note. A hiss, and the paper flew from his fingers and the machine burbled.

Walter fished a betting slip from his pocket and handed it over.

Reginald peered at the slip. "The horse is *A Moment's Consideration,* and the race was yesterday. How did you do it?"

"Your note arrived three days ago. I read it and bet on the horse."

Reggie nodded and frowned.

"And this," announced Walter, "is your note."

Reggie took the sheet, held it up to the light, and squinted. "It's my handwriting, I'll grant you, but the words are different: 'Consider for a Moment whether betting is good for you.' That's all there is. And there's no signature, but it's definitely my writing. It's the same ink and everything."

Walter beamed. "The machine changed your words to disguise their meaning."

"Take care, Walter. This is a frightening thing." His eyes darted to the guttering fire. "I have to be going."

Walter walked him to the door. "Come back tomorrow and we'll have another go."

Reginald stepped into the neat garden, nodded, shivered, raised his collar, and looked up. Smoke from the chimney rose into a clear and jet-less sky.

The next morning, Reginald returned to Walter's house and hesitated at the front door. Then he straightened his back, cleared his throat, and knocked.

There was a shuffling in the hallway and the door rattled open. Walter smiled. "Come in. I hope you slept well."

Two armchairs stood before the desk, bracketing an occasional table set with tea and biscuits. Walter took the left chair, and Reginald the right.

The machine gave out a faint electrical hum, and its cogs inched round. It ticked like an old clock, and blue oil bubbled in a glass tube.

"How could you possibly know how to build this machine?"

Walter munched on a biscuit and washed it down with weak tea. "It's not my design at all." He took another sip, stood up, arched his back, sniffed, stepped over to the bookcase, and extracted a thin volume. "Take a look at this."

Reginald squinted at the red leather cover and its gold-leaf time machine. Its title was *Walter's Temporal Telegraph*.

"I found it in the shop down the road," said Walter, lowering himself back into his chair, "and the title intrigued me."

Reginald frowned, harrumphed, and nodded for Walter to continue.

"I had to buy it. Then I raced home, made a pot of tea, and tore open the wrapper. It was a delightful story about a time machine—full of mystery and coincidence. When I'd finished, it was dark outside and my tea was cold."

Reginald cleared his throat. "Mysteries are one thing, but too many coincidences make a story implausible."

"They weren't coincidences in the *plot;* they were references to real life. The fictional machine was used on the twentieth of December, a hundred years from now. As you know, the twentieth of December is *my* birthday. And characters had the names of my relatives and friends." He grinned. "There was even a Reggie..."

Reginald nodded, as one might nod to a friend who'd lost his reason. "Please go on."

"There were place names I recognised, too. And the inventor —the main character, the *Walter* of the title—entered the numbers 86145351711 into his fictional machine. They're house numbers—*my* house numbers. The author wanted me to know that the fictional Walter represented me."

Reginald's eyes widened. "I see..."

"I read it again and again," said Walter, "and I made drawings and notes about the time machine." He leant forwards. "And each time, the descriptions in the book got more detailed..."

"You mean you understood more?" asked Reginald.

"No, there was progressively more information about the machine, and the rest of the novel shrank to make room. The book—hitherto a lovely thing of quirks and conversation— turned into a straightforward instruction manual. It lost its plot, its characters, its dialogue, and its settings..."

"That's impossible," said Reginald.

"I know. And now it's changed back into a novel. But it's a weaker thing. The instructions have gone, and the personal references have vanished. The book broke its link to me and became mundane."

"It's still called *Walter's Temporal Telegraph*," said Reginald. "It left that."

Walter snorted. "Merely to taunt."

Reginald leafed through the peculiar book. "But you still had your notes?"

"Yes, and I could work from those..." Walter stared into a strange and receding yesterday. "Most of the stuff I needed was just lying around the house. It was easy to build a time machine —strange as that might sound. Although growing the branching fibres that lie at its heart, was tricky. But as you saw, it works."

Reginald froze. "What did you do with your diagrams? Where did you put your notes?"

Walter simpered. "I followed the instructions—written in my own hand—and I fed them into the machine."

"What came out?"

"Nothing," Walter whispered. "Nothing at all..."

The humming stopped, leaving a hollow silence. The cogs clicked and came to rest. And a lone bubble floated to the surface of the blue oil and popped.

Walter jumped up and grabbed the knobs and bashed the dials. He pulled the wires and tapped the glass and thumped the table. But the machine was dead.

Two hundred years ago—a century before Walter and Reginald played the horses—Father O'Farrell sits hunched over his desk, absorbed in a book. It's a slender thing, bound in green leather, with its title—*Patrick's Eternal Clock*—stamped in gold. The priest shakes, and his lips move, and his cheeks glow red. He crumples pages as he races through the book. Then he stops at a diagram and presses the paper flat, his stubby fingers ironing out the creases. He leans forward, squints at the etching, pops out his tongue, grabs a pen, and scribbles in the margin.

The Great Mind hovered in the damp night. A truck—painted brown with creamy script, and full of mahogany furniture—tore along the motorway.

The Great Mind reached out and touched the driver's brain, and the truck jackknifed across three lanes. Eight vehicles—bunched together on the drizzled blacktop—tried to stop. The truck's metal side guillotined the would-be bomber of the plane, sending his head into the back seat. His three accomplices, following in a white van, got torn apart. Six more hammer-blows, then hollow quiet. Red tail lights twinkled, and the crippled truck's main beams shone across the emergency lane and onto the blighted grass of the embankment.

The driver of the approaching fuel tanker—revolving on a recent rape—took a fraction too long to interpret the scene picked out by his lights. He turned left, braked hard, and aimed for the gap. Had he been on a motorbike, or even in a small car, he might have succeeded, but his tanker was too big, and no amount of technology could stop his half-filled rig from slewing round and smashing into the waiting vehicles.

Viewed from above, it was pleasingly symmetrical: eight smaller vehicles bracketed by parallel trucks. The Great Mind lingered for a moment, savouring its art.

Then physics resumed. With a boom—satisfyingly reminiscent of the now averted plane explosion—the whole collection of metal, glass, wood, rubber, plastic, fuel, and flesh, detonated.

The Great Mind had twisted many histories into this beautiful assassination—this cleansing ballet of steel and fire—and it felt no remorse.

Deleting the terrorists changed history: the bomb never reached the plane, and Dr Olivia Fox, her friend Lisa, her colleagues, the other passengers, the crew, and a few animals, survived.

Seconds after the plane didn't explode, events a century earlier also changed. *Walter's Temporal Telegraph,* the singular red book, snuffed out of existence, and Walter's finger slid into the new gap on the shelf. He blinked, shrugged, and wandered off shaking his head.

Several moments after Walter's book vanished, and a hundred years further back, the green volume entitled *Patrick's Eternal Clock,* disappeared. Father O'Farrell shifted from his desk and his feverish labours and found himself strolling around the village, with an untroubled mind, and pink cheeks. Back in his house, the floor of his cramped office snapped clean, as scrunched-up pages vanished.

The Great Mind relaxed and contemplated the horrid time-virus it had just blocked. This vengeful knot of consciousness came from the death pulses of Olivia, Lisa, and a pissed-off entrepreneur in first class. It had emerged from the exploding plane like a bad mood from a mob, and then it had hurtled back a hundred years. A century was its limit, and so it had recruited Walter. The unfortunate man, in the thrall of the viral book, had built his time machine and slipped his diagrams and notes into its metal mouth. The machine had digested the information and pulsed the viral code back in time. It had arrived a hundred years earlier, printed on creamy paper and encased in fine leather, and it had fallen into the hands of Father O'Farrell.

197

The Great Mind suspected that there were more victims, but it lacked the will to look, and it tried to forget the troublesome germ. Managing forward causality was hard enough, but stamping out retroactive time-viruses was impossible. These mini-nightmares propagated backwards in time, and so should threaten their own genesis—but they survived. Most were mild, and the Great Mind wondered how many lay quietly embedded in history. And it wondered how many outrages—and history is full of outrages—had spawned such creatures. It imagined mass executions, and sinking ships, and it imagined the viral instructions arcing back from these events—like scorpion tales stabbing the past—to re-work history.

The Great Mind felt ambivalent, for it too was built from death pulses—albeit on a grand scale—and, just like a time-virus, its job was to change history...

Three hundred years ago, Gerald Ashman, an English master in a small provincial school, stared at a thick blue book entitled *Gerald's One-Hundred-Year Diary,* which had landed on his desk.

His pupils had gone, and the classroom was silent. Late afternoon sun from the high windows made the blue leather glow and the golden letters waver. The book was rich and enticing, and Mr Ashman picked it up...

Germ of an Idea

"Visiting the past is impossible," concluded the professor, fighting to keep awake, "which is just as well, since it would cause all sorts of problems. Things are best left in, um, in place. In their places. But maybe, as I suggested earlier, *ideas* can go back..." he swayed and grabbed the desk, "...in fact..."

But the students were leaving, hefting their bags and chattering. They'd absorbed enough, and their minds were elsewhere. They were oblivious to Professor Ned Knight's haunted look, and to his stumbling delivery, for at sixty-one he belonged to another species—one they could never imagine themselves becoming.

The Great Mind hung in the lecture theatre, like an invisible airship. It stared at the professor's stooped figure and wondered how he could know about time viruses. As the last of the students filed out, it entered the professor's head. The man's brain was, by human standards, remarkable but there was no hint of a viral infection—just the germ of an idea.

Ned sat in the refectory warming his hands around an extra-hot double-shot latte. He glanced down at a slice of carrot cake. Half was missing, but he had no memory of eating it. He stared vacantly at the crumbs in his lap, shook his head, and sipped his coffee.

People milled around with piled plates. At the next table, five engineering students chomped through mountains of Asian food. They jabbered, laughed, slurped, forked, and checked messages. And just beyond, nestled in a glassy corner, two girls stared into each other's eyes. Ned edged around to get a better look. Their loose black and grey clothing marked them as arts students. One whispered something in the other's ear, and they interlaced hands, and Ned had to look away.

He pulled out a notepad and riffled through to the last entry —dated that day at 3.47am. Symbols, boxes, arrows, circles, squiggles, and blocks of spidery script filled the pages. Even here, in the bustling café, his nighttime thoughts on retroactive ideas—mind viruses that could travel back in time—retained their icy beauty. His logic was flawless, sparse, and poetic. He rubbed his forehead. A massive headache was building, like a summer storm, dark and damp and electric. He closed the notebook and left the refectory. He turned right and then left, and tottered down the concrete ramp, keeping to the side and grasping the rail. At the bottom, he paused as if he'd lost his way. After some frowning and finger waving, he headed left towards a bench. As he wobbled down the avenue, a cyclist flew past with a rush and a hiss. Ned staggered in the slipstream and looked round. The idiot cyclist swerved around a bunch of students— who weren't in the least bothered—and powered into town.

Ned reached the bench. Feverish and shaking, he grabbed the armrest and lowered himself onto the hard slats, keeping his head level. He pulled out his notebook and stared at his scribbles, hoping to rein in his frantic thoughts—much as one might pick up a book on a restless night.

The Great Mind poured more of itself into Ned's brain. The man's eyes closed, his head lolled back, and he let out a long sigh. He lay like this for several minutes, relishing the peace, and the morphine-like relief, and—in his augmented mind—the germ grew.

Ned looked up. Busy campus people flashed past, all blurred colours and abstract shapes. He slapped his thighs, shook his head, levered himself up, and headed home.

He stood outside his flat, whimpering and groaning, then he dug in his pocket, grunted, pulled out a key, aimed for the keyhole, and missed. "Bollocks," he said, and leant against the door frame like a cartoon drunkard, with his tongue out and his brow furrowed. He tried again, and the key slipped in, and he fell into the hall, stumbled into the lounge room, and landed on the settee. He curled up, clutched his head, and wept.

Ten minutes later, he stomped up to the bathroom, splashed water on his face, and stared into the mirror. "Fuck me," he said, pulling his lower eyelids down. He opened the cabinet. The bottom shelf had shaving foam and a razor; the top shelf had pills and creams. "Bastard stuff," he shouted. "Useless, *bastard* stuff." He tore everything out, scattering it across the floor. And then he stood and sobbed.

Andy knocked on Ned's front door, but there was no reaction, so he let himself in. "Hello?" he called down the hallway. "Are you here?" But there was no reply, so Andy headed to the kitchen, grabbed a beer, wandered into the lounge, and stared at the ammonite on the mantlepiece. He broke wind, sniffed, and swigged his drink. "Why did you call?" he muttered, then he shrugged, put down his bottle, and headed for the bathroom.

A body—and for a moment, Andy didn't know whose—lay on the tiled floor with its head pressed against the toilet bowl. Water ran from the cold tap, pills were scattered everywhere, plastic containers lay against the bath, and shards of glass lay under the sink. Andy knelt down. "What have you done, you stupid, *stupid, bastard?*" He felt his brother's neck and put his ear to his mouth. Then he stood up, pulled out his phone, and called an ambulance.

Ned opened his eyes, looked up, frowned, and gurgled.

"Quick, he's waking up," Andy yelled into the phone. He edged forward. "Are you OK?"

Ned reached out, grinned, and punched the floor. Andy jumped back, with his jaws and his scrotum clenched. Then Ned arched and twisted, and smashed his head against the toilet bowl.

"Ned?" said Andy, as he stared at the blood on the porcelain, trying to connect the red and white shapes with his brother, trying to weave the mad impressions into some kind of understanding. "Ned?"

Ned's jaw worked away, but no words came, just a thin and rasping gibber. Andy reached out, but Ned's mouth slammed shut, cracking teeth. Then his eyes rolled back.

Nurse Julie popped in at tea time. "How are we today, Professor Knight?" she asked, but she didn't expect an answer. She edged towards his bed and pursed her lips. And the machines kept watch, blinking and beeping.

Ned sat up, gurgled, tilted his head, flapped his tongue, raised his arm, and pointed at the nurse. Julie screamed and dropped her tray. Ned frowned, as if puzzled by her reaction, and then he fell back. He was dead—in the conventional sense—when his head hit the pillow. During that short collapse, a thought-bundle had escaped. It was part Ned, part time-virus,

202

and part Great Mind. And it barrelled into the past, heading for fifty years ago, and a new host.

The virus struck Helen at night, and her five-year-old mind raced. A dream locomotive roared across her curtain rail, and faces with shifting features floated around her bed. She twisted and turned, and thrashed about, and fought see-through monsters that grinned and gibbered and danced.

Morning came, and the slippery thoughts faded, and the world clicked back to normal. The fish on the curtains glowed yellow and pink and blue, as sunlight lit the fabric. Helen rolled onto her side and stared at the toys piled high on the dresser. She sniffed, swung out of bed, and marched over. "I want you to behave when I go," she said, wagging her finger. "And no funny business."

The stuffed animals, squeezed together at funny angles, stared back.

Helen trudged downstairs and slumped at the kitchen table. She stirred her breakfast and stared at the cereal packet's grinning cartoons. And the cartoons stared back. And one winked.

Her mother reached across and brushed back curls from Helen's sticky brow. "What's up, Darling?"

"Neddy's in my head."

Old Dr Bell had an impressive-looking certificate on his wall. Helen squinted at it, but the words were long, and curling, and difficult to understand, and the light from the French windows glared in the picture glass. Below, was a cabinet of glinting bottles and funny instruments. And high on another wall, was a print of a stag, proud on its mountain, and Helen tried to lose herself in its mists.

"OK," said Dr Bell, coming round his wooden desk. "Let's have a look."

He peered through funny half-moon spectacles at Helen's face. She looked up, pursed her lips, and did her best to keep still.

He felt around her neck and under her jaw. "No glands," he said. "Now, open wide and say ahhh."

"Ahhh," sang Helen.

The doctor shone a light down Helen's throat, harrumphed, sat back, and turned to Helen's mother. "It's probably a virus."

"Should I keep her off school?"

"It's up to you. I don't think she's infectious, but she could do with some rest."

"Any medicine?"

"No, just plenty of fluids, *and lots of sleep.*" He looked over his spectacles at Helen's mother. "No television, *and in bed by seven.* If she's no better by the end of the week, bring her back. Thank you Mrs Harper."

They filed out from the surgery.

"That boy's called Neddy," said Helen, tugging her mother's arm and pointing at a spindly kid in the waiting room. "Is *he* the one in my head?"

The boy looked up, massaged his throat, and stared at Helen. Their eyes met, and the time-virus hopped, like a psychic flea, from Helen's fevered mind to the spindly boy's head. "Don't point," said her mother. "And no, people can't get into your head. Let's get an ice cream."

They ate as they walked along the park's edge. And beside them, people in white played tennis in neglected courts, a little dog tore along after a big yellow ball, and a young boy threw a toy aeroplane.

"His mum called him Neddy. That's how I know his name. What's wrong with him, Mummy?"

"Maybe tonsillitis, I really don't know."

Helen looked up from her cone. "The doctor had a nice room, didn't he?"

"Yes, dear, now let's get you home."

Seven o'clock arrived, and Helen—a worn-out waif in a monkey nightgown—stood at the foot of the stairs. "Neddy's gone and I'm better."

"Yes, darling, I'm sure he is, but you look exhausted. Now go to bed, and I'll bring you some juice."

Helen nodded and clambered up the stairs, and climbed into bed, and she was fast asleep when her drink arrived. Her face was smooth, her mind was free, and her favourite toy—an ugly creature called 'Friend'—nestled against her cheek. Her mother closed the door, smiled, and tiptoed away.

Miss Angela Fernlee watched 1K, her class of eleven-year-olds, and chewed her lip. At twenty-six, she was still new to teaching, but she felt that even old Mrs Anderson, her favourite teacher in high school, would baulk at this. Miss Fernlee squared her shoulders, cleared her throat, and addressed the class. "Please turn to page fifty-four."

No one moved. The children looked pale, and haunted, and distracted. And at the back of the class—his textbook open, his pen poised, and his spectacles askew—a spindly boy called Neddy Knight massaged his throat.

There was no chatter or playfulness in this class, and smudgy eyes tracked Angela's every move. The young teacher sat at her desk and marked the work. At eleven o'clock, the children trooped out for morning tea. Their footsteps clumped down the corridor, and no one ran or sang, or chattered.

When the footsteps stopped, Angela walked to the staff room and made herself a strong tea. She stirred in three sugars and, in her nervousness, rattled her cup against her saucer, and Ben, the tweedy history master, and Alf who taught remedial English, looked up. She gave a thin smile and reached for a biscuit.

Angela returned to class and found the children already in their seats and staring at the blackboard, where someone had drawn a ball with blobs and radiating lines. Her history notes had been rubbed out, and the chalk duster lay on her desk in a halo of dust, like a smoking gun.

"Who's the artist?"

No one answered. No one giggled or pointed fingers. The children sat taut, like radio masts in a field, and the air thrummed. She rubbed her arms, sat down, and pretended to mark the history test. After ten minutes, she looked up. And the children looked back.

The school day finally ended, and Angela arrived home. She shut the front door of her little terraced house, leant against its solid wood, rested her head on its frosted glass, sighed, and waited for her heart to slow.

"OK," she muttered and set off along the narrow passage. She brushed past the bulky winter coats and stepped into the kitchen. She switched on the kettle, drummed her fingers on the counter, and stared through the window at the ancient holly bush and the dank and mossy garden wall. Behind the wall, the neighbour's house rose like a factory side, with bricked-up windows and iron pipes. She wanted to move to a newer suburb, to a semi-detached house with wide lawns and sweeping paths. But today, her cramped kitchen, her tiny garden, her blighted bush, her neighbour's ugly house, and all the huddled brick, made her feel safe.

Angela took her tea to the front room, drew the curtains against the late afternoon, and settled down with her novel. But the letters swam. She blinked and scrunched her eyes, but nothing helped. Beyond the dusty golden drapes, footsteps clattered, and cars droned, and a distant motorbike worked through its gears, and Angela wondered what sorts of lives they had, those outside people.

She ate a light supper, fretted, watched TV, sipped brandy, and took herself to bed, where she lay, wide-eyed, until morning. She got up, stumbled downstairs, sipped black coffee, gazed at her holly bush, and left for school with no makeup.

The class of 1K was silent. The crystalline array of boys and girls glared as the mind-virus circulated. Then the virus detached from the children and torpedoed into the teacher's tired head.

Miss Fernlee walked out of the classroom, past the office with its muted chatter and hard clack of typewriters, through the main doors, and into the street. She blinked in the sunlight, then marched down the avenue, turned right, and pretended to look in the dress shop window. The number 12 bus appeared, and she stepped out. Angela's death pulse—and its viral cargo—shot back fifty years and slipped into the mind of a sleeping child. Little Dorothy's brain offered no resistance, and by early morning she was sick with future thoughts...

Miss Fernlee wasn't missed until lunchtime, when Alf, the remedial English teacher, wandered past her noisy classroom. He tapped the door and popped his head inside, expecting that Miss Fernlee was trying something experimental. A pencil flew past his eye and clattered against the wall.

Alf screamed.

Silence.

He pointed at the nearest pupil. "You boy!"

A tousled-haired child, tie on one side, and ink stains down his shirt, got up. "Sir?"

A strangled squeal came from the back.

"What the hell's going on in here?"

"It's Miss Fernlee, Sir, she's gone, Sir." The boy smirked, and a titter ran round the class.

Alf turned purple. More giggles. He was used to difficult children—the disadvantaged, the slow, the bloody-minded, and the plain stupid—but these kids were exultant. He sniffed, turned on his heels, and marched to the headmaster's office.

The class erupted into laughter. The virus had gone, and the air had cleared, as if someone had thrown open the tall windows of a stifling sanatorium.

Morning assembly the next day was sombre. The Headmaster stood on the stage, flanked by his staff. He cleared his throat and called for quiet. A stifled sob, and a teenaged girl ran out, surrounded by several friends. The music teacher struck the piano keys, and the school sang. 1K stood together at the front of the hall, and amongst them, a spindly boy—one Neddy Knight— massaged his throat, and smiled, as the germ of an idea formed...

Grimoire

In the Mind Library, there was a book of spells that worked. It *might* be hiding in plain sight, faded, broken, and unremarkable, slipped between volumes of fiction, or next to an outdated almanac. Or it might lie buried in the mountains of discarded works. Or it might pretend to be something else.

Alarmed

Jason hated mornings, but he hated his alarm clock even more; it had been a gift from his mother and so he felt obliged to keep it, although it was big, ugly, loud, and unreliable. And it was getting worse. He rolled over and swore. The bloody thing had gained twenty minutes since last night, which was bad by anyone's reckoning. He knew it was wrong, and by exactly how much, because his radio said 6.40. The radio came on every morning at seven, but without the alarm clock, Jason would sleep through its static-filled news, blending its death and destruction into his dreams. But the hated alarm clock smashed through any sleep. It might take a few seconds—during which time its bell became a fire alarm at his primary school, or a remembered ambulance—but it *would* wake him.

He reached over, bashed its button, and lay there fuming, determined to stay in bed until seven. But the clock went off again, louder than ever. He slammed it. Silence. It rang again, and this time Jason tingled. And the more annoyed he got, the more awake he got. He crossed his arms and thrashed his legs. He swore, rolled out of bed, and raised his fist above the little clock. "I'm going to get my hammer," he explained to the empty room, "and smash that *fucking* clock to *fucking* bits." The alarm stopped. And Jason's anger drained away.

He stumbled around, fighting his clothes. Then he wandered into the kitchen, filled the kettle, and emptied the dishwasher. This was his daily routine. It took the same time to empty the dishwasher as it did to boil the water—a little synchronisation that geared him up to face his day. But he dropped a wine glass, and as he cleaned it up, the kettle boiled. The dishwasher—uncoupled in time from the boiling kettle—still gleamed with cutlery and spotless plates.

He ignored the call of the dishwasher, warmed the coffee pot, spooned in the coffee, added boiling water, stirred the peaty mix, and left it to stand. He put his cereal and frozen fruit into the microwave and stabbed in three minutes—enough time to let the coffee brew.

Jason took his warm and sticky cereal to the table, pushed down the coffee plunger, slumped in his chair, and took a long and scorching drink. At the first spoonful of oats, the house moved, roaring and shuddering like a train crash wrapped in an earthquake.

Jason flew up, spilling oats and fruit and coffee. Panting too hard to swear, his heart thumping, his chest heaving, and his fists clenched, he raced to the front door, fought its handle, and fell onto the porch. And into diesel fumes and dust. He grasped the railings and stared across the wreck of his garden. The truck was huge. And its front-end—the entire cab—was buried in his bedroom. He tilted his head and frowned, and thought of all the other demolition work in his suburb. Then he thought that he should have bought a different house—one that didn't sit at the bottom of a fast and downhill road. Finally, he realised that he'd cheated death. Happy at his luck, he trotted down his steps and smiled at all his neighbours.

Ben from next door ran up. "Are you all right, mate?"

Jason grinned.

"Mate," said Ben, "I think you're in shock."

Jason's grin got bigger.

"Come inside," said Ben. "I'll make you a coffee. You need to sit down."

A huge man, covered in dust, emerged from the hole in Tom's house, stared at his truck, and scratched his head.

"You go in," said Ben. "I'll see if the driver's OK."

Jason wandered into his neighbour's house and sat down. A distant siren sounded. And the seven o'clock news came on.

That night, Jason rang his mother.

"Hello Mum, I just—"

"I saw the doctor today..."

Jason held the phone away from his ear. His mother paused, mid-bulletin, and Jason jumped in. "Thanks for the alarm clock."

"That's all right, dear. Glad you like it."

"The thing is, it broke, and I wondered if you could get me another one?"

"Um, well, I'm not sure..."

"I'll pay for it."

"It's not that. The shop I got it from changed."

"Changed hands?"

"No, I don't think so. The same man's still there, although, like the rest of us, he's getting older—"

"And?"

"It's gone fancy," she said. "There are no more alarm clocks —it's all pearls and diamonds, and showy watches."

"Let me know where it is. I'll buy a watch—one with an alarm."

"Funny you should say that. I was in there recently, and the man—he's very nice you know, I think his name's Bernie, or something like that—tried to sell me a watch. He said *an alarm on your arm is better...*"

212

The Punishment Man

Rex climbed from his small yellow car, sniffed the air, and opened the rear hatch. He glanced down at the blacktop at his feet and noticed shards of glass near the back wheels.

"Some lowlife left a bottle there, some thoughtless *fucker*." He rummaged in the boot and grabbed a stained bag. "I might need a new tyre—and all because a *fucking* lowlife dropped a *fucking* bottle." He slammed the hatch and marched off, twitching and sniffing, to the post office.

Rex thought back to when he'd cut his foot on a long-ago beach, when he was a seven-year-old kid paddling in the sea. He'd stepped on the bottom of a smashed bottle, whose jagged edges pointed up, like an evil glass crown. He was carried off, still bleeding, to the local surgery. Rex remembered the clinic's window, and the sunlight slanting through its Venetian blinds, and how his dad had said he needed stitches in his sole and ankle. And how his mother had held him down on the hard couch. "Try to keep still, Rex," she'd said. "Be brave."

He'd listened to the busy sounds, and grown-up voices, and the clatter of a metal bowl, and a distant laugh. And he'd smelt the sharp stench of disinfectant. He'd stared at the white ceiling for ages, until a doctor appeared at his feet. Rex had looked past the white coat and concentrated on the window, doing his best to be brave. The needle jabbed his sole, and the pane's bright oblong shattered into twenty window-ghosts.

Hard to believe it happened fifty years ago. It was another life, another *low*-life, another discarded bottle.

Rex opened his post-office box, peered inside, and pulled out a handwritten envelope which had two lizard stamps, a smudged postmark, and no return address. He looked around frowning.

Chatter floated across from the café next door. Two skeletal blondes in designer gym-wear picked at rocket salads. A young man chomped on a dripping gourmet-sandwich and reached, without looking, for a long black coffee. And a slender man— bearded, and formal, and of indeterminate age—looked up.

Rex sniffed. It was too early for lunch, and café meals were expensive. He locked his box and walked away.

The concrete paving by the shops glared in the sun. Rex squinted and looked away, and he thought about the bearded man who looked like a refugee from eighty years ago. In those days, it was impossible to tell a person's age, because people became adults in a moment, and they stayed that way for years in a kind of suspended middle-age, before suddenly getting old. Rex wondered why. Had bodies changed, or was it fashion, or the way old films were lit?

A spaniel strained to reach him, knocking water from a stainless steel bowl. Someone called the dog and tried to make conversation with Rex. But Rex didn't chat to dog owners. Instead, he hurried past and peered in the newsagent's window. Seeing no papers, he continued walking, negotiating another café, whose tables spilled onto the path. The last obstacle was a charity stall, shadowed by the overhang of the supermarket. An eager girl thrust a yellow paper flag at Rex, while her companion, a lanky, acned youth, busied himself with the display. Rex looked away, turned right, and slipped into the coolness of the shop.

The Italian loaves smelt wonderful, and he poked around until he found a warm one. Then he stashed it in his stained bag, and headed for the alcohol section, where he inspected the wine racks, as he did every morning, for specials. He grabbed a dark Merlot and nodded at its bronze awards. Then he joined the queue and thought about his peculiar letter.

"Next please," called a girl in black.

Rex handed over the exact money, had a minor argument over the discount on the wine—which he won—and then he left. And as he left, he had the strangest feeling that the girl had been toying with him. It was a nice feeling, and he smiled at the sunshine. And in this state of bliss, he continued around the block, avoiding the stall, the coffee drinkers, and the friendly dog. Then he clambered into his little car, reversed over the broken glass, and drove off.

A truck pulled out from a side road, straight through a stop sign. Rex slammed on his brakes and leant on the horn. A stubby finger, at the end of a hairy arm, appeared out of the truck's window, and a fat and stubbly face mouthed off at him.

"Thoughtless bastard," screamed Rex. "Hit a tree and die."

Rex remembered nothing of the rest of the journey, and he found himself in his kitchen, his hands trembling, and the shopping bag on the floor. After composing himself, he pulled out his bargain Merlot and stood it on the worktop. It looked full of dark and velvet promise, and he would open it at seven and sip it while he fried the garlic...

215

But now, it was lunchtime, so he cut his bread, sliced his cheese, and washed his salad. Then he stirred his black coffee and thought about the letter; it was an intriguing thing, but it would keep until he'd eaten...

Rex slit the envelope and pulled out the letter, causing a sachet of powder to fall onto the worktop. The message was handwritten in green ink. Rex steadied himself against the counter and began to read.

Dear Rex,

I trust this letter finds you well—and not too agitated. I have enclosed some special dust. Use it sparingly to visit the past and punish those who've wronged you. Make them suffer in closed-off bubbles—private hells that you can decorate as you wish. You are the Punishment Man.

Try the powder and let me know what you think.

Cheers,

Rick

Rex closed the letter and frowned. Rick, whoever Rick was, understood him, and understood his need for revenge. Rex opened the sachet and inserted a finger, like a television cop checking for drugs. Then he lurched in sudden drunkenness and grabbed the counter, and fine dust scattered. He stared at his rippling finger, and then he gawped as his hand, and then his whole arm, wavered. How stupid, he thought, to touch an unknown powder.

The room tilted, and blackness, like spilt ink, swamped the kitchen floor. Rex pitched forward, but instead of hitting the ground, he hovered over a dark and heaving sea. Waves broke

216

behind him, and he rotated, like a blimp on a wire, and faced the shore. Street lights twinkled on the promenade, and below the sea wall, several boys stood on the beach. A crash of glass, and a sharp tinkle of laughter. Then an arm swung, and another bottle crashed against the wall. The boys whooped with delight.

"Thoughtless bastards," muttered Rex. "Children will play there tomorrow."

Dark groynes stretched into the sea, and something stirred in Rex: this was his childhood beach. *He was back fifty years.*

Were these the boys who broke the glass that cut his foot?

"Yes," he said, with dreamy conviction. "They were..." He skimmed the surf and flew across the sand.

Three of the yobs were skinny, with narrow, gormless faces, and empty, uncaring expressions. The fourth was tall, with a glint of low cunning in his eyes, while the fifth was squat and stupid, and stood apart. Rex hovered at shoulder height and stared at the idiot faces. "You stupid bastards!"

The yobs looked around. Tall Boy walked over and punched Squat Boy in the shoulder and laughed. "Are you a fucking comedian, or what?"

"No," said Squat Boy. "I can't do voices, *not like that.*"

Tall and Squat glared at each other. And, as if to defuse the tension, one of the skinny yobs opened a beer while the other two lit cigarettes.

Rex smelt the thin and poisonous smoke, and fury filled him. He clenched his fists and fired up the engines of this nightmare place, and the groynes rose up like prison walls. They slid across the sand, and thick fog trailed them, hanging from the sky, like privacy curtains. More fog poured in from the land, coiling over the sea wall, and blocking the lights, and boxing them in. This place, this patch of soiled sand and yobs, was hell.

Rex knew that the fog held nothing. There was no world beyond its vapours, no horizon, no stars, no promenade, and no town. "Pick up the glass, you bastards," he said.

The boys looked round, and muttered, and shrugged, and stubbed out cigarettes.

Rex floated up. *"Now!"* he shouted.

A skinny boy giggled, girlish and hysterical. Squat Boy made a dash for the groyne, and scrabbled up its blackened wood, but he slipped and cut his shin. And he wept and limped away.

"Pick it up, you stupid bastards!" yelled Rex. "Or things will get worse."

"Fuck you," said Tall Boy, "whoever you are."

The groynes moved closer; the bubble-beach was shrinking.

"Time's running out," said Rex. *"Pick it up."*

The boys formed a loose circle and watched the groynes advance from left and right. The great weed-encrusted timbers pushed the litter across the beach, creating a dirty bow wave of cigarette butts, bottles, cartons, and condoms. And evil shards of broken glass rose from the spitting sand. Then the grinding stopped, and the bubble-hell paused.

"Pick up the glass. *With your lips.*"

"Fuck you," said Tall Boy, but his voice trembled.

The groyne-wood moved again, and the three skinny young men put their mouths to the ground.

"That's good," said Rex, "very good. But you've got to *pick it up*, not just kiss it!"

Squat Boy got down on all fours and chomped through sand and glass. "It hurts," he said. "It's cutting me."

"Good, perhaps you'll learn something. *Now eat!*"

Tall Boy reclined on the rocks, dragged on a cigarette, and smirked.

Rex stared at the bright red dot cupped in the young man's hand, and noted the curled lip. "You too, smart-arse, you too."

The tall one gave his invisible tormentor a V-sign.

"We've moved on from lips!" shrieked Rex. "It's eyelids now."

A heavy section of timber detached itself from the eastern groyne and slammed into Tall Boy, knocking him forwards, and ramming his face into the dirty sand. He pulled his head out, and shards of glass poked from his eyes.

"No, no, no," he wept. A fish hook pierced his cheek, and a condom hung from his lips, like a thin rubber tongue.

"Get down. Pick up every bit!" screamed Rex.

The other boys looked up, like cows disturbed at pasture, and then they returned to munching glass. The fog closed in, and the bubble-hell vanished.

Rex was back in his kitchen, a wide smile across his face. "That was good. That was *great*. That was *fucking brilliant*." He sighed. "Now for that finger-giving bastard of a truck driver."

Rex scattered more magic dust, and flashes danced in the air, and sparkles settled, and the light went milky, as thick fog descended outside. But the house stayed level, and the kitchen floor remained.

A cough.

Rex span round. "Who's there?"

"Remember that scrawny boy from primary school?" a voice behind him asked. "The one you stopped at the gates..."

"Who are you? And *where* the fuck are you?"

"I'm that kid. I'm Rick."

Rex frowned and rubbed his brow. Then his mouth fell. "You're that snotty-nosed kid. The bony little shit with cheap glasses..."

"The very same," the voice whispered in Rex's ear. "I'm your victim from long ago, and your correspondent from last week—boy and man."

"But that was *years* ago."

"*You* don't forgive, *I* don't forgive," said the invisible Rick.

Rex sniffed. "You mean the bottle-boys were a test?"

"Yes. And you failed."

"But—"

"They were more than just a test," continued Rick, "they were a taste of what's to come. For you, that is."

Rex gulped, and a tear welled. Something struck the kitchen window, cracked the glass, and left a smear.

"The groynes," observed Rick, "were a nice touch—closing round those stupid boys, like timber jaws. You're quite the artist."

"It was the dust. The *magic* dust did it—*your* dust did it."

"No," said Rick. "*You* made it happen. *You* made a hell. And as an artist, you'll appreciate the hell I've built for you."

The floor of Rex's kitchen turned to asphalt. Not the blacktop of the road into which the idiot truck driver had pulled, but the gritty tar of the long-ago playground from the school where Rex had tormented Rick. Sweet papers blew around, an invisible skipping rope slapped the ground, and unseen girls giggled.

"The litter's good, isn't it? The wrappers are authentic, you know."

"Brilliant, you're a fucking genius."

"Notice the chewing gum on the ground. It'll make running harder. *Your shoes will stick.*"

"Can't we just forget it?" begged Rex. "It was so long ago. I was so young…"

"No, now stop snivelling and get through those school gates *before they close for good.*"

Rex looked up. Giant gates blocked the kitchen doorway. Their planks were dark and drenched, and crusted with barnacles, and draped in seaweed. And they creaked.

"You stole my groynes," moaned Rex.

"Yes, how naughty of me. And they're closing fast because it's going-home time, so *run!*"

But Rex's feet were stuck to years of gum. He pitched forwards, his hands flew out to break his fall, and the blacktop hit. He hunched and sobbed and picked the grit from his palms, and blood welled up.

And just beyond, and out of reach, the gates slammed shut, and fog—the bubble's edge—closed in.

The Doctor Redacted

Dr Walden, absorbed and prim, scribbled at his desk, putting the finishing touches to his paper. The door flew open, and he turned his skull-like head and forced a smile. "Derek," he said, "do come in."

A small and sprightly man—who could have been a jockey in a different world—stood panting in the entrance. He clutched pages to his chest and jiggled.

"Let's see," said Walden.

Derek ambled across and handed over the crumpled sheets. He took a step back and waited. The psychiatrist smiled, smoothed the pages with his delicate fingers, and peered at the writing through his gold-rimmed spectacles. His pen darted across the lined sheets, pausing now and then to tick a word. Derek cackled and wrung his hands.

Walden grinned. "Brilliant, Derek, you've done it again." He aligned the pages and stapled them together. "This will take me a while to go through. Let's speak tomorrow. Will you have more stuff for me by then?"

Derek shuffled out, nodding and twitching. Walden waited until the latch had closed, then he tugged at his top drawer. Pages bulged out, and Derek's note from yesterday fell onto the floor. Walden added the latest offering, pressed down on the pile, and closed the drawer. He gave a long sigh and gazed through his office window at the asylum gardens. There was a wide lawn, lush after recent rain, surrounded by thick hedges and high brick walls, and clouds—torn and shredded—ran across the sky. He sucked on his pen, and he let his mind wander...

A madhouse was the right place to study the psyche. The insane saw things differently, and sometimes they saw things that no one else could see. The future, for instance. Precognition had interested Walden since medical school, and now he studied it in his mental patients. This was a rich seam, unrecognised and unworked, and he had met many talented subjects. But Derek was the star. The poor man was small and twitchy and confused, and he babbled and gibbered, and stared into space. But Derek could write, and write well, although he took hours to put down a few lines. He would sit in his favourite corner with his tongue sticking out, carefully forming each word. His letters were big, and neat, and round, and equally spaced, and they sat on the lines of the paper like fat bottoms on a wall. Derek had never mastered joined-up writing, and sometimes it was hard to know where one word ended and another began. And there was no punctuation. And it was in code.

Walden understood Derek's writing, and he admired its brevity, clarity, and precision—he knew that you don't waste words when you take dictation from the future. He shifted gear and thought about a December evening, *the day he understood*. His eureka moment came, appropriately enough, in the bath. He closed his eyes, and leant back in his office chair, imagining himself reclining against the curved enamel of his bath. And the tick of the office clock became the drip of a tap, and he felt hot water touch his skin. He squeezed his remembered sponge and felt its softness, and he saw its pale porous surface crunch in his fist, and he watched its tiny golden mouths spew water. That was when he had understood, and he had lain transfixed in his bath, until the water had cooled.

He remembered the aching, bone-deep chill, and how he had clambered out, his skin waterlogged and covered in goose pimples. He shivered at his desk, and the sense-memory jolted him awake. But he wanted more...

He closed his eyes and wriggled his shoulders against the chair to get comfortable. He returned to his moment of inspiration for a replay—this time as a hovering observer. He watched his gangly body soak in the hot, soapy water. He saw his eyes on the sponge. And he saw his idea hang in the moist air and glisten, and twinkle, and swirl around his balding head, and coil down his arm, and orbit the clenched sponge. His idea—his *new* idea—was that brains leak into time because of their complexity. Brains are too busy and too intricate to stay in the paper-thin present. The *now* is too small to hold a mind, and so the mind spills out...

He watched his body whiten in the cooling water. And he watched his mouth move, and his blue lips purse, and his head shake. And then his mind's eye rose through the plaster ceiling, through the beams and tiles, and through the rain, and through the clouds, and into the starry night.

And the stars became bright babbling cells, their fast-shifting states and countless connections creating an invisible ectoplasm. This cell-spun gossamer spread over time and spawned souls, and angels, and demons, and gods.

He dropped his viewpoint, shifting to a few metres above his own rain-slicked roof. Time, he realised, as he hung suspended in the darkness, was stranger than we thought. Time-leaking minds broke the tyranny of an ever-advancing now, and the

224

present was no longer special. The past was real, and the dead are with us—or in their yesterdays. And everything was OK.

He felt a warm rush of comfort and emerged from his reverie, in a kind of birthing.

He glanced back at the asylum grounds, and the greenery cleared his head. Derek was outside, trudging through the grass, then he jumped and span—mad and completely, gloriously, happy.

Walden's back ached, for he'd been motionless too long. He hobbled around his desk and massaged his spine. Then he sat back down and reread the introduction to his paper. It was ready to submit. *Precognition in the Insane* had a nice ring to it, but the editors would object. They'd want a longer title that skirted round the madness. And they'd dilute *Precognition* with other words. It didn't matter. The paper was written merely to publish his time-leaking ideas. To prove precedence. He imagined the journal, and he saw his paper with its new and rambling heading. And he imagined that pompous title typeset in Derek's fat-bottomed letters…

He sighed, opened the overstuffed drawer, and retrieved Derek's latest offering. He flattened the crumpled sheets and peered at the neat lines of letters. Most of it was typical Derek code but the last line of the last page—framed in a haze of tiny squiggles and dots—was plain English: "Walden will be redacted."

But *redacted* was not a word that Derek would use.

There was a sharp knock at the door.

"Come," said Walden.

A huge orderly brought in the new patient. The subject was tall and broad-shouldered, and his hospital robe hung open at the back. The orderly nodded and slipped out.

"Hello, Mike," said Walden. "Please take a seat."

The man sat bolt upright and glared at the psychiatrist.

"I'd like to confirm a few details," said Walden.

Mike nodded. The doctor checked Mike's date of birth, next of kin (none), and the name of his doctor. Walden peered at the referral letter and then looked out at the trees.

Mike smiled, showing a line of brilliant white. "My brain's leaking," he said.

Walden jumped and his fountain pen shot from his hand, splashing ink across his soon-to-be-published paper.

Mike tilted his head and stared at the blue spatter, as if looking for meaning. Then he watched Walden, as a crow might watch a passerby.

A sharp click, and Walden stiffened. The French doors swung open, and a slight breeze ruffled the papers on his desk. Sounds from the gardens and beyond—a twittering bird, wind in the trees, and distant traffic—wafted in.

Derek ambled across the lawn, and he looked up and down and all around, like a hick in a big city. He peered at the grass and then at a tree. And then he pointed at a bird and waved, and grinned.

A woman in a faded, floral dress picked up a leaf and dropped it into a wheelbarrow. She stirred the leaves with her arm, wiped her hand on her dress, shook her head, muttered, walked two paces, and grabbed another leaf.

Mike continued, "My brain's spilling into time. Are you familiar with that," he looked around, as if searching for the right word, *"problem?"*

Walden fought to keep his expression neutral. "I *have* heard of similar cases…"

"*I* heard," snarled Mike, "that you have a theory. Is that true?"

"Well, yes. I'm working on an idea about time and brains. It's not published yet, but I think my insights could help my patients…"

Mike smirked and twitched. "Does anyone else know about these ideas?"

Walden gulped.

Mike's arm levitated and pointed at Derek. "Does your tiny friend know?"

"Derek's a promising case, but he understands very little. He knows nothing of my theory."

Mike's gaze sharpened, as if a hundred minds peered through his flinty eyes. His body grew, and his skin, and his hair, and his gown blurred and wavered, as if he were wrapped in a mirage.

Walden was familiar with the unnerving gaze of psychopaths, but nothing had prepared him for the implacable super-mind sitting opposite. The demon stared at Walden, and Walden stared back.

Mike looked away and laughed. "Sorry, Doc. It's a new trick. I tried it on the other inmates. *And it fuckin' terrified 'em.*"

Derek danced in the grass, with soft footfalls and bright yelps. The Wheelbarrow Lady returned with a stick which she dropped in the barrow, and then she grinned at Walden, as if sharing a joke.

Mike edged around the desk. Then his hand flashed out, grabbed the pen, and drove it deep into Walden's neck. Walden gasped and pulled it out, and blood spurted, like a tilted red fountain spraying across the formal garden of his office. And Derek, beyond the windows, screamed.

Mike picked up Derek's latest note and nodded, then he rolled up the pages and walked out through the French doors. Derek ran up to Mike and thumped Mike's broad and heedless back. But Mike just stared ahead and squelched across the lawns, his gown flapping, his arse poking out, his head held high, and Derek's pages—with their code, and funny quote—clutched in his fist like a diploma.

The Wheelbarrow Lady beamed at Mike and curtsied. The wind picked up, making the leaves rustle, and Mike smiled at the imaginary applause.

A giant male orderly burst into Walden's office as Derek tumbled in through the French doors.

"What the bloody hell's going on in here?" said Walden, putting down his pen. For a moment, the term *fountain pen* intruded into his thoughts, and he saw a splash of red on white. Then he was back, fully in the moment, and keenly aware of his office and its unexpected visitors.

Derek gibbered and punched himself in the neck, again, and again, and again. The nurse surged over and frogmarched him out.

Walden shook his head as the footsteps and cries echoed down the corridor. Now he'd forgotten where he was. He ran his finger down the typed sheet, grunted, and made a small notation in the margin. Then he leant back, stared through the windows at the turbulent sky, and sighed. His paper, *History of an Asylum,* was going well, despite all the interruptions.

Walden glanced at the carpet. Derek's old note, the one that had fallen from the drawer, lay crumpled under his desk. He picked it up and pressed it flat. The letters were round and neat, and they sat on the lines like cartoon carriages on a railway, but they made no sense. Walden scrunched up the sheet and threw it in the bin.

Bestiary

Many books in the Mind Library were torn and stained, but one stood out; it was a magnificent thing; it was as big as a family Bible, and its edges were chewed by time. Its cover had a painting of a wolf with its head turned, and its teeth bared. There were poisonous yellows, and burning reds, and carbon blacks, and the background was hammered gold. A dwarf dragon, framed by winding greenery, sank its teeth into the wolf's neck. And beneath the wolf's feet, amongst the roots in the sectioned ground, the worms waited, as they always do.

Worms & Frogs

Diving scorpions infested the balmy coastal waters of GhorMan-11. These nightmare creatures reached two metres, not counting their arching sting-tails. And they were fast. Even at a gentle amble, they outran the lumbering sea worms. The walrus-sized worms—segmented, slippery, and maggot-like—grazed on the blue seaweed, scraping it from the rocks with their serrated disk-mouths until they were full, when they'd rest on the sandy sea floor near their burrows.

When a scorpion found a worm, its spiked claws would snap out and grab the leathery flank. The worm would twist, and the scorpion would sting, sending poison into the worm's nerves. And the nerves would pulse their warning back in time. The earlier worm would lumber off to its burrow, avoiding the attack, and the scorpion would stab at empty water, and thrash in empty sand. Then the scorpion would scuttle to the burrow, glimpse the worm's tail, and scratch and dig. And then give up.

The fabric of time suffered with each undone kill—not enough to tear reality, but enough to keep the worms, and their lagging predators, under surveillance. They were watched by the Great Mind who was worried that the scorpions might develop precognition. If that happened, predator and prey would race around in a vicious time-circle—like a dog chasing its tail—faster and faster, until the resulting vortex detonated.

It might seem unlikely that a scorpion would evolve such an ability, but funny things happen after repeated exposure to reality jumps. Especially when death and food are involved. But it happened twenty million years ago on the planet EldersHap-17. Squat frogs would wait under shady palms for juicy birds, but they never caught one, for the sparkling birds were precognitive, and always escaped.

One day, a frog—after years of frustration—saw three seconds into the future, and grabbed a bird. They chased each other in an accelerating time loop, until local reality exploded and destroyed the galaxy.

The Great Mind had reached back in time to five years before the frog's moment of clairvoyance—and wiped out the birds. It spared the frogs who, with no frustration to egg them on, never evolved precognition. The frogs then made do with the fat, chitinous hoppers that favoured the shady palms. And eventually, the frogs died out, as all species do.

The Great Mind felt a special regret about exterminating the innocent birds, but it knew that any species that became too precognitive would have to be destroyed—sooner or later. The Great Mind remembered the gorgeous birds as it considered the ugly worms. A giant precognitive scorpion was far worse than a clairvoyant frog. And such a frog had destroyed a galaxy...

It would take enormous effort to watch over the worms and scorpions. The Great Mind told itself that its decision had nothing to do with aesthetics, and everything to do with efficiency. It said it was doing the right thing as it deleted both species. And perhaps it was.

Lagovarians

The average Lagovarian could have designed a cathedral, written a symphony, or painted a Madonna and Child. But instead, it thought only about sex. Lagovarian brains were pure erotic circuitry, with no sublimation of the libido into the arts whatsoever. The species lived on a group of low islands in the warm seas of the planet Ah-Bing-145. Food was plentiful on the shorelines, and on the lush plains, and in the dripping forests of this ancient archipelago. The Lagovarians had only to reach out their prehensile tongues to collect the fleshy meat of beached shellfish, or to pull the ripe fruit that hung from the soft-barked milk trees. They gorged for hours each morning, and they spent the long, hot afternoons fornicating prodigiously and indiscriminately.

Evening was the time for birthing. The wailings of newborn Lagovarians pierced the night, as they cried for milk, which they could get from any adult. No full-grown Lagovarian could resist the sound, and so the babies were over-fed, like cats with several homes.

The species originated on an outer island. Entangled groups, too occupied by their passions to notice danger, fell into the sea and were carried by the gentle currents to the neighbouring islands. The bracing swim in the salty water, and the sight of virgin territory, sent them into fresh breeding frenzies, and within two years, Lagovarian flesh coated the entire archipelago.

Overcrowding and erotic intensity created a local spike of consciousness that stressed time. But the sex-drenched Lagovarians wouldn't listen to reason, and they rebuffed the Great Mind. No venereally inclined microbes existed, and none could be engineered. There were no adjustable predators, and the planet was seismically quiet, leaving no hope of triggering a volcano or tsunami.

The Great Mind reached back tens of millions of years and perturbed geology. The islands vanished, and the warm seas rippled as they always had. Slow currents carried clouds of plankton in streams where the islands might have been, and the Lagovarians existed only as an aching regret in the memory of the Great Mind.

Periodically, the Great Mind would trawl up this memory and wonder if the Lagovarians had ever existed, or if they were a dream—and if there was any difference.

The Great Mind was capable of soaring philosophy, bitter yearning, and the most abyssal angst but it was, above all, pragmatic. Real or not, the Lagovarians were perfect material for cautionary tales. If a species became too self-absorbed and lubricious, then it would fashion a mind-virus and send it hurtling towards them. Their lusts would shrivel, or at least be redirected, and another temporal disaster would be averted.

Dogged Days

Oliver Wilson kissed his wife and daughter goodbye. For them, it was a normal day, and they had no inkling how many times they might have lived it.

He climbed into the taxi, which smelt of old sweat and cheap air-freshener, and he waved. His little family stood framed in the porch, and waved back.

"Bye, Daddy," shouted Ella.

His wife nodded, her mouth set.

The taxi reversed out of the driveway and lurched forwards. Oliver twisted round. His daughter waved frantically, getting smaller and smaller. He blew her a kiss, then he slumped in his seat and stared out as gum trees, embassies, and office blocks streamed by.

Oliver stood for a moment and admired the new airport. The concourse was slick and airy, with walls of patterned glass, and all around him, normal people walked or hobbled along. He sighed and joined the queue, and he wondered how many times he'd done exactly the same thing, with exactly the same people, in this perpetually new airport.

A lithe couple stood in front, chatting in Spanish. They wore baggy clothes, and their battered canvas luggage lay on the floor by their feet. Ahead of them, a suave crowd nodded and smiled and frowned. And a stout American, the only person actually checking in, was arguing with the girl behind the counter.

A woman with three young children arrived behind Oliver. Two more desks opened, and the smart group surged forward to the right-hand desk, and the young couple moved to the left-hand desk. A fourth desk opened, and Oliver walked over, his eyes darting around. He handed over his documents and hefted his pink case onto the scales. He stared at the bag—and all the fairy and flower stickers that his daughter had added—and sucked in his cheeks. When check-in was over, he edged away, straining to hear the increasingly irate American.

It was a quick hop to Sydney, and the journey helped prepare Oliver for the long flight ahead. There's an inertia to travel, he thought, as he shot along in the sky. It's hard to begin a journey, but once you start, it's easy to keep going. Oliver's bag was going straight to London, leaving him free and unfettered, and he should use the time to ready himself for the challenge, but he just stared out as the brown earth scrolled along below.

The plane landed, and he emerged, dazed and preoccupied. He navigated through the international airport and settled down in the boarding area. Except for an elderly couple who stared into the distance, everyone was absorbed in a book or an electronic device.

A voice—once human, but now booming and distorted—called Oliver's row, and he forced himself up and headed down the jet bridge. He perked up at the sharp smell of the aviation fuel that leaked round the entrance hatch, and, with his head flung back, he stepped aboard.

The jet was nearly empty, so he spread out, claiming four adjacent seats. He frowned at the safety instructions, hoping to be ignored.

"Mr Wilson?"

He nodded and swallowed hard.

"You've been upgraded to first class, please come with me and I'll show you to your new seat."

He clambered from his row, grabbed his bag, and followed the flight attendant's swaying hips down the gangway. He kept quiet, scared to derail his unexpected upgrade.

The first-class cabin was empty except for a blonde-haired woman several seats in front who didn't turn her head.

The flight attendant indicated Oliver's seat. "Champagne, Sir?" she asked.

Oliver nodded, terrified that speaking would break the spell, and have him sent back to economy.

His drink arrived, not in the delicate fingers of the attractive girl, but clutched in the spade-like hand of a dishevelled and portly man. And it was red, not white.

"It's a long flight," said Bert, "and I thought you'd like the company. Here, take this, it's sparkling Shiraz, your favourite."

Bert was the one who'd shown him how it would work. He'd explained about closing the time loop, and how Oliver must visit a front garden on the other side of the world. And face a dog. Bert had explained things well, but still...

"Perfect," said Oliver. "Cheers."

Oliver arrived in Leicester at eleven o'clock on an oppressively hot Tuesday morning. It felt like a new day, but it was probably just another Terminal-Tuesday. He stood in the driveway and patted his pocket. The book was still there. The instructions had been specific, and Oliver knew them by heart, but having them to hand was reassuring. In case he forgot. In case his mind, under all this stress, cracked wide open.

A growl.

Oliver turned to face the Rottweiler, and their eyes locked. The dog was black and tan, and bristling—all muscle, and bone, and vicious stupidity—a real bastard of a creature. Oliver stood between the dog and its home, a mad but necessary position. He'd been preparing for this moment for months, but he hadn't expected things to feel so real.

Oliver's mind swelled—reaching past his skull—trying to bridge the moments. The dog leapt. And teeth, and hair, and skull, and face collided in a train-smash of pain and blood. Oliver's head hit the concrete, and his death pulse—a ball of searing emotion and crucial information—thumped back in time, and crafted its message as it flew...

Bert grabbed the red paperback. It smelt old, and the paper was yellow. But the stories looked promising. They were short and optimistic, with trips to Mars, and monsters with tentacles, and mad professors with impossible machines. Bert paid and left.

Run to Sirius was the best story. The main character was Bert, and he explained everything to the reader. The real Bert liked that. He also liked the plot—a recurring trip to Sirius. Over and over, Bert and his hapless companion Oliver took the rocket to the stars. It was a class III Freighter with small windows and a giant, shielded hold. Their cargo was a menacing time grinder, a hulking thing in olive grey. It was powered down for the journey, but it still thrummed and ticked, and tiny lights flashed along its sides. Bert and Oliver had to ferry it around Sirius and back. And then do it all again. And no one could remember why. Space ships, and time travel, and characters trapped in looping destinies. It was a perfect story. But what really grabbed Bert's attention were the coincidences. Bert the character mirrored the real-life Bert, and place names were familiar. Numbers jumped out from the pages because they matched important ages, birthdays, pass-codes, house numbers, and dates. He read it, again and again, trying to work out its message.

Although it had kept its central mystery, the story had yielded enough clues to find the real Oliver. And together, Bert and Oliver pored over every line, trying to analyse *Run to Sirius*. But despite their efforts, the tale's meaning, and what they should do about it, remained elusive.

Bert slammed the book on the pub table. "I've had it." Peanuts scattered everywhere, and a damp beer mat teetered and fell. "Sod it all." Bert swept the paperback onto the dirty wooden floor, crossed his arms, and stared out at the gathering clouds.

The barmaid, dressed entirely in black, glanced up. Her only customers looked like a couple having a tiff, but she knew better.

Oliver reached down and picked up the little book. It was still open at the Dog Star story. And its spine was broken.

He stared as the heading, *Run to Sirius*, flickered and shrank to *Sirius*. Beneath the shortened title, the text blurred, and the tiny black letters ran like busy ants. Oliver heard the clatter of a faraway typewriter, and he cocked his head and sniffed, and he smelt the thin stench of an old cigarette, and the fat aroma of cheap whiskey.

He returned to the book. The letters skittered across the paper and bumped into each other, and jolted and jumped and bounced, and strings of them ran off the page, like toy trains plunging over a white cliff.

At last, the frantic words settled, and the invisible typist fell silent. Imagined smoke hung in the air, and the story had shrunk to half a page. Oliver twitched and pouted, and his eyes stung. His finger trembled as it rubbed and smudged the fresh ink. He cleared his throat, and squared his shoulders, and forced himself to read the impossible story. His lips moved—like the lips of a child lost in a fairytale—until he reached the end. And then he looked up.

There were no spaceships, or stars, or time grinders left in this magically redacted tale. And only one character, the fictional Oliver, endured. This man, his namesake, was caught in a steely destiny that looped, forever catching a plane and meeting a dog...

Barking Mad

Street light leaked around the curtains, and Tom could just make out vague shapes in his bedroom. He glanced at the clock radio. It was ten past two, and the fucking dog was barking. He turned his head left and right, trying to work out where the animal lived, but it was no use, because the sound came through a single window, and so lost its direction. Plenty of dogs barked at him on his way to the shops and gym, but he couldn't be sure if one of those daytime dogs was his nighttime tormentor.

He stared at the ceiling and fumed. The barking wasn't loud, but it was loud enough. Inconsiderate, selfish bastards, he thought. Who would leave a dog out all night? Can't they hear it bark? Perhaps they're deaf. Perhaps they've gone away. After all, the barking happened mainly at weekends. That would explain it. The stupid fuckers had piled themselves, and their crop-haired, wide-faced kids, into their diesel-chugging wagon and headed off to God knows where, leaving their stupid dog to guard their run-down house. Tom smiled at his profiling, based as it was on the sound of an unknown dog in a distant garden.

The relentless barking drove shards of pain into Tom's head. He'd taken an aspirin, as he did every night, but that was to clear his blood vessels, not to stop headaches. He contemplated something stronger, but he decided that he lacked the energy to get up, put on his spectacles, fumble through the medicine box, read the instructions—lest he overdose—and swallow the pills. And he resented drugging himself because a thoughtless bastard had a dog. How could someone that stupid afford to live around here, he wondered, *and* go away every weekend?

He thought about installing double glazing—expensive, *evacuated* double glazing—to piss himself off even more. And it worked. The prospect of emptying his wallet because of his idiot neighbour drove him to new heights of fury. He wriggled and tingled and twitched, and he conjured dark magical fantasies— sharp voodoo playlets of revenge. He imagined sneaking down the street in a hooded jacket, a ray gun in his hand:

All the windows were dark, and there was no one around. He found the house.

"Here boy!" he called. An ugly dog—black and tan, and squat, and growling—padded over.

He aimed between its eyes. His ray gun throbbed, and laser light shot out, lancing the dog. The animal lit up, crackled like popcorn, and exploded—leaving nothing but a pink mist and a sticky stain. Tom sneaked home and climbed back into bed.

For his next fantasy, he left with a cloak and a surgical bag, like an evil doctor on a midnight house call:

He stood at the fence, his hands on the peeling paint, and called. The dog scampered over, eyed Tom, and woofed. It sounded friendly, and Tom threw it some sweets. The dog cocked its head, leant forward, gobbled up the laced goodies, whined, and keeled over.

Tom checked the neighbourhood. Everything was dark, and nothing stirred. He dropped his bag into the dog's garden and clambered in after it. Then he crouched and put his ear on the animal's flank. Tom nodded, satisfied that the creature was asleep, and then he reached into his bag and pulled out a silvery globe. He weighed it in his hand, like a metal cricket ball. It was heavy, dense with hidden machinery, and its surface was polished and unbroken. He pushed it against the dog's throat, and the ball opened tiny doors on either side, and metal watch-strap things flew out. The straps encircled the dog's furry neck and tightened, and the ball hummed and jiggled. There was a grinding, a snip, and a buzz, then the straps shot back, and the machine detached, falling from the dog like a sated tick.

Tom pulled a towel from his bag and wiped the blood from the dog's fur. Then he cleaned the ball and dropped it into his bag, stuffed the towel on top, and snapped the clasp. He lowered the bag into the street, climbed out of the sleeping dog's garden, picked up the bag, and strolled home, smiling at the thought of surgically quietened dogs and soon-to-be-mystified neighbours.

Of course, these were only wishes, and the barking continued. In the real world, there were no ray guns or alien balls, and Tom grew more irate. He flipped on his side, scrunched up, and yelled, "Bastards."

Then came a yelp and a snarl.

He threw off the duvet, stormed down the hallway, flung open the lounge room door, hit the light switch, slumped into his armchair, crossed his arms, and muttered obscenities.

The barking continued. Woof, woof, woof...

Tom picked up a book and flipped through. The dog barked again. Tom shivered. Then he swore and slammed the book onto the coffee table.

Woof, woof, woof...

Another dog answered. The little bastards were having a conversation, woof, yelp, woof, woof, yelp, howl...

The dogs were far away. What do the nearer neighbours think? It was three in the morning, and life must be hell for them. He returned to bed and fell into a twitching sleep.

Tom woke to a dismal Saturday and peered through the window. The clouds were heavy and threatened rain. Incredibly, the dog was still barking. Tom swore and staggered off to the kitchen. He sat at his breakfast bar, sipped his coffee, and stared at his fish tank. It was a spectacular setup—a small chunk of bright and bubbling sea—with electric-coloured fish, lurid rocks, dead coral, and swaying plants.

He rubbed his brow, poured another coffee, and reached for the croissants and blueberry jam. He slurped and munched. And then he smiled, as the caffeine and sugar worked their magic and brightened his mood. And the dog sounded further away. He focused on the aquarium, and the barking became fainter still. But he needed to get out of the house and give himself a treat.

The man in the pet shop was vague. "It's exotic and good for the water," he explained. "It *purifies* things."

Tom stared at the yellow blob and nodded as if deeply impressed. "How much is it?"

"Two hundred."

Tom had no idea what sponges, exotic or otherwise, were worth. "OK," he said, "I'll take it."

Tom named his sponge Cecil, *Sessile* Cecil. The little creature sat on his rock and grew. Periodically, he clenched and spurted oil. Ten days later, Cecil had doubled in size, the water was swimming-pool blue, and the fish were in hiding. It was late afternoon, and Tom was contemplating his aquarium. He's beautiful, my sponge, thought Tom. And bewitched, he nodded off.

Two blocks away, Wesley came home in his new utility truck and kicked open his gate. Jack launched at his master. Wesley hugged his dog and blew into his nose. "Miss me, you old bastard?"

Jack sneezed and squirmed, and licked the beloved face, tonguing the pockmarked skin.

In his house and in his dream, Tom tasted Wesley's greasy skin and felt his tickling beard. Wesley's smell hit Tom like a soggy quilt, and Tom retched, and a small piece of himself flew into Wesley's face.

Freezing-water pain shot up Wesley's sinuses. He staggered back, swearing, and tearing at his hair. Something scraped his inner skull, and blue lights flashed, and his windpipe locked shut.

The pain, and panic, and choking, stopped, and the garden lay broken by the prisms of his tears. "Fuck me," Wesley sobbed. "*Fuck me.*" He blinked and wiped his eyes. He forced himself to calm down, and he took a long, slow breath. My God, he thought, the garden smells good. It must've cleared my nose— that bastard pain's pushed out the snot. Well, *fuck me again.*

Jack raced around his human's feet, barking and squirming. Wesley trudged up the garden path, put his key into the front door, and stepped into a sick, stale smell. Brooke better do some fucking cleaning, he thought, it's never smelt this bad before. He headed to the kitchen, filled the kettle, leant against the counter, and ran his hand through his hair. As Wesley relaxed, Jack skidded across the floor, whining and grizzling, and headed outside.

Brooke pouted one last time at the illuminated passenger mirror, put her makeup away, and clambered out. "Bin a good boy?" she asked.

Jack's tail beat against the vehicle's gleaming side and, squirming, he led her to the house.

Brooke made tea, while Jack—happy to have his humans back—ran around the garden, barking non-stop.

Wesley worked hard that week, and dreamt of the weekend. At three o'clock on Friday afternoon, Wesley and Brooke reversed out of their driveway. At the end of the street, Wesley dropped to second gear, did a cursory check, and turned right.

"Sounds like Jack," he said, after they'd been driving for twenty minutes.

"You what?" asked Brooke, squinting through the windscreen. She pulled out an earphone.

"I said," replied Wesley, leaving gaps between his words, "that I heard a dog that sounded like Jack."

"Mmm." She replaced her earphone, and they drove in silence—Brooke occupied with her tunes, and Wesley with his thoughts.

Outside town, the road straightened and rose. The engine growled, and Wesley shook his head. "I can hear him again."

Brooke paused her music and turned.

Wesley's face was set, and his brow was furrowed. "He's still barking," he said. "It sounds like Jack, and he won't stop. It's really loud."

Brooke poked him in the ribs. "Don't be so daft."

Wesley looked away, clenched his jaws, and rammed the accelerator. Brooke tensed as they flew over a short bridge. Then she removed her earphones and listened, but no dogs barked. They drove without speaking for an hour, then swept into a small town and cruised past a sleepy pub, and past a disused mill, and past a long-dead bank.

"I need a piss," announced Wesley. He stopped at the park, tore out the key, booted the door, and ran for the urinal. And didn't look back.

Brooke watched him disappear into the concrete toilet block. She grabbed her bag, climbed out, and looked around. The world was normal. Without Wesley, the world was *perfectly* normal. A battered white estate car ground up the road, tugging an enormous caravan, and she could smell the fumes from its struggling engine. A black terrier raced around the playground and yapped. A couple in their sixties sat at a table, munching their way through a pile of takeaway packets. And a little girl squealed as her big brother pushed her on a swing. Brooke leant against the utility, bit her lip, and waited for Wesley.

The elderly couple gobbled the last of their meal and walked to their beige saloon. They climbed in, and one side sank and then the other. Then the engine roared. A puff of smoke, and they reversed out and meandered down the road.

Wesley was still in the toilets, so Brooke pushed herself from the vehicle and walked over.

"You OK, Wes?" she asked.

A moan, a retch, and a *fuck off*.

Brooke shook her head and stepped into the female toilets. The metal mirror showed her lank blonde hair and hollow cheeks. She grinned to inspect her teeth, but the reflection was blurry and distorted. Then she thought of Wesley, and her hands shook. A wave of nausea hit, and she dry heaved. "Christ, Wesley," she muttered, wiping her eyes. "What the *hell's* wrong with you?"

She turned to face the cubicles. Two were occupied. The third was vacant, but its lock was gone. She pushed the door and stared at the stained seat and spattered bowl. Paper lay strewn across the floor, and a cheap earring lay in a dirty groove. "Nice," she said. "I'll wait."

Brooke stepped outside, unrelieved, and found Wesley standing in the grass and staring at the sky. She walked up and put a hand on his shoulder.

He flinched. "I can still hear him," he moaned. "Jack's still barking."

Brooke shrugged. "I can't hear him. He's miles away at home. I bet he's chasing birds. It *can't* be him."

He turned to face her. "Are you saying I'm mad?"

She grabbed his hand. "Maybe you got that tinny thing? You know, ringing in the ears?"

"It's not ringing, it's fucking barking. And it won't stop. It can't be Jack, because he's at home. But it *sounds* like him." His mouth turned down as if he were ready to blubber. "Let's go." He held out the car keys. "Can you drive?"

"Sure. Do you want a coffee first?"

"Nah, let's just go."

Wesley screwed up his eyes, fastened his seat belt, and wriggled. Brooke let out a long sigh, started the engine, reversed out, and merged with the coast-bound traffic.

"Shall I try the radio?" she asked.

Wesley nodded. The station was running a competition, and people were phoning in. She changed channel. A soft rock song poured out, annoying in its polished familiarity. Wesley smiled, leant back, shut his eyes, and panted.

Brooke focused on the road as another bad song came on. She glanced across at Wesley. He looked peaceful, but then he twitched, as if dreaming. She sighed and stared ahead, and clenched her jaws.

An hour later, they pulled up at the flat. Wesley staggered in and threw himself on the couch. Brooke dashed to the toilet and let the roar of the fan soothe her. The white noise made her think of jets and faraway places, and for a while, it blocked out the world.

She brought in the luggage and checked on Wesley. "I need to go shopping. You can stay here if you like."

Wesley grunted.

"Well?" she prompted.

"Yeah, I'll stay. I need a beer. I've got a *bastard* of a headache."

He wriggled in the cushions, flicked the remote, and watched an advert for a 4-wheel drive.

Brooke returned to find him asleep and the TV still on. She pressed mute, unloaded the shopping, tidied the kitchen, fried the fish, and made a salad.

"It's on the table!" she announced.

Wesley opened his eyes, grumbled, staggered to the fridge, grabbed a beer, and slumped into his chair. And they ate in silence, watching flickering adverts and nodding presenters.

At the end of the meal, Brooke parked her cutlery. "How do you feel?" she asked.

"I can still hear barks and whimpers." He played with the remains of his dinner, circling his fork in the vinegar and olive oil, and watching the patterns. "I'll see the quack if it carries on."

Brooke cleared up and put the kettle on. "Let's watch a film, it'll take your mind off things."

Wesley prepared himself with another cold beer, and Brooke switched off the mute. They snuggled together on the settee, and Brooke selected a movie.

A minute later, Wesley was asleep, and Brooke extracted the bottle from his hand.

He twisted, flinched, made a sound halfway between a sob and a snore, and kicked out. "Shut the fuck up," he muttered. "Shut—" Then came a choke, a spasm, and a grunt. Finally, he settled, all twisted, with his legs drawn in, his head thrown back, and his mouth slack. He looked too uncomfortable to sleep—the way that children look when they doze in cars or pushchairs. Then he drooled.

The TV flashed, and throbbed, and filled the room with gunfire. There were screams, and screeching tyres, and something exploded, then a van slewed through an intersection, chased by wallowing police cars. When the helicopter arrived, Brooke clicked the remote. She faced the dark screen, breathed in, and clutched her belly. Then she rolled her shoulders, stretched, stood up, took the bottle to the sink, put a duvet over Wesley, and switched off the lights.

She lay in the double bed and frowned at her paperback, but the words stayed on the page and refused to go into her mind. She closed the book and stroked its scarlet embossing. Behind the coiling script, the muscular torso and the firm and stubbly chin promised so much...

"Hopeless," she said, and switched off the bedside light. At last she drifted until a distant thudding—a rock-band bass from the pub in town—brought her back. "Inconsiderate fuckers..."

She looked around, wide-eyed and alert. The curtains glowed pale cream, and she frowned, and wondered if it was moonlight.

Then she forced herself to lie straight, with her arms at her sides. This was her normal going-to-sleep position, but tonight it didn't help. She stared at the picture directly ahead. The two painted parrots were dark and flat, their daylight gaudiness drained away. And the leaves were clumped and black, like a nighttime forest. But instead of being relaxing, the picture—which was a daytime thing—was threatening and disturbing.

Brooke turned onto her side and worried about Wesley. And the more she worried, the more awake she got. And the louder the pub got.

After an hour, she slept and dreamt she was in a car—a tiny, unknown car—climbing up a muddy hill. The tyres were slipping, and the hill got steeper, and the car slid, and the hill became a cliff, and the cliff tipped her backwards into a black and freezing reservoir. She fought the wheel, but nothing helped, and the water was rising. But it was rising the wrong way. She was upside down, and she beat on the window and wrenched the handle.

Then she was in her mother's house, but it looked like Sarah's house, and they were all having dinner, and she was explaining how Wesley had barking dogs in his head. Then Jack ran over, and she rubbed his back and he yelped.

Her eyes flew open.

Wesley was standing over her. "The dog's back," he said.

"I dreamt of Sarah," she mumbled, pushing herself up, "and Jack."

"Can you hear him?"

"No." She lay down and sighed.

251

Wesley peered at the curtains. "It's worse than ever," he said, "like my head's a tin shed and Jack's inside. He's going spare, barking like a bastard."

"I wonder what he's up to," mused Brooke.

"Who?"

"Jack. I wonder what he's doing?"

"How the fuck should I know? He must be asleep. Christ, it's nearly two in the morning." Wesley shook his head, and tears welled up.

But Jack was very much awake and barking—an incessant yapping, howling, and woofing—calling for his master.

His mate Bozo from two doors down sympathised with high-pitched yelps. And Fred, the springer from next door, grizzled in his lobby, miserable and alone.

Not too far away, Tom lay in his bed, listening to the incessant barking, a broad smile across his face. He got up, pulled the curtains back and opened the window a little wider. The yelps and howls were clearer now, like beautiful music. He snuggled back under the covers and thought of the yellow sponge in the fish tank. Cecil was a beautiful creature, he thought. The perfect pet...

Lycanthropy

Moonlight streamed in, and something stirred in Tom's belly. He flung off the sheets, jumped out of bed, stalked down the dark hallway, brushed against the line of coats, grabbed a winter fur, pulled it over his pyjamas, opened the front door, stepped into the night, sniffed the crisp and fragrant air, and stared at the moon. The door behind banged shut and rattled open. And in the distance, a dog barked.

Tom grasped his lapels with his right hand and ran. The fur flapped behind him like a cloak, and his bare feet padded on the cold pavement, and he ran hunched, his left arm swinging, as if, at any moment, he might drop to all fours. He glanced at the claws on his fingers and the hairs on his wrists. And he was happy and aroused. And ready to hunt...

Dr Walden glanced at the hunched man. The patient was slender, and balding, and twitchy.

"Are you a *werewolf?*" asked Walden.

"Of course I'm bloody not," said Tom.

"You were in a neighbour's garden, cuddling their dead cat. And chewing their rabbit."

Tom sniffed. "Werewolves don't exist." He held out his scratched hands and shrugged. "I'm a part-time *dog*—and that's what dogs do…"

"Dog, you say?"

"Dog," affirmed Tom.

Walden tapped his lips. "How did it start?"

"With a sponge in my fish tank…"

Walden gazed beyond Tom's left ear, as Tom's lips moved. Something was trying to surface in Walden's mind, but it was quick, and slippery, and impossible to catch, like a fat carp in a dark lake.

"…and it's more than just a sponge," continued Tom, his drone resolving into words, and breaking into Walden's reverie. "It spurts oil. The fish hate it…"

Walden nodded. "Where did you get it?"

"At a pet shop for exotic animals. But I'd never seen sponges there before, not till I got Cecil…"

"Cecil?" asked Walden, raising an eyebrow.

"I named him because I felt a connection…"

"And the fish?"

"I didn't give them names."

"I understand," replied Walden. "About sponges, I mean, not naming pets." He tapped his bottom teeth with his pen. "Let me look into this. I think we're onto something." Walden pushed his chair back, signalling the end of the session. "Let's meet in a week. In the meantime, try these visualisation exercises."

Tom grabbed the photocopied pages and loped away.

Scents of Futility

That night, Tom sniffed the air. He understood the problem—he felt it in his bones and in his dog-keen nose. He had to talk to Dr Walden, *and soon*. He couldn't wait a week, *not for this*. The psychiatrist was a smart man, and he'd know what to do. Tom wriggled in his bed, stretched his limbs, grizzled, and fell asleep.

The next morning, he wolfed down his breakfast and picked up the phone.

"The doctor can see you this afternoon," the lady said, "at three."

"Thanks." Tom nodded furiously. He wrote down the time and hung up. He looked around and stroked his chin, and paced about. He was lucky to see Walden so soon. It was almost as if the receptionist had been waiting for his call...

Tom arrived ten minutes early and was admitted to Walden's wood-panelled office as the clock struck three. He sat on the patient's chair, the hard one facing the desk, and looked up at the psychiatrist. They exchanged pleasantries and fell silent.

Tom looked around and fidgeted. He glanced at the clock and watched its hand sweep across five seconds, then he looked at the certificates with all their swirling script and coloured stamps. Then he took a deep breath. "You know how dogs piddle against lamp posts?"

Walden nodded gravely. "Indeed, I do."

"They do it to warn other dogs, and to mark their territory. That's fine, because other dogs can move away. But imagine if they couldn't."

"Couldn't pee?" asked Walden, with a smile.

"Couldn't walk away," said Tom, grinning.

"In that case," said Walden, "I suppose they might get aggrieved."

"Exactly," said Tom, jiggling, "very aggrieved. And if it continued—if they had to smell another dog for weeks—what then?"

"They'd get distraught, depressed even..."

Tom hunched. "It's happening, *as we speak.*"

Walden frowned. "I'm not sure I follow."

"Everyone lacks motivation," said Tom. "You must've noticed the idle young and the defeated old. It's not the economy or the internet—it's more fundamental than that." Tom tapped his nose and winked. "We're depressed because of something like dog piss."

Walden raised his eyebrows. "Is someone spreading it?"

"Yes..."

"Can you smell it?" asked Walden.

"Yes, but it's not a normal scent, and I can't get a proper fix. It's everywhere." Tom twisted in his chair and looked out through the French doors. He sniffed in rapid bursts, as if hankering after a walk. "And it's draining the life out of people."

"I'll give your idea some serious thought," said Walden. "It's fascinating."

"Thanks, Doc. I'll think about it too."

"Good, let's meet next week. You already have an appointment."

"OK," said Tom, and scurried out.

Walden sucked his fountain pen, frowned, and cleared his throat. He'd written *lycanthropy* in big round letters and framed it with clouds of squiggles and stars—decorations that he didn't remember making. He'd assumed that Tom was insane, but madness didn't explain his insight. For a slim, maddening moment, Walden thought that Tom's mind really could enter a dog's head—and vice versa. It was ludicrous, but...

Six days later, Tom sat in the chair, with his hands in his lap, and his shoulders hunched.

Walden's wide-bodied pen hung poised over a fresh sheet of paper. "Last time, you said this substance was being deliberately released. Why would anyone do that?"

"To control people," replied Tom. *"To reduce competition..."*

"Who would do it?"

"The elite. *You know what elites are like...*"

Walden nodded. "Go on."

"The rich want to get richer, and chemical control would help."

"Maybe the rich naturally release these substances because they're powerful people—like dominant dogs. Imagine a factory owner marching across the shop floor. Molecules waft from his skin, and the workers pick up his scent and stay compliant, and too depressed to strike."

"It's not an accidental or natural release." Tom leant forward. "Someone's *making* the stuff." He coughed. "And *selling* it."

"It would be *very* marketable." Walden grinned. "I have several colleagues who should sniff it..."

257

They laughed and struck an alliance, and Walden felt his professional standards slip, like a pair of falling trousers.

"Tom, you're cured." He span to face the window. "And I'd like us to work together on this—as colleagues."

"That's fantastic, I'm ready to sniff out the chemical as soon as I change and my nose is strong."

A bright blue creature arced over the asylum gardens—its dusty wake tugged and shredded by the breeze—and landed in the hedge with a thud.

"See that bird?" asked Walden.

Tom raced to the French doors and scrabbled against the glass. Walden walked over and unlatched them, releasing his patient. Tom bolted across the lawn like an excited spaniel and sniffed the bushes. Then he yelped and recoiled, rubbed his face, sneezed, and looked around. But his eyes had lost their shine, and his body sagged, and he shuffled back to Walden.

Squamafly powder drifted—like poison from a crop-duster—across the lawns and into the psychiatrist's nose. The time-leaking particles burrowed into his brain and interfered with his consciousness-field, and his ambitions drained away, and he clenched and unclenched his weakening fists, and his tears welled up.

In the bushes, the fly—as fat as an armoured pigeon—raised its abdomen and shook. And as it shook, it shed more dust.

Numbers

Most books are full of words—words that make stories. But beneath the words are numbers.

The Numerology Machine

Brian stared at Alice across the common room. He pushed out his lower lip, scratched his gut with his stubby fingers, and flared his nostrils. As head of department and full professor, he outranked her, but he could never have her. He sipped his milky tea and tried to imagine a fairer world.

As Alice leafed through a newspaper, Brian slipped out. He scuttled down the corridor, down the concrete steps, and down the passage to Alice's office. Hunched and furtive, like a comic burglar playing to an unseen audience, he checked over his shoulder and let himself in. Warming to his part—and as obvious and ugly as a pantomime dame—he took an exaggerated breath and exclaimed, "Damp leather and perfume!" Then he waddled to the bookcase, slid his finger between two pink folders, licked his lips, and pulled out a diary. He grinned, turned to the first page, memorised it, and moved on.

"Brian!"

He turned, feigning sympathy and concern, the diary held behind his back. "Alice, I'm *so* glad you're here. You'd better call security. I heard a noise and came to check. Your door was open, so you'd better see what's missing."

Alice punched numbers into her phone. "Finance? What? No, I need security." She tried again.

Brian slipped the diary back into the bookcase and reversed into the corridor, staring at Alice's shapely hips. He rapped on the open door.

Alice turned. "Please hold a moment." She put her hand over the mouthpiece. *"Yes?"*

"Security, Alice, is *everyone's* business. *Keep the door locked.*"

"Sorry," said Alice into the phone.

Brian slid from view and mimed her call. He flounced, and pouted, and wiggled, and minced, and giggled. And his flank shook, and his tongue flapped out.

Alice's phone smashed down.

Brian half covered his mouth and gasped and stepped away. Then he stopped and cocked his head.

Alice was sobbing and swearing and pacing about.

Brian swaggered off, recalling as he did so—and with photographic clarity—the pages of her diary. There were jottings about staff (for ammunition), unrecognised names and numbers (for investigation), and childish doodles (useless and typical). But the last page was best: it had her name, with a number beneath each letter. It looked like a kid's game, but it was numerology. You're a stupid woman, he thought, a witchy fool. He grinned, dug into his left nostril, inspected the result, rolled it up, and stuck it on the wall.

Back in his office, Brian locked his door, eased his bulk into his chair, grunted, started his computer, and opened a browser. Ruining someone, he reflected, was easy. First, you stripped them of their credibility—that was the best bit, the public unravelling—then you whispered in certain ears. But first, he had to look things up...

Alice got home to screaming.

"Calm down, Mr S," she called. "I'm coming." She closed the door and sighed.

The screaming got louder.

She marched over and stooped down. He jumped on her shoulder, twittered, and manoeuvred onto her chest. She held the cockatiel's tiny yellow head and stroked his beak. "You know, Mr S, it's been a bastard of a day."

He squawked and flapped.

"Brian was in my office."

But the bird was in bliss, and had stopped listening.

"It was like finding a toad squatting in my panties drawer."

Mr S climbed back onto her shoulder and dug under his wing, scattering dander and feathers. He paused, extended his backside, and crapped down her coat.

"You're an incontinent bugger."

She went over to his cage, and the bird stepped delicately onto his perch, cocked his head, and stared at Alice.

"And pompous, too."

She walked into the kitchen, withdrew yesterday's dinner and a bottle of white wine from the fridge, put the dinner in the microwave, and the wine on the counter. She poured a large glass, let out a long sigh, slumped onto the settee, and took a swig. The wine was resinous and icy, and condensation coated the glass, and she drew a circle in the droplets. The microwave hummed, and the smell of reheating lasagne filtered out. Grabbing the remote, she switched on the TV, and moments later, the microwave beeped.

Alice ate as she watched the news. There were politicians, emergency workers, and grieving relatives. Then, an ageing celebrity couple discussed their reproductive challenges, while a blonde in a blinding-red dress nodded and frowned.

"As if she'd know," said Alice, through a mouthful of dinner.

A sports presenter—thick of arm, and thick of neck—came on. Alice turned the television off, dumped her plate in the sink, leant on the worktop, opened her diary, and flipped to the last page. Frowning, and counting under her breath, she added up the numbers beneath her name, reached for a pencil, and wrote 68. She added six and eight to make fourteen, then she added one and four to make five. She tapped the pencil on her lip and smiled. This was fortune telling with maths—and she could automate it. Alice enjoyed programming, and coding a numerology calculator would be fun—and it would help her to forget about Brian.

At last, the work was done, and Alice leant back and smiled. The cursor blinked. She sniffed and typed her name, and the just-finished program replaced each letter with a number. Then it calculated the digital root—the number five.

"OK, that worked." She entered her name, including her middle initials, and got the number nine. She checked the result with a pencil. "Good," she breathed. She tried her four names and got the answer three. Her mother's full maiden name gave one, and her married name gave three. And her father's full name gave seven. Other relatives followed—those she could remember—and figures from history, including generals, artists, scientists, musicians, and writers. The program wrote the names in one column, the equivalent numbers in another, and the digital root in the third column.

She stared at the list, tilted her head, pursed her lips, and frowned. Then she sorted the names, first by their equivalent numbers, and then by their digital roots, but there were no obvious patterns. Of course, no connections between names, numbers, and destinies were possible, not in any rational universe—and certainly not in this one. Numerology was useless —and the program told no fortunes—but it distracted her, and she went to bed happy.

That night she dreamt of giant clocks, and having tea with Grandma. She trudged through sleepy, stagnant pools—funny-shaped, half-drained, and full of dead things—and squeezed through pipes and curtained sluices. Then she emerged—filthy, scratched, and naked—onto the university quad. The staff and students pointed, and Brian laughed. And then she woke.

Alice spent the morning gazing through her office window. She wandered in the quad at lunchtime, suffered a recall of her dream, and returned to her desk. At three o'clock, she gave up, gathered her things, locked her office, and left. She put her head round the secretary's door. "I think I'm coming down with something, but I should be back tomorrow."

"Fine," said the nodding blonde. "I'll let the others know."

Alice stopped at the shops to buy a bottle of red wine and a packet of mixed creams—the same biscuits that her dead grandmother had served in her now remembered dream.

She opened her door to screams. *"Be quiet,* you stupid bird."

But he was dancing from foot to foot, desperate for attention.

"Wait, I'm putting the kettle on."

She emptied the biscuits onto a plate, picked one up and nibbled.

Mr S retreated into his cage to sulk.

"OK, be like that," she said, and she took her tea and biscuits to her computer. Alice chewed and slurped, and hammered code, and the numerology program grew and grew. Hours later, she wrote the last line and set the software running. And names scrolled down, and numbers flickered as the computer searched for patterns…

Bang!

Alice looked up. The lounge room curtains were open, and the windows were black. She stared at the darkness outside, willing it to be empty. But a shape emerged as she knew it must. A hulking figure, dark grey against the black, stood in the middle of her lawn. He was facing away and watching her gate. He opened and closed his hands, and rocked from foot to foot.

Bang! The gate slammed shut against its post and juddered open.

He's guarding me, she thought, from things outside. *Because I didn't lock my gate.* "I must be ill," she whispered, trying to breathe in shallow gasps. She tried to stand, but slipped. Her hand shot out, and cold tea flew.

It was only a slight sound, but the figure twitched. "I thought I heard a noise," it screamed. "I think you should call security, Alice. *Call security!*"

Fist to mouth, she stumbled from her desk, and bashed her knee, and yelped.

The figure slid to the window and kissed the glass, and then the fat lips pulled away. "*Now* Alice!" said the lips. "*Call them Now!*"

She jumped onto the settee and tugged the curtains closed. The voice stopped, leaving a hollow silence, and she sank into the soft leather, gasping and heaving.

She rubbed her knee, wiped her tears, and forced her legs to move. "I must shut the others," she mumbled. "Shut this one." And she pulled the curtains across the side window. "Shut this one." And she lowered the kitchen blinds. She returned to the settee and hugged a cushion. "All shut," she said, and rocked. "All shut."

The doorbell rang, and then a knock. She screamed, raced upstairs, and buried her head under a pillow.

Alice woke to find the bedroom curtains open, and darkness outside. The radio said 8:30. She slumped back, stared at the ceiling, and forced her breathing down. It was dinner time, and a whole day had gone. She threw off the duvet, staggered downstairs, and lurched to her computer. She dropped into her chair and tapped a key, and the screen lit up. Alice scrolled through thousands of names and numbers, but the program had found nothing—there were no patterns. It's all random, she thought, nature won't play. "I should give up," she muttered. That would be rational, but rational didn't work any more, not for Alice.

She sat at the kitchen counter sipping tea and munching biscuits. It's the letter-to-number swap, she realised, A, B, C, to 1, 2, 3, is too simple—the universe would pick something fancier. She stared at the screen. Where to begin? Pi was an obvious choice, A=3, B=1, C=4, D=1. And so was the golden ratio. And dozens of physical constants could also work...

For hours she typed code, building a program that could search for interesting number-maps to test. When it was finished, she set it going, stood up, stretched, yawned, and went to bed.

At ten-thirty the next morning, Alice swung into the common room and poured a long black coffee.

Brian looked up from his newspaper. "Welcome back…" he said with a sneer.

She sat down and nodded at the other three staff. The two senior mathematicians ignored Alice, and the postdoc squinted, and shifted, and looked away.

Brian folded his paper and stared at her. "You should get help." He pushed himself up. "I think you should see someone, Alice. *And sort yourself out.*"

As she watched him go, her cheeks flushed, her throat knotted, and she wheezed. She gulped coffee, but it scalded, and she spat it out. Then she cleared her throat, returned her mug, walked out of the room, out of the building, and drove straight home.

Alice put on her staying-in dress, picked up the bird, slumped in front of the television, and flicked through the channels. Mr S wandered across her chest, asking for cuddles.

"I should have published more," she said, staring into the bird's beady eyes. "I really should. Still, my students like me…"

Mr S squawked, and Alice stroked his crest.

"I think you should see someone," she mumbled. I'm a bloody idiot, she thought, that's the problem. And it's time to grow up—before Brian gets me fired. She marched across the room and popped Mr S on his cage. He ruffled his feathers and lunged at her. "*Behave*, Mr S. And be a good bird while I try to work."

Alice tapped the keyboard, and the computer lit up. The program had stopped and was flashing an alert. Her hands twitched and clenched. "Yes," she panted. "Yes, yes, YES!" She reached behind and pulled up the chair, keeping her eyes fixed on the screen. This latest version of her program had been running for less than a day, and the result—twenty-six digits long—glowed red. This number was the key to the universe. And below that magic string, were hundreds of names grouped by their numbers. The first lot was artists, then came composers, and chemists, and mathematicians. Her finger stroked the display above the maths group, and she mouthed their names. Brian was not amongst them. "Bloody right!" she said, and then she scrolled past architects, and poets, and stopped at thieves. And Brian's name was top. "That's odd," she said, and her eyes widened. But she *had* caught him in her office, and he *had* been glib and made it all her fault. She wondered what he'd stolen, and then she reddened as she thought of her diary, and his photographic memory. She leant back and exhaled. "You bastard…"

Alice considered a photographic memory a handicap, something that cluttered the mind. Maths needed clarity and judicious forgetting, but Brian had succeeded with a trivia-clogged head, and no originality.

Thief…

She scrolled down. The final group was *Victims*, and the first was Heather Doyle.

"I knew it," she muttered. "I bloody knew it."

Brian had hounded Heather and sacked her for a minor expense claim. After that, no other university would touch her, and she'd left academia. Six months later, Brian had his epiphany, his brilliant idea, his *Conjecture*. No one knew how. Now Alice knew: he'd stolen it from Heather. She drummed her fingers. "I wonder where Heather is now. I bet she'd like to see my program…"

The letter-to-number map—the program's key—still glowed. Alice jotted down the twenty-six digits, and added six random

268

numbers at the beginning and end. Then she folded the note and slipped it into her purse. After that, she copied the key into her private email, added six false numbers on either side, stared at the screen, pursed her lips, and clicked send. Then she leant back, sighed, and defocused.

Deep inside her machine, an alien time-circuit—without which, the computer would have taken a billion years to find the key—melted. The instability spread, and more components died, as the failure of one led to the breakdown of another. White smoke coiled from the vents, carrying the smell of burning plastic, and then the image froze. A bang, like a child's cap gun firing, and the screen went black.

Alice frowned. "Time for a new computer." She leant back and grinned. "I'll get something sleek—and impossibly fast."

Mr S squawked and bobbed on his perch.

"I know, Mr S, I know."

The bird went frantic. He nodded at the window, his eyes bulged, and his body stretched out.

"There's nothing out there, you stupid bird. Now, calm down."

Nothing could dampen her victory. Alice knew that the universe played games. She knew Brian was a lecher, a woman-hater, and a destroyer of lives—and a thief. She'd contact Heather, and together they'd take Brian's life apart, piece by slimy piece. Alice would have to write another program, but that was trivial, for she already had the 26-digit key.

Alice had a definite swing in her step as she marched out into the bright afternoon.

Mr S—who normally relaxed when abandoned—became hysterical.

Two men in matching blue overalls sat in a delivery van and watched her go. "She looks happy," said one.

"Let's go," said the other.

They walked up Alice's path and slipped in through a side door.

Mr S hopped from foot to foot and chirped away. The men ignored him and crept across the kitchen. Then they stood on either side of Alice's computer and grasped its base.

"Wait." The first man sniffed the machine. "It smells bad." He touched the top. "And it's hot." He tapped some keys and pressed the power button, but nothing happened. He took out his phone. "Rick," he said, "there's something wrong. The computer's dead…"

"Bring it anyway," said Rick, and he stared at his collection of dismantled computers and hung up.

Pseudonym

Heather stared out through the grubby window of her home office. She'd begun her novel last year, and it had started out promisingly enough—full of verve and stinging rebuke—but now she was stuck. Failure had drained her energy and mired her in the past. Fighting Brian had been unwise. He'd stolen her mathematical idea, but he outranked her. And he was a ruthless bastard. She should have moved on. Now she just bobbed in his fucking wake. Heather looked up from her computer. Sixty-thousand words was good, but not good enough. The dining-room phone rang, and she trudged over. "Hello?"

"Heather, it's Alice."

"Alice?"

"Of bastard-Brian fame," said Alice. "How are you?"

"Is he dead?" asked Heather, perking up.

"No. In fact, he's a bigger shit than ever. Can we meet?"

"Sure, come round. I'm always here. I'm writing the great novel—or rather, not writing it—and I'd love an excuse to stop. Well, I've already stopped..."

"Great. I'll come this afternoon. About three?"

"Perfect." Heather put down the phone and smiled. "Alice," she said, tapping her lower lip. "I wonder..."

She stood in front of the hall mirror, untied her hair, and shook her head, sending red curls cascading over her strong shoulders. "The dishevelled pre-Raphaelite look should do it." She pouted, then she changed her top and applied a hint of mascara.

That afternoon, they stood in the kitchen holding mugs of scalding coffee. The floor was dirty, and dishes filled the sink—and Alice pretended not to notice.

"Tell me about that fat fuck," said Heather. "What's he up to now?"

"I caught him snooping in my office. It was as creepy as hell…"

"I bet. My God, the *thought* of it."

"He's out to get me—like he got you."

"He stole from me, *then* he destroyed me." Heather glared at the memory. "The *bastard*."

"He took your conjecture and made it his."

Heather's eyes widened. "You guessed?"

Alice nodded. "I've got an idea too, but it's not one that Brian would nick."

"Brian can steal anything. Sit down and tell me more."

Alice perched on the edge of the settee and sipped her coffee. "It's very New Age, so you might not approve."

Heather leant back and sighed. "I'll believe anything now. Fire away."

"Numerology works."

Heather slurped her drink and smiled. "*Do* go on."

The two mathematicians faced each other. It was an awkward moment, charged and sweet—like a first kiss on a first date.

"I wrote a program that discovered a key, twenty-six digits long, that turns names into numbers in a meaningful way," said Alice. "There are patterns everywhere. *Numerology really works.*"

"Impossible, but intriguing."

"The program tested names and classified them. Accurately..."

"So, it put me under *Failure?*"

Alice coloured. *"Victim,* actually—it's not the same thing. Brian came under *Thief...*"

Heather roared with laughter. "It must work then."

"It seems impossible, and I wanted your advice. And my computer broke, *then* someone stole it."

"Can I use the idea?" asked Heather.

"About the stolen computer?"

"Well, yes, but I was thinking more of the numerology thing."

"Be my guest."

Heather grinned. "Brilliant!"

Alice leant forward and frowned. "How can numerology possibly work?"

"I don't know. But if it's true, then everything changes. For a start, it means that something designed the universe—or modified it."

"You're serious?"

"Well, yes..." Heather leant close and tapped Alice's knee. "It means that names echo structure, and poetry infuses reality. There may be cosmic jokes, and a deep intelligence..."

Alice stared open-mouthed. "A god? You mean I've proven there's a god?"

"I wouldn't go that far, but you've shown that words and numbers are embedded in the universe—at least locally."

Heather looked out of her window, as if she expected to see figures in the clouds.

"God's signature in twenty-six numbers…" mused Alice.

Heather nodded. She gave a quick smile, and then her face dropped. "I'm a determinist, as you know. Which means I'll be a victim forever…"

"I hadn't thought of it like that."

"I could always change my name and escape my destiny…"

"Not allowed," said Alice. "You can't go around changing the future by deed poll. It wouldn't be right."

"Authors do it all the time. That's legit…" Heather's eyes widened. "Fuck me. Wait a second." She launched from the settee and ran to her office. She returned clutching a manuscript and thrust it at Alice. "That's my pseudonym. Can you run it through your program?"

Determined to Succeed

Heather stared through her blurry window at the withered brown below and felt the vertigo of success. She was flying back from a Sydney book event with an aching jaw, an aching wrist, and an aching back. The numerology story was loved and disbelieved across the globe. And her pen name—chosen before meeting Alice—had guaranteed sales. She pressed the call button.

"Yes, Madam?"

"Gin and tonic, please."

More brown fields passed below, and a small town came and went. Another jet flew past, and then the gin arrived. She took a sip, and the spirit hit, and an idea grew: Alice should start a business—and name it for success. Then she could leave the university and escape Brian...

The Business of Names

Alice read the email for the fifth time. Heather's idea was brilliant. But Alice had beaten her to it. She'd already created a company and bought the domain. It was a powerful name, chosen by the numerology machine. And it burned reality and twisted time. But the universe had recoiled. It hates meddlers, and had fought back. Registering the business took weeks, and buying the domain was a nightmare of frozen computers and misbehaving banks; things got lost, and equipment failed. And Alice wept. A lot. But the name won. The *numbers* won. As they always do.

Alice typed her reply, thanking Heather and giving her the credit. She grinned and pressed send.

They met at the pub to baptise the business, and above the background chatter, their glasses clinked. "Here's to your new venture," said Heather.

Alice smiled. "Thanks, but it was your idea and your money..."

"I have to park my royalties somewhere..."

"I thought you only drank champagne," said Alice, "now that you're a famous writer."

"I'd rather have a dark beer with you..."

Alice blushed and took a long sip. "Tell me about the new book."

"Based on you, obviously. Nerd makes good with magic name. Immeasurably evil bastard gets his comeuppance, and brilliant friend guides nerd to market dominance." Heather pushed out her bottom lip. "What do you think?"

Alice smiled. "Nice, but will it work? It's a strange plot..."

"Yes," said Heather. "What can possibly go wrong?"

Stranger than Fiction

Heather stood on the stage, book in hand, and the crowd cheered. And Alice smiled. They were a literary sensation—Heather the artist, and Alice her muse.

The signing was over, and the last book lay face down on the table. Heather grinned from the back cover, and Alice ran her finger over the photo. The book was their child, conceived over coffee and beer, and nurtured, and prodded, and named with care. She turned it over and stroked its title. And flinched.

That night they drank French Champagne, and Heather proposed.

Millions read the book, and then the film came out. The story was everywhere—and the hidden-number-magic behind its words tore at the world. The stock market—exquisitely sensitive to such things—crashed. Anomalies bubbled, and causality fractured. And reality snapped.

Heather looked up from her computer. Sixty-thousand words was good, but not good enough. The dining-room phone rang, and she trudged over. "Hello?"

"Heather, it's Alice."

"Alice?"

"Of bastard-Brian fame," said Alice. "How are you?"

"Is he dead?" asked Heather, perking up.

The Great Mind was pleased with its numerology game. It was hard to stitch names and numbers into destiny, but the result was satisfying—like holding puppet strings. And a working numerology made people believe in a cosmic poet, and the Great Mind—artist that it was—enjoyed the recognition. But numerology had broken reality, and everything had snapped back and reset. The Great Mind watched the story loop—the endless stitch and crash. Then it got bored. It was time to uncouple destiny from letters and numbers, and time to let Alice and Heather get off the treadmill. It was time to make reality simple again. *Much simpler...*

Dead End

Alice dug into her pizza, took a swig of beer, and grinned. "The pizzas here are brilliant."

"Agreed," said Heather, "and yet the place is empty."

"They all go next door," said Alice, waving her fork at the entrance.

Heather twisted round to face the front of the restaurant. A family trooped past, led by a muscular and grim-faced father in bright green shorts and a tradesman's tee shirt. Then came a stout mother in an over-tight floral dress, followed by two teenage daughters. The girls were pretty, and slender, and twittery, like excited birds trailing pachyderms.

Alice sipped her beer. "I must have watched fifty people go by. They ignore this place and head straight for the grill next door. I can't understand it. They don't even glance in this direction."

Heather waved at the waitress. "Two more beers, please."

The girl in black arrived with foaming bottles and frosted glasses. "Anything else?"

"No thanks," said Heather, "that's perfect."

280

"I love empty restaurants," said Alice. "I like the mix of comfort and desolation—and the fast service. But it feels artificial..."

"As if we're in a cheap film," said Heather, "and they can't afford enough actors."

"Just those hungry extras outside..."

"It makes us special," said Heather, and smiled.

"We *are* special—and in a good way. But it seems like no one else exists."

"The girl in black exists. She's real. *Very* real..." Heather ogled the waitress.

"Enough of that."

"You're only jealous."

"Maybe..." said Alice.

"Maybe the slinky girl's a pleasure robot..."

"I wish," said Alice, but her mouth turned down.

Heather pursed her lips and frowned. "You *are* serious, aren't you?"

"Yes, the feeling's getting stronger—*and the world's getting sketchier.*"

"You think it's too computationally expensive to add more diners to this pizza place?" asked Heather. "That it would strain the engine of our universe?"

"Something like that. If it populated the restaurant, then the pizzas might lose their taste, and the beers lose their froth. You can't have everything. As you say, it's too computationally expensive."

Heather ran her fingers over the wooden table. "Is this a crack in the stage set—a fault line in our world?"

"It's laminated wood; the grain *never* matches up."

"Yes, but the seam goes right through. *Look, there's a split in the floor.*"

Alice whitened.

"Joking," said Heather. "Don't take things so seriously."

They paid, and Heather left a tip.

"That girl in black gave you a funny look," said Alice, as they pushed through the glass door. "Maybe she heard you call her a robot."

"I meant it as a compliment," said Heather, staring back into the empty pizzeria.

The cook switched off the oven, and the waitress stared into the night, her eyes glinting green.

"Let's check the place next door and see how busy it is," said Alice. "I wonder what they serve. Whatever it is, it's popular."

But the restaurant was dark. Heather walked up to the window, cupped her hands, and peered inside. "There's no one in there. It's shut."

Alice twitched. *"Nobody left.* I was facing the street. *And no one left."*

"Beats me," said Heather. "It's a dead end. They must've passed our window, there's no other way out. I'll ask the girl in black, *she'll* know."

"Any excuse."

But the pizzeria was dark as well. Heather rattled the door. "It's locked, and she didn't leave—not through here, anyway. Perhaps they're robots after all, the waitress and the cook. They might be parked out the back, recharging their batteries..." Heather stared into darkness, her jaws clenched and her fingers wide.

"No," wailed, Alice, "not you too."

"Got you!" shrieked Heather.

A tear ran down Alice's cheek.

"Sorry darling," said Heather, "I didn't mean to scare you."

They walked up the concrete stairs to the main road. The evening was clear, with no wind, and no rain, and no sound.

"I would suggest that we get a taxi," said Alice, staring towards town, "but there's no traffic. And no people."

Heather's eyes flashed green. "Too computationally expensive…"

Alice turned to her friend. But Heather had gone.

"No," wailed Alice, *"don't scare me again."*

Inside Out

This was the strangest book. Its covers had been torn off and glued together, and forced between the pages. It was an inside-out book, and the unprotected pages, which ran in reverse order, were damp and stained.

Read Me

"You can read minds with this stuff," Rick had explained, as he'd handed Morris a spool of spongy material. "But be discreet. Stitch it inside a hat and let me know what happens."

Morris had lined his old fedora with the felt, and then he'd wandered through the town to try it out, but nothing had happened.

He rang Denise. "Fancy trying on a special hat, courtesy of Rick?"

She was there in five minutes.

"It's *your* old hat," she said, pulling it over her auburn curls.

"Yes, but I added—"

"What the hell?" She tore it off and glared at Morris, her face white. "What the *fuck* just happened?"

"I added telepathic felt."

"I *saw* things," said Denise, *"private* things. *You try."*

"Rick said it reads minds, but it didn't work for me—"

"Here."

"OK, OK." His eyes widened.

"Well?"

He panted. "It works. It didn't before. I spent hours in town and got nothing…"

"Maybe Rick tuned it just for us."

"No, he said *minds*."

"Maybe we need more of the stuff to see into other people's heads," said Denise.

"OK," said Morris, "I'll make headbands. And I'll make them several layers thick. That should give us enough power."

With the headbands, they saw more clearly into each other's minds. But they still couldn't read anyone else. They *saw* things though—ghostly things that ran away. And they *heard* their phantom thoughts...

They jogged to the graveyard and stopped at the padlocked gate. Morris adjusted his headband, and the murmuring of the dead grew louder. Their voices rose and fell, like the ocean against the sea wall from long ago. He grasped the rusty palings and peered at the graves. The undergrowth rippled, and glassy figures darted between the headstones. Morris took a deep breath and wondered what the hell he'd done. Then he ripped off the felt, and the voices stopped, and the ghosts vanished. He sighed and stared at Denise. Sweat dotted her brow, and her face was set. And her eyes bulged, fixed on a tilted cross beyond the fence. He pulled off her headband and her shoulders fell.

"What do we do?" asked Denise.

"I don't know—we're not meant to see the dead."

They walked away, and Denise glanced over her shoulder for a last look at the quiet graves. Then they carried on along the road, they passed under a glassed-in pedestrian bridge, and turned left at the intersection.

"Is it safe to put them back on?" asked Denise.

"No, we're still too close."

They continued for several minutes, walked under a railway bridge, and stopped at a set of lights.

"Now?" asked Denise.

"Soon."

The lights beeped, the walking man lit up, and they crossed to the park.

"OK," said Morris. "It should be safe now."

They refitted their headbands and fell into step.

"Here's one," said Morris. "Let's try her."

A stooped lady with a halo of white hair tottered towards them. She looked up at Denise, and her wrinkled face broke into a smile.

"Do you see anything inside?" he asked.

Denise shook her head.

"We should be picking up *something*," said Morris. "I'll ask Rick."

"Be careful what you tell him. Be vague. We need to know what we're dealing with. He said nothing about ghosts. He thought we'd be able to read *everyone's* mind."

A young couple jogged past in bright outfits and designer shoes. Morris and Denise looked at each other and shook their heads.

Rick had chosen a fashionable café for his meeting with Morris. The place was all shadows and dark wood, and it smelt like a chocolate box. Rick sat in the corner, gazing through the window at the people outside. On the table was a tall coffee, a pot of melted chocolate, and a bowl of strawberries. He speared a lip-red fruit, dipped it in the chocolate, and popped it into his mouth. He closed his eyes in appreciation, and then he dabbed his lips with a cloth napkin. "Hello Morris," he said. "I've ordered for you."

Morris lowered himself into the chair, crossed his legs, arched an eyebrow, and leant forward. "Did you remember my cake, Rick?"

A girl in dark brown arrived with a silver tray. "Double-shot latte and a pecan pie?"

Morris nodded. "That's for me, thanks." He smiled at Rick. "I see that you did!"

Rick sipped his coffee. "How did the mind reading go?"

"It works on Denise—just."

"The felt needed more work, so I tweaked a few things." Rick pulled out a strip of pink, fluffy material and spread it on the table. "This is from the new batch, and it's got finer fibres. Here, touch it."

Morris stroked the fabric and nodded. "So, it's more powerful?"

Rick grinned and popped another chocolate-coated strawberry into his mouth.

Morris tried to look casual. "*How* does it work?"

"The fibres are so fine, and they branch so much, that they leak into time and detect the ripples of consciousness. They are time aerials—*mind aerials…*"

Morris frowned. "So, the finer the better?"

Rick nodded. "Come back to the factory, and I'll give you a whole sheet."

Rick's building occupied an entire block in central Leicester, and its brick sides rose like cliffs from the narrow pavements, and along those pathways, people scurried, all hunched and preoccupied. And beyond the pavements, the traffic surged and roared.

Rick and Morris climbed the corner steps and pushed through the corner door, and the modern grind of cars and trucks gave way to the clack of mills. Great timber engines filled the factory floor, and—despite their spin and smack—the dusty air was oddly still, as if time had slowed inside those walls.

A woman in white adjusted a dial, straightened, waved, and coughed. Morris waved back, but the woman turned and retched.

"Is she OK?" asked Morris.

"She's a long-time smoker..."

Rick led the way down a side corridor, up four flights of clanking stairs, and into a storage area. The room was empty except for a metal chest pushed against the far wall. Rick unlocked it and pocketed the key. He flung open the lid, slamming it against the wall, and then he pulled out sheets of coloured felt, soft pink, and green, and blue, and dust swirled around his head. "Sorry about the powder..."

Morris stepped back. "It's not like asbestos, is it?"

"No, it's perfectly safe."

"Mmm..."

"Each batch is colour-coded," continued Rick.

Morris edged closer, keeping his breathing shallow.

"Yours is the pink sheet—it's from the latest run and it has the finest fibres." Rick grinned. "It's my best work." A cloud passed over his face, and he frowned, as if chasing memories. "But be careful, this stuff's dynamite."

Morris held his breath, took the felt, and backed away. Rick rammed the green and blue sheets back into the chest, and more dust rose. Then he slammed the lid and turned and retched.

The evening light had gone, and the traffic had started. Denise swivelled in Morris's chair, drummed her fingers on his bench, and watched him unwrap the bundle. He spread out the pink felt across the workbench and pulled the lamp down, and the fabric glowed and shimmered, and dancing motes hung in the air.

289

"It's dusty," he advised, "so try not to breathe it in."

Denise edged forward and ran her fingers over the velvety material. "It's softer than the last lot. Will it work better?"

"Rick thinks so. His new process makes the fibres even finer." He held out his hand. "Scissors, please."

Morris snipped away, tongue poked out, and eyebrows knotted, like a child doing craft. He cut seven strips and stacked them. Then he stitched and cut and folded until the two headbands were ready. "Here goes," he said and slipped one on.

He gasped and recoiled, and moaned, and retched. Hunched up, he held out the other headband, like a desperado thrusting out a shot of whiskey. "Here," he said, "you try it."

She pulled it over her hair, and her eyes widened, and she grabbed the side of the table. "God, I feel sick. *All that stuff in your mind…*"

He grinned. "Likewise." He took off his band and shook his head. "Let's go for a beer, and see how it works in the pub."

Morris pushed against the door of The Rolling Lizard and stepped into warm and beery air. Thursday night was always busy, and the usual crush of bodies hogged the bar. The chatter was loud, and something familiar, but unplaceable, screamed from the jukebox. Morris pointed at a table near the door, and Denise stepped over to claim it.

Morris wove back with a pint in each hand and a packet of nuts in each pocket. Denise patted the seat, and he slid in next to her.

"Cheers," said Morris.

Denise glanced through the window, distracted. "Cheers." Traffic roared past in the dark, making the pub even cosier. She opened her nuts and sighed.

As they sipped their beers, Morris scanned the room. "If you stare at people too long, they look weird—like aliens."

"When you stare in a mirror too long, you see a demon," said Denise. "And repeating words makes them strange. Perhaps we overload our filters, and then we see what's *really* there. Scary, eh?" She took out the headbands. "OK, let's find out what the people in here think…"

They sat like awkward Christmas guests in paper hats, but no one paid them any attention. A group of girls at the next table shrieked and giggled over a shared photo. Morris shook his head.

Total radio silence.

They stared in parallel, with their hands in their laps, like an old married couple long past talking.

Denise sipped her beer, coughed, and pushed her glass away. "It's not working," she said. "Let's take them off."

She popped the bands into her bag and snapped it shut. And at the sound, the chatter stopped, and the noisy girls looked round with hollow eyes.

A moment later, the jabber restarted, and Denise elbowed Morris. They edged around the table, hoping that no one had noticed their unfinished beers, and they slipped into the street.

He shivered. "Unfriendly, weren't they?"

Denise nodded. "We didn't belong, and I've never felt that before—*not at the Lizard.*"

"And I've never left a beer before…"

"It happens in the movies," said Denise, "all the time."

"The emphatic half-finished drink." He sniffed. "Like the emphatic half-finished shave, when the hero hears the doorbell and wipes away the foam…"

"We're heroes, then, with our abandoned drinks…"

"No," he said, "we ran."

A group of young men wandered along the pavement, joking, and shouting, and pushing each other into the road. Further along, a drunken pensioner belched. Denise handed Morris his headband and fitted her own. A car hissed by, and a cyclist—middle aged and puffing—wobbled in its wake. They watched the cycle's red light flicker. And they watched the youths jostle and scream. And they watched the old man totter and retch. And Morris shook his head. "Nothing," he said. *"I can't read any of them."*

She took his hand. "Come on, let's go."

The path in the park was dotted with street lamps—like a toy road in a toy garden—and they walked from one bright patch to the next, holding hands like fairytale children, with the prison looming on their left, like an evil castle.

They reached the intersection at the far side of the park, and the walking light flashed green, and the beeping started. They crossed a wide and empty road and walked beneath the railway bridge—but no train clattered overhead to finish the scene. A few minutes later, they turned right, past the sullen university blocks, and back to the graveyard.

Denise squeezed Morris's hand. "It's starting," she said. "I'm picking up the ghosts again."

"Me too," he whispered. "But they're friendly—nicer than those hollow bastards back at the pub."

"We belong with the dead..."

He shivered. "Don't joke."

"I wasn't."

In the middle of town, in his factory suite, Rick thumped his brow. "Penny, I need help. *Now!*"

A tall blonde swept in. "You called?"

He squinted. "Can you remember who we tried the felt on?"

Penny shrugged. "Just Morris and his girlfriend, I believe."

He frowned. "Did *you* try it?"

"I can't remember. I don't think so…"

"Anyone else?" he asked.

"No."

"It's bloody odd," said Rick, and swivelled in his chair. "I can't find any records in the computer…"

Penny leant over his shoulder, tapped the keyboard, and shrugged. "There's nothing there."

He twitched. "I can't remember a bloody thing. Can you get the felt?"

"Of course."

"Hold on, I'm coming too."

Rick flung open the chest, like a manic pirate going after treasure. "I gave the top sheet to Morris, so these will have to do." He handed the green one to Penny. "Try it on," he said, and then he coughed and wiped his eye.

She wrapped the felt around her head like a turban, and Rick did the same with his. Up there, in the storage space, they looked like overgrown kids dressing up in an attic.

"Do you feel anything?" he asked.

"No. What about you?"

He shook his head. "Maybe the felt got damp."

Penny pulled off her dry and dusty sheet. "I don't think so. Here—"

He grabbed it, tore the sheet from his own head, clumped off, and kicked the door. "Useless, *bastard* stuff!"

Penny caught up with him in his private suite. "What now?"

"I'm going after Morris," he said, scrunching his fabric. *"Tonight."*

In the darkness, beside the cemetery, the car hissed to a stop, and Rick thrashed and bounced in the back, like a crazed dog. Then his face, swaddled in cloth, pressed against the window. "It works," he said. "The signal's stronger, and I can read their minds. They're watching the ghosts, and they have no idea we're here."

Penny glanced in the mirror, her eyes all small and steely. "What are they thinking?"

Rick frowned and moved his head, as if he were trying to pinpoint a distant sound. "They're scared and alone."

"It's a graveyard at night, so they're bound to be spooked. And they *are* alone."

Rick scrunched his eyes. "Yes, but they're not scared of the ghosts." He tensed. "They're happy with the dead, *because the dead have souls.*"

Penny twisted round. "Something doesn't feel right."

Rick nodded and opened the door. "Yes, I know."

Penny clenched the wheel and set her mouth and watched him storm across the road. And tears streamed down her face.

Rick stopped behind Morris and Denise, adjusted his sheet, and coughed.

Morris turned. And his jaw dropped. "Rick," he blurted. "What are you doing here?"

Rick twitched. "I'm watching you. *I can see the dead, too.*"

Morris fingered his headband, as if he were twiddling a radio knob.

"There's nothing inside him, Morris," Denise whispered in his mind. "Be careful."

"I *heard* that, Denise!" yelled Rick. "I *heard* your thoughts." His voice rose to a scream. "I can *read* you, Denise."

"Then read this Rick. What the *fuck* are you? And why can't I read your mind?"

"I'm not like you." He pointed at the spirits cowering by the stones. "Or them—*the bastard dead with souls.*"

Penny leant against the car's bonnet with her arms crossed. She was frowning and watching the unfolding drama, like a mother watching a soccer game that was spiralling into violence.

Rick ran to the railings and reached through, clutching at the spectres. But the spirits swirled away. "Bastards!" he screamed, as he thrashed against the rusty palings. Then he climbed.

Morris and Denise stepped back and watched him scale the fence. He gashed his leg on a spike, and his blood ran dark. He jumped down on the other side, looked around, sniffed, yelped, and ran at the graves. The spectres fled, and the smaller ones— the children—cried.

Morris—fists clenched and legs wide—stood frozen on the spot.

Rick paused by a stone cross, bobbed his felt-wrapped head, shot forward, and hit the ground.

A sharp cry made Morris wince.

Rick clutched the soul, which thrashed and slithered in his arms. Then he fell, ripping his cheek and breaking his teeth on a grave's hard edge. The soul arched and shrieked, but Rick held on, pinning it down, as it sobbed and quivered—a phantom child clamped to a stony bed. Rick gazed down—in a parody of a caring parent—and opened his mouth. Wide. Then wider still. His lower jaw detached with a sickening pop, and he worked his broken teeth over the slime, and the jelly-thing sighed and slipped inside.

In a flash, Morris read Rick's mind—and saw a hollow hunger satisfied. Then contact stopped. The ghost was all used up, and Rick's brief soul had gone. Rick—back to his dark and empty self—waved and then collapsed.

Morris listened, but there was nothing. His mind reached out for Denise. "He's gone."

"Yes," she answered in his head. "They've all gone."

They crossed the road and stood by the car. Penny still leant on the bonnet, her arms crossed, her shoulders hunched, and her eyes wet.

"How long have you known?" asked Morris.

Penny shrugged. "I got worried when we couldn't remember how we got the felt. Things were missing, and the world was wrong. *Rick* was wrong." She stared across the road at the broken man lying on the grave. "He realised that he lacked a soul, and he seethed—jealous of you *and* of the ghosts. It's funny, really, how badly he reacted. But then, he was *never* normal…"

Denise grabbed Penny's hand. "But *you* feel warm. *You're normal.*"

"Can you read me?" Penny asked. "Is there anything inside my head?"

Denise turned to Morris.

He shrugged. "We only see each other's minds. Maybe it's tuned to us. Maybe we're soulmates. Maybe…"

Penny's eyes went blank. Behind her perfect teeth, behind her painted lips and quiet tongue, the clockwork froze.

Denise dropped Penny's switched-off hand, and pulled away, and gasped.

Morris held Denise's shoulders and looked her in the eyes. "She's gone," he said, and sniffed.

"They've both gone." She shrugged. "If they were ever here…"

Morris let go of Denise's shoulders. "Come on, give me a hand. We can't leave her standing like this."

And together, they carried the rigid Penny out of the road and propped her against a low wall, like a lost manikin.

"Let's go," said Morris, and he opened the passenger door for Denise.

"OK," she said. "I've had enough."

Morris walked around Rick's car, climbed into the driver's seat—*Penny's* seat—and ran his finger over the dashboard. "It's not walnut," he said, and turned the key. The engine roared. "I'm not picking anything up—the felt's stopped working. But at least the engine started. I didn't expect it to..." He touched the dials, getting comfort from the just-animated machine. "What a day! What do you think?"

But Denise stared straight ahead. Her eyes were blank, her back was rigid, and her face was frozen.

"Denise?" he cried. *"Denise?"*

The Book of The Great Mind

Miles frowned and tried to ignore the sounds beyond his window. It was hard to concentrate these days, hard to keep things straight. The world had changed, and the stories in his beloved books were changing, too. Miles squirmed in his armchair. He opened the faded red paperback, and the spine cracked. He sniffed the dust and glue and ran his fingers over the paper. The pages *felt* the same, but the text was different. He pursed his lips. It might help if he *spoke* the words—hearing them might pin the story down. And so he read aloud:

Reality exploded. Quadrillions died as space and time were ripped apart. Each dying mind tried to warn its earlier self, and quadrillions of death pulses thumped back through time. But the earlier selves couldn't run from the catastrophe, and they died again, and so the pulses circled in those final moments. They iterated, but they couldn't escape. Instead, the pulses shoaled together and formed the Ghost at the End of Time.

This Ghost, this Great Mind, this Sum of the Dead, coiled against the high rafters of history and peered down into the inky past. Its awareness grew, and it saw deeper into time. It saw the bright traces of earlier minds, for each scrap of consciousness had twisted time and left a gleaming trail. And the wide, frozen

298

tracks of time machines—and the welded folds and buckles in history that they had stapled in their wakes—cut across this glowing scene, but they were rare, like vapour trails in a summer sky.

The Great Mind found the symmetry thrilling: how consciousness and time travel had broken the universe—and created the ultimate consciousness. The Great Mind reached back in time and repaired the damage...

History updated, and the Great Mind was reborn—a phoenix at the end of time, but a phoenix with a memory. It saw the fatal flaw in geometry: how everything leaks into time; how every rock and piece of interstellar grit, and every wisp of gas, seeps into the fourth dimension. Such leakage was barely noticeable until life appeared. Life was far more complex than a rock, and life leaked further. And brains leaked most of all.

Death pulses—the very fabric of the Great Mind—were temporal reflexes, made possible by this leakage. From the earliest times, creatures with death pulses thrived. They had a kind of temporal eye that watched for the flash of future death, and this gave them a powerful advantage, and it drove the evolution of minds, and the flowering of consciousness. But consciousness broke causality, and that broke everything else— full circle.

Miles looked up from the book. He smacked his lips and took a sip of water. Outside, the shuffling got louder.

Great Mind interventions could be simple, like crushing the Squamafly Eve, or complex, like a multi-vehicle collision. But whenever it intervened, whenever it changed history, strange bubble-worlds pinched off. Not full-blown universes, or alternate realities, or fresh time-lines, but cul-de-sac worlds, stagnant oxbow lakes in history that captured a fragment of reality at the point of change. They were half-formed places, low-fidelity copies, shallow and thinly populated. Alison got caught in a bubble world once, a simple place with no cars or driveways...

Miles thought about Alison and the squamaflies, and the other stories in his book—stories that had vanished. Outside, the groans got louder. He focused on the page.

Minds usually flipped back to their new histories, as Alison's had, but sometimes they'd stay trapped, like a forgotten locomotive in a siding.

The bubbles were just temporal pollution, an annoying foam on the trunk of history, and the Great Mind ignored them, for it had bigger fish to fry. It had whole enterprises to undo—except for the last one. The sponge-books were a different animal. They were a business to end all businesses. Sponge-books held everyone in lovely dreams, and the real world lost its magic.

The Great Mind liked the idea of dream books so much that it built a library—a Mind Library—a place of the imagination, where it could read the books and read the minds. And write them, too. Some were speculation, and some were autobiographical...

Reanimation in Black

Miles shut the book and fixed his wife with a penetrating stare. "Well, what do you think?"

Christine squirmed and ran a finger under her necklace. "It all sounds plausible, but..."

"But, what?"

"It seems complicated and unnecessary. I mean, why invoke a god at the end of time to explain all this..." She indicated the horrors outside the window. Rotting and leering faces pushed against the glass, leaving tendrils of spittle and pus and plasma. A pane cracked, and something moaned, and Christine took another gulp of brandy.

For days, Miles had buried himself in his book. It was written in happier times. It had branching time-aerials, and monster insects, and crazed entrepreneurs with impossible machines, and fierce robots, and cunning time-travellers, and retro-assassins. The stories consoled him, even the last one about the Great Mind—the story that explained everything. That's why he'd read it to Chris. But his lovely wife was beyond help. Her remains gaped at the dead beyond the window, and her black dress—she always wore black—was stained and torn.

He cradled the paperback and thought about that final story. Yesterday, it was about a mad scientist who was using a reanimation machine on his cousins and aunties and nieces. These relatives were all killed in car crashes, one after another. Bang. Bang. Bang. Cars were more dangerous in the fifties, but still... And why animate mangled corpses? Miles knew the answer, which is why he faced the apocalypse so bravely. The story was crass and obvious. And designed to stick in his head. Today, when it turned into *The Book of the Great Mind*, the author was talking to him—speaking through the shifting words. The Great Mind—author and subject—was giving him clues: if stories can change, and if the dead can rise, then this is not reality. The Great Mind was dreaming or having sport, but it had the courtesy to let Miles know that his world, and his apocalypse, were imaginary.

Christine teetered over Miles. Her rotting fingers twitched, and her tumbler fell. It shattered, but no drink spilled. For she had died and stopped drinking days ago, and her glass was dry. Her eyes were cloudy, and she grinned vacantly. Tendrils of spittle and pus and plasma dribbled down her chin. She took the paperback from Miles's outstretched hand and tilted her head. Then, like a destructive toddler, she ripped the pages out, one by one. His lovely girl—once perfect and mysterious—stomped her stained and stockinged feet, and gurgled, as the pages drifted down.

Miles scrabbled over the floor, grabbing the crumpled pages and holding them to his chest. He took them to the coffee table and tried to sort them out, and press them flat. "My story," he sobbed. "My clues." But the pages had no numbers and—except for pink and yellow stains—were blank. "Don't fall apart on me now," he said. And he giggled. And the giggle became a laugh. And the laugh became a bray. He tried to speak, but his mouth was drier than Christine's glass, and no words came.

Christine covered her milky eyes with mottled hands, and then she started counting, "One, two, three…" She jigged, like a huge and rotted child. This was a horror-show version of hide-and-seek—and she was in.

Outside, the risen dead scurried off to hide. Three bodies jostled for cover behind the car, and two leered from behind a narrow tree trunk.

Giant flies buzzed around. Then one, fatter than the rest, flew at the window. Its crispy abdomen split apart, and an orange sac —full of twisting comma-babies—fell out. One of the partly hidden dead cocked her head. The lady was portly, and middle-aged, and she wore a stained white hat, as if she'd died playing bowls. Her corpse stumbled across the lawn and stared at the insect on the glass. She pushed up her hat with a pale green finger, as if to get a better view, like a shopper inspecting a brooch, then she picked up the broken abdomen and put it in her mouth and munched. Her dead eyes looked down and watched the orange sac as it inched over the windowsill. She squealed, grabbed it as it throbbed, tilted her head, and swallowed it whole —as if it were an oyster—complete with flakes of paint and thrashing babies. She let out a belch, and then—legs wide apart and bent—she shuffled round to face the street. Miles watched the erstwhile bowler make her painful way through the garden. She snagged her skirt on a prickly bush, tugged it free, continued into the road, and marched away.

Miles knew, he just *knew*, that the fly babies were still alive. The mother fly *wanted* its children to be eaten. God help me, he thought, part of its life cycle involves passage through a dead bowel. The white-hatted corpse arrived at a neighbour's garden, rotated to face Miles, lifted its skirts, squatted by a bush, and grinned.

A spindly gentleman in a stained suit wandered over to look at White Hat. He stooped down, planting his large grey hands on his knees, and he watched enraptured, as luminous insects issued from under her skirts. And he listened through his dead ears to the faint buzz of baby wings, and the stuttering blasts of dead bowels.

An old man—cadaverous even in life—sat on the porch opposite, a glinting axe head in one hand, and a wooden handle in the other. He tried to fit them together, clink, tap, clink, tap, but he failed, time and time again.

Some bodies were still playing hide-and-seek. Others had lost interest and swayed and gawped, captivated by the glowing trails of squamaflies. A young man's corpse grabbed at a fly. And missed.

"It's not real," Miles sobbed. "Let me wake up, for fuck's sake."

The girl in black—the postmortem Christine, and avatar of the Great Mind—stared out through the grubby window. She was the most elegant of the dead, even in her stained and ruined garments. Then she raised an arm and pointed. Something luminous and blurry was coming out of the clouds, aiming right for her.

Through the Window

It hit the window with a thud and the glass melted. Then another blurry flier struck. For a moment, the Great Mind thought it was the start of a full-scale squamafly attack, and that poor Miles would have even more to cope with—more than having a dead wife standing in his lounge room, and an apocalypse beyond his window. But things had shifted.

Miles and Christine had vanished, and the deserted garden stretched much further. On the far side of the road, where the white-hatted corpse had squatted to birth her squamafly babies, the earth was piled up, as foundations—or a grave—were dug. The turned soil smelt sweet and heady, but the giant excavators stood idle, canted and reaching out, like dinosaurs frozen in the act of nest building. And the house—the cottage where Miles had hidden from the apocalypse—was now much grander. The sash windows, hitherto small-paned, and modest, and dirty, now stretched—high and gleaming—into a vaulted ceiling.

The Great Mind felt alone and besieged, like Alison in her lab. But these were not squamaflies that were striking the window of the Mind Library, they were Extirpators. Everyone had gone home, and the invasion had begun.

With that realisation, the floor, the walls, the windows, and the high ceiling vanished, and the Great Mind peered down into the inky past. It saw the bright traces of all the minds that had gone before, and it saw the wide frozen tracks of time machines. And it saw the glowing trails of the Extirpator robots as they smashed their way through history, erasing memories and deleting consciousness.

The robots arrived at the end of time and invaded the Great Mind, their protein tails catching in its networks like sticky tinsel. The murmuring time field screamed, and the Great Mind tried to escape, to burrow into the past where the world was bright, and clean, and safe. But the billions of time aerials that made up the Great Mind were dying, and their withering branches were retracting, pulling out of time. And the past was out of reach.

The Great Mind shut down, and its death pulse thumped back in time.

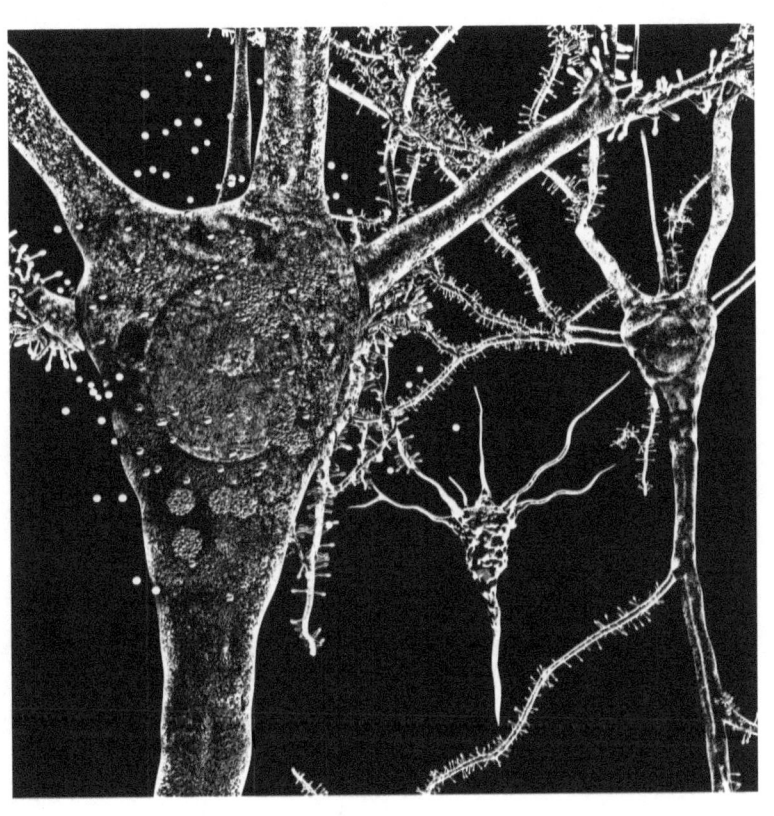

www.ingramcontent.com/pod-product-compliance
Lightning Source LLC
Chambersburg PA
CBHW031218120726
47905CB00002B/379